The Killing Bottle

CLASSIC ENGLISH SHORT STORIES

The Killing Bottle

—

CLASSIC ENGLISH SHORT STORIES

SELECTED BY
DAN DAVIN

Oxford   New York
OXFORD UNIVERSITY PRESS
1988

Oxford University Press, Walton Street, Oxford OX2 6DP

Oxford New York Toronto
Delhi Bombay Calcutta Madras Karachi
Petaling Jaya Singapore Hong Kong Tokyo
Nairobi Dar es Salaam Cape Town
Melbourne Auckland

and associated companies in
Beirut Berlin Ibadan Nicosia

Oxford is a trademark of Oxford University Press

Preface and Selection
© The English Association 1958

First published as English Short Stories of Today, Second Series 1958
First issued, with the title The Killing
Bottle, as an Oxford University Press paperback 1988

British Library Cataloguing-in-Publication data:
[English short stories of today. 2nd series]
The Killing bottle : classic English short
stories.
I. Davin, Dan
823'.01'08 [FS]
ISBN 0-19-828149-0

Library of Congress Cataloging-in-Publication Data
English short stories of today. Second Series.
The Killing bottle : classic English short stories / selected by
Dan Davin. p. cm.
Originally published: English short stories of today : London :
Oxford University Press for the English Association, 1976.
1. Short stories, English. 2. English fiction—20th century.
I. Davin, Dan, 1913– . II. Title.
PR1309.S5E534 1988 823'.01'08—dc 19
ISBN 0-19-282149-0 (pbk.)

Printed in Great Britain by
The Guernsey Press Co. Ltd.
Guernsey, Channel Islands

PREFACE

A SHORT story may be described as the brief relation of a fictitious event. It will usually be about persons and the 'event' narrated may belong to the world of external reality, or it may exist in the thoughts or emotions of the characters. It can be distinguished from an anecdote, on the one hand, by being long enough to light up and define the characters whom it concerns—seldom less, say, than 2,000 words; and it will differ from the novel, on the other hand, by recounting a single episode or situation rather than a complex sequence of events where the characters are only gradually displayed. A story of such length as Conrad's *Heart of Darkness*—about 40,000 words—begins to verge towards the novel.

This is hardly enough, however, to convey all that is meant by the form. A short story is a work of art and all art should enlarge life by creating and communicating an experience. The reader should be able to identify himself with one or all of the characters and experience through them what happens. But since the life, the experience, comes from the writer the story will depend for its intensity and its value on the quality of the story's creator. And a good story, as distinct from one meant merely to entertain, should leave the reader with his sympathies or his vision or his understanding enlarged by what he has read.

A short story, because it is short, is easily seen as a whole. This means that any flaws are more readily detected and so the writing and construction has to be very careful. The plot must be simple and the characters few, because there is not the space or the time for complexities. Irrelevance and digression cannot be concealed and so all detail must be significant and the development must be clear. And because the writer is usually trying to convey one central experience in a very small space he must pursue the maximum of meaning with the minimum of words. He must stimulate the reader into inferring what there is not room to say, use bold transitions in passing from one part of the narrative to the next, and aim at a kind of echo, or resonance, so that the reader when he reaches the end will find the experience vibrating in his memory like music.

The present selection is intended to show something of the methods by which a few contemporary writers in the form approach its problems and to give some idea of how rich and flexible the form can be.

The stories have also been chosen with a view to their use in schools.

CONTENTS

ELIZABETH BOWEN

Ivy Gripped the Steps

Ivy gripped and sucked at the flight of steps, down which with such a deceptive wildness it seemed to be flowing like a cascade. Ivy matted the door at the top and amassed in bushes above and below the porch. More, it has covered, or one might feel consumed, one entire half of the high double-fronted house, from the basement up to a spiked gable: it had attained about half-way up to the girth and more than the density of a tree, and was sagging outward under its own weight. One was left to guess at the size and the number of windows hidden by looking at those in the other side. But these, though in sight, had been made effectively sightless: sheets of some dark composition that looked like metal were sealed closely into their frames. The house, not old, was of dull red brick with stone trimmings.

To crown all, the ivy was now in fruit, clustered over with fleshy pale green berries. There was something brutal about its fecundity. It was hard to credit that such a harvest could have been nourished only on brick and stone. Had not reason insisted that the lost windows must, like their fellows, have been made fast, so that the suckers for all their seeking voracity could not enter, one could have convinced oneself that the ivy must be feeding on something inside the house.

The process of strangulation could be felt: one wondered how many more years of war would be necessary for this to complete itself. And, the conventionality of the house, the remains, at least, of ordering its surroundings made what was happening more and more an anomaly. Mrs. Nicholson's house had always enjoyed distinction—that of being detached, while its neighbours though equally 'good', had been erected in couples or even in blocks of four; that of being the last in the avenue; that of having on one hand as neighbour the theatre, to whose façade its front was at right angles. The theatre, set back behind shallow semi-circular gardens, at once crowned and terminated the avenue, which ran from it to the Promenade overhanging the sea. And the house, apart from the prestige of standing just where it stood, had the air of reserving something quite of its own. It was thus perhaps just, or not unfitting, that it should have been singled out for this gothic fate.

This was, or had been, one of the best residential avenues in Southstone, into which private hotels intruded only with the most breathless, costly discretion: if it was not that now it was nothing else, for there was nothing else for it to be. Lines of chestnut trees had been planted along the pavements, along the railed strip of lawn that divided the avenue down the centre—now, the railings were, with all other ironwork, gone; and where the lawn was very long, rusty grass grew up into the tangles of rusty barbed wire. On to this, as on to the concrete pyramids—which, in the course of four years of waiting to be pushed out to obstruct the invader, had sunk some inches into the soil—the chestnuts were now dropping their leaves.

The decline dated from the exodus of the summer of 1940, when Southstone had been declared to be in the front line. The houses at the sea end of the avenue had, like those on the Promenade, been requisitioned; but some of those at the theatre end stayed empty. Here and there portions of porches or balustrades had fallen into front gardens, crushing their overgrowth; but there were no complete ruins; no bomb or shell had arrived immediately here, and effects of blast, though common to all of Southstone, were less evident than desuetude and decay. It was now the September of 1944; and, for some reason, the turn of the tide of war, the accumulation of the Invasion victories, gave Southstone its final air of defeat. The withdrawal of most of the soldiers, during the summer, had drained off adventitious vitality. The A.A. batteries, this month, were on the move to another part of the coast. And, within the very last few days, the silencing of the guns across the Channel had ended the tentative love affair with death: Southstone's life, no longer kept to at least a pitch by shelling warnings, now had nothing but an etiolated

slowness. In the shuttered shopping streets, along the Promenade, in the intersecting avenues, squares and crescents,
vacuum mounted up. The lifting of the ban on the area had,
so far, brought few visitors in.

This afternoon, for minutes together, not a soul, not even a
soldier crossed the avenue: Gavin Doddington stood to regard
the ivy in what was, virtually, solitude. The sky being clouded,
though not dark, a timeless flat light fell on to everything.
Outside the theatre a very few soldiers stood grouped about;
some moodily, some in no more than apathy. The theatre
gardens had been cemented over to make a lorry park; and
the engine of one of the lorries was being run.

Mrs. Nicholson could not be blamed for the ivy: *her* absence
from Southstone was of long standing, for she had died in
1912—two years before the outbreak of what Gavin still
thought of as Admiral Concannon's war. After her death, the
house had been put up for auction by her executors: since
then, it might well have changed hands two or three times.
Probably few of the residents dislodged in 1940 had so much as
heard Mrs. Nicholson's name. In its condition, today, the
house was a paradox: having been closed and sealed up with
extreme care, it had been abandoned in a manner no less
extreme. It had been nobody's business to check the ivy. Nor
apparently, has there been anybody to authorize a patriotic
sacrifice of the railings—Gavin Doddington, prodding
between the strands of ivy, confirmed his impression that that
iron lacework still topped the parapet of the front garden. He
could pursue with his finger, though not see, the pattern that
with other details of the house, outside and in, had long ago
been branded into his memory. Looking up at the windows
on the exposed half he saw, still in position along the sills,
miniature reproductions of this pattern, for the support of
window boxes. Those, which were gone, had been flowery in
her day.

The assumption was that, as lately as 1940, Mrs. Nicholson's
house *had* belonged to someone, but that it belonged to nobody
now. The late owner's death in some other part of England
must have given effect to a will not brought up to date, by

which the property passed to an heir who could not be found—
to somebody not heard of since Singapore fell or not yet
reported anything more than 'missing' after a raid on London
or a battle abroad. Legal hold-ups dotted the world-wide
mess. . . . So reasoning, Gavin Doddington gave rein to what
had been his infant and was now his infantile passion for
explanation. But also he attached himself to the story as to
something that had nothing to do with him; and did so with
the intensity of a person who must think lest he should begin
to feel.

His passion for explanation had been, when he knew Mrs.
Nicholson, raised by her power of silently baulking it into the
principal reason for suffering. It had been among the stigmata
of his extreme youth—he had been eight when he met her,
ten when she died. He had not been back to Southstone since
his last stay with her.

Now, the lifting of the official ban on the area had had
the effect of bringing him straight back—why? When what
one has refused is put out of reach, when what one has
avoided becomes forbidden, some lessening of the inhibition
may well occur. The ban had so acted on his reluctance that,
when the one was removed, the other came away with it—as a
scab, adhering, comes off with a wad of lint. The transmuta-
tion, due to the fall of France, of his '*I* cannot go back to
Southstone' into '*One* cannot go there' must have been salutary,
or, at least, exteriorizing. It so happened that when the ban
came off he had been due for a few days' leave from the
Ministry. He had at once booked a room at one of the few
hotels that remained at the visitor's disposition.

Arriving at Southstone yesterday evening, he had confined
his stroll in the hazy marine dusk to the cracked, vacant and
wire-looped Promenade—from which he returned with little
more than the wish that he had, after all, brought somebody
down here with him. Amorist since his teens, he had not often
set off on a holiday uncompanioned. The idea of this as a
pilgrimage revolted him: he remained in the bar till it closed.
This morning he had no more than stalked the house, approaching it in wavering circles closing through the vaguer

Southstone areas of association. He had fixed for the actual confrontation that hour, deadline for feeling, immediately after lunch.

The story originated in a friendship between two young girls in their Dresden finishing year. Edith and Lilian had kept in touch throughout later lives that ran very widely apart—their letters, regularly exchanged, were perhaps more confidential than their infrequent meetings. Edith had married a country gentleman, Lilian a business man. Jimmie Nicholson had bought the Southstone house for his wife in 1907, not long before his death, which had been the result of a stroke. He had been her senior by about fifteen years: their one child, a daughter, had died at birth.

Edith Doddington, who had never been quite at ease on the subject of Lilian's marriage, came to stay more often now her friend was a widow, but still could not come as often as both would have liked. Edith's own married life was one of contrivance and of anxiety. After money, the most pressing of Edith's worries centred round the health of her second son: Gavin had been from birth a delicate little boy. The damp of his native county, inland and low-lying, did not suit him: there was the constant question of change of air—till his health stabilized, he could not go away to school. It was natural that Lilian, upon discovering this, should write inviting Gavin to stay at Southstone—ideally, of course, let his mother bring him; but if Edith could not be free, let him come alone. Mrs. Nicholson hoped he and she, who had not yet met, would not, or would not for long, be shy of each other. Her maid Rockham was, at any rate, good with children.

Gavin had heard of Southstone as the scene of his mother's only exotic pleasure. The maid Rockham was sent to London to meet him: the two concluded their journey with the absurdly short drive, in an open victoria, from the station to Mrs. Nicholson's house. It was early in what was a blazing June; the awnings over the windows rippled, the marguerites in the window boxes undulated, in a hot breeze coming down the avenue from the sea. From the awnings the rooms inside took a tense bright dusk. In the sea-blue drawing-room, up whose walls reared mirrors framed in ivory brackets, Gavin was left to await Mrs. Nicholson. He had time to marvel at the variety of the bric-à-brac crowding brackets and tables, the multitude of cut crystal vases, the earliness of the purple and white sweet pea—at the Doddingtons' sweet peas did not flower before July. Mrs. Nicholson then entered: to his surprise she did not kiss him.

Instead, she stood looking down at him—she was tall—with a glittering charming air of uncertainty. Her head bent a little lower, during consideration not so much of Gavin as of the moment. Her coiffure was like spun sugar: that its crisp upward waves should seem to have been splashed with silvery powder added, only, marquise-like glowing youth to her face.

The summery light-like fullness of her dress was accentuated by the taut belt with coral-inlaid clasp; from that small start the skirts flowed down to dissipate and spread where they touched the floor. Tentatively she extended her right hand, which he, without again raising his eyes, shook. 'Well . . . Gavin,' she said, 'I hope you had a good journey? I am so very glad you could come.'

He said: 'And my mother sends you her love.'

'Does she?' Sitting down, sinking an elbow into the sofa cushions, she added: 'How *is* Edith—how is your mother?'

'Oh, she is very well.'

She vaguely glanced round her drawing-room, as though seeing it from his angle, and, therefore herself seeing it for the first time. The alternatives it offered could be distracting: she soon asked him her first intimate question—'Where do you think you would like to sit?'

Not that afternoon, nor, indeed, until some way on into this first visit did Gavin distinguish at all sharply between Mrs. Nicholson and her life. Not till the knife of love gained sufficient edge could he cut out her figure from its surroundings. Southstone was, for the poor landowner's son, the first glimpse of the enchanted existence of the *rentier*. Everything was effortless; and, to him, consequently, seemed stamped with style. This society gained by smallness: it could be comprehended. People here, the company that she kept, commanded everything they desired, were charged with nothing they did not. The expenditure of their incomes—expenditure calculated so long ago and so nicely that it could now seem artless—occupied them. What there was to show for it showed at every turn; though at no turn too much, for it was not too much. Such light, lofty, smooth-running houses were to be found, quite likely, in no capital city. A word to the livery stables brought an imposing carriage to any door: in the afternoons one drove, in a little party, to reflect on a Roman ruin or to admire a village church. In the Promenade's glare, at the end of the shaded avenue, parasols passed and repassed in a rhythm of leisure. Just inland were the attentive shops. There were meetings for good causes in cool drawing-rooms, afternoon concerts in the hotel ball-rooms; and there was always the theatre, where applause continued long after Gavin had gone to bed. Best of all, there were no poor to be seen.

The plan of this part of Southstone (a plateau backed by the downs and overhanging the sea) was masterful. Its architecture was ostentatious, fiddling, bulky and mixed. Gavin was happy enough to be at an age to admire the one, to be unaware of the other—he was elated, rather than not, by this exhibition of gimcrack size; and bows, bays, balustrades, glazed-in balconies and French-type mansardes not slowly took up their parts in the fairy tale. As strongly was he impressed by the strong raying out, from such points as station and theatre, of avenues; each of which crossed obliquely, just less wide residential roads. Lavishness appeared in the public flowers, the municipal seats with their sofa-like curving backs, the flagpoles, cliff grottoes, perspectives of lawn. There was a climate here that change from season to season, the roughest Channel gale blowing, could not disturb. This town without function fascinated him—outside it, down to the port or into the fishing quarter, 'old Southstone', he did not attempt to stray. Such tameness might have been found odd in a little boy: Mrs. Nicholson never thought of it twice.

Gavin's estimation of Southstone—as he understood much

later—coincided with that of a dead man. When Jimmie Nicholson bought the house for his wife here, Southstone was the high dream of his particular world. It was as Lilian's husband he made the choice: alone, he might not have felt capable of this polished leisure. His death left it uncertain whether, even *as* Lilian's husband, he could have made the grade. The golf course had been his object: failing that he was not, perhaps, so badly placed in the cemetery, which was also outside the town. For, for Southstone, dividends kept their mystic origin: they were as punctual as Divine grace, as unmentioned as children still in wombs. Thick-set Jimmie, with his pursuant reek of the City, could have been a distasteful reminder of money's source.

Gavin, like his dead host, beheld Southstone with all the ardour of an outsider. His own family had a touch of the brutishness that comes from any dependence upon land. Mr. and Mrs. Doddington were constantly in wet clothes, constantly fatigued, constantly depressed. Nothing new appeared in the squire's home; and what was old had acquired a sort of fog from being ignored. An austere, religious idea of their own standing not so much inspired as preyed upon Gavin's parents. Caps touched to them in the village could not console them for the letters they got from their bank. Money for them was like a spring in a marsh, feebly thrusting its way up to be absorbed again: any profit forced from the home farm, any rents received for outlying lands, went back again into upkeep, rates, gates, hedging, draining, repairs to cottages and renewal of stock. There was nothing, no nothing ever, to show. In the society round them they played no part to which their position did not compel them: they were poor gentry, in fact, at a period when poverty could not be laughed away. Their lot was less enviable than that of any of their employees or tenants, whose faces, naked in their dejection, and voices pitched to complaints they could at least utter, had disconcerted Gavin since babyhood, at the Hall door. Had the Doddingtons been told that their kind would die out, they would have expressed little more than surprise that such complicated troubles could end so simply.

Always towards the end of a stay at Southstone Gavin's senses began to be haunted by the anticipation of going back. So much so that to tread the heat-softened asphalt was to feel once more the suck of a sticky lane. *Here*, day and night he breathed with ease that was still a subconscious joy: the thought of the Midlands made his lungs contract and deaden —such was the old cold air, sequestered by musty baize doors, of the corridors all the way to his room at home.

His room *here* was on the second floor, in front, looking on to the avenue. It had a frieze of violets knotted along a ribbon: as dusk deepened, these turned gradually black. Later, a lamp from the avenue cast a tree's shifting shadow on to the ceiling above his bed; and the same light pierced the Swiss skirts of the dressing-table. Mrs. Nicholson, on the first occasion when she came as far as his door to say good-night, deprecated the 'silliness' of this little room. Rockham, it seemed, had thought it suitable for his age—she, Rockham, had her quarters on the same floor—Mrs. Nicholson, though she did not say so, seemed to feel it to be unsuitable for his sex. 'Because I don't suppose,' she said, 'that you really ever *are* lonely in the night?'

Propped upright against his pillows, gripping his glass of milk, he replied: 'I am never frightened.'

'But, lonely—what makes you lonely, then?'

'I don't know. I suppose, thoughts.'

'Oh, but why,' she said, 'don't you like them?'

'When I am here the night seems a sort of waste, and I don't like to think what a waste it is.'

Mrs. Nicholson, who was on her way out to dinner, paused in the act of looping a gauze scarf over her hair and once again round her throat. 'Only tell me,' she said, 'that you're not more lonely, Gavin, because I am going out? Up here, you don't know if I am in the house or not.'

'I do know.'

'Perhaps,' she suggested humbly, 'you'll go to sleep? They all say it is right for you, going to bed so early, but I wish it did not make days so short—I must go.'

'The carriage hasn't come round yet.'

'No, it won't; it hasn't been ordered. It is so lovely this evening, I thought I would like to walk.' She spoke, though, as though the project were spoiled for her: she could not help seeing, as much as he did, the unkindness of leaving him with this picture. She came, even, further into the room to adjust her scarf at his mirror, for it was not yet dark. 'Just once, one evening perhaps, you could stay up late. Do you think it would matter? I'll ask Rockham.'

Rockham remained the arbiter: it was she who was left to exercise anything so nearly harsh as authority. In, even, the affairs of her own house Mrs. Nicholson was not heard giving an order: what could not be thought to be conjured into existence must be part of the clockwork wound up at the start by Jimmie and showing no sign of beginning to run down yet. The dishes that came to table seemed to surprise her as much, and as pleasingly, as they did Gavin. Yet the effect she gave was not of idleness but of preoccupation: what she did with her days Gavin did not ask himself—when he did ask himself, later, it was too late. They continued to take her colour— those days she did nothing with.

It was Rockham who worked out the daily programme, devised to keep the little boy out of Madam's way. 'Because Madam,' she said, 'is not accustomed to children.' It was by Rockham that, every morning, he was taken down to play by the sea: the beach, undulations of orange shingle, was fine-combed with breakwaters, against one of which sat Rockham, reading a magazine. Now and then she would look up, now and then she would call. These relegations to Rockham sent Gavin to angry extremes of infantilism: he tried to drape sea-weed streamers around her hat; he plagued to have pebbles taken out of his shoe. There was a literal feeling of degradation about this descent from the plateau to the cliff's foot. From close up, the sea, with its heaving mackerel vacancy, bored him—most of the time he stood with his back to it, shading his eyes and staring up at the heights. From right down here, though Southstone could not be seen—any more than objects set back on a high shelf can be seen by somebody standing immediately underneath it—its illusion, its magical artificiality, was to be savoured as from nowhere else. Tiny, the flags of the Promenade's edge, the figures leaning along the railings, stood out against a dazzle of sky. And he never looked up at these looking down without an interrupted heartbeat—might she not be among them?

The rule was that they, Rockham and Gavin, walked zigzag down by the cliff path, but travelled up in the lift. But one day fate made Rockham forget her purse. They had therefore to undertake the ascent. The path's artful gradients, hand-railed, were broken by flights of steps and by niched seats, upon every one of which Rockham plumped herself down to regain breath. The heat of midday, the glare from the flowered cliff beat up Gavin into a sort of fever. As though a dropped plummet had struck him between the eyes he looked up, to see Mrs. Nicholson's face above him against the blue. The face, its colour rendered transparent by the transparent silk of a parasol, was inclined forward: he had the experience of seeing straight up into eyes that did not see him. Her look was pitched into space: she was not only not seeing him, she was seeing nothing. She was listening, but not attending, while someone talked.

Gavin, gripping the handrail, bracing his spine against it, leaned out backwards over the handrail into the void, in the hopes of intercepting her line of view. But in vain. He tore off clumps of sea pinks and cast the too-light flowers outwards into the air, but her pupils never once flickered down. Despair, the idea that his doom must be never, never to reach her, not only now but ever, gripped him and gripped his limbs as he took the rest of the path—the two more bends and few more steps to the top. He clawed his way up the rail, which shook in its socket.

The path, when it landed Gavin on to the Promenade, did so some yards from where Mrs. Nicholson and her companion stood. Her companion was Admiral Concannon. 'Hello, hello,' said the Admiral, stepping back to see clear of the parasol. 'Where have *you* sprung from?'

'Oh, but Gavin,' exclaimed Mrs. Nicholson, also turning, 'why not come up in the lift? I thought you liked it.'

'Lift?' said the Admiral. 'Lift, at his age? What, has the boy got a dicky heart?'

'No, indeed!' she said, and looked at Gavin so proudly that he became the image of health and strength.

'In that case,' said the Admiral, 'do him good.' There was something, in the main, not unflattering about this co-equal masculine brusqueness. Mrs. Nicholson, looking over the railings, perceived the labouring top of her maid's hat. 'It's poor Rockham,' she said, 'that I am thinking about; she hasn't got a heart but she has attacks.—How hazy it is,' she said, indicating the horizon with a gloved hand. 'It seems to be days since we saw France. I don't believe Gavin believes it is really there.'

'It is there all right,' said the Admiral, frowning slightly.

'Why, Rockham,' she interposed, 'you look hot. Whatever made you walk up on a day like this?'

'Well, I cannot fly, can I, Madam; and I overlooked my purse.'

'Admiral Concannon says we may all be flying. What are you waiting for?'

'I was waiting for Master Gavin to come along.'

'I don't see why he should, really—which would you rather, Gavin?'

Admiral Concannon's expression did not easily change, and did not change now. His features were severely clear cut; his figure was nervy and spare; and he had an air of eating himself—due, possibly, to his retirement. His manners of walking, talking and standing, though all to be recognized at a distance, were vehemently impersonal. When in anything that could be called repose he usually kept his hands in his pockets—the abrupt extraction of one hand, for the purpose of clicking thumb and finger together, was the nearest thing to a gesture he ever made. His voice and step had become familiar, among the few nocturnal sounds of the avenue, some time before Gavin had seen his face, for he escorted Mrs. Nicholson home from parties to which she had been wilful enough to walk. Looking out one night, after the hall door shut, Gavin had seen the head of a cigarette, immobile, pulsating sharply under the dark trees. The Concannons had settled at South-stone for Mrs. Concannon's health's sake: their two daughters attended one of the schools.

Liberated into this blue height, Gavin could afford to look down in triumph at the sea by whose edge he had lately stood. But the Admiral said: 'Another short turn, perhaps?'—since they were to *be* three, they had better be three in motion. Mrs. Nicholson raised her parasol, and the three moved off down the Promenade with the dignified aimlessness of swans. Ahead, the distance dissolved, the asphalt quivered in heat; and she, by walking between her two companions, produced a democracy of masculine trouble into which age did not enter at all. As they passed the bandstand she said to Gavin: 'Admiral Concannon has just been saying that there is going to be a war.'

Gavin glanced across at the Admiral, who remained in profile. Unassisted and puzzled, he said: 'Why?'

'Why, indeed?' she agreed. 'There!' she said to the Admiral. 'It's no good trying to tease me, because I never believe you.' She glanced around her and added: 'After all, we live in the present day! History is quite far back; it is sad, of course, but it does seem silly. I never even cared for history at school; I was glad when we came to the end of it.'

'And when, my dear, did you come to the end of history?'

'The year I put up my hair. It had begun to be not so bad from the time we started catching up with the present; and I was glad I had stayed at school long enough to be sure that it had all ended happily. But oh, those unfortunate people in the past! It seems unkind to say so, but can it have been their faults? They can have been no more like us than cats and dogs. I suppose there *is* one reason for learning history—one sees how long it has taken to make the world nice. Who on earth could want to upset things now?—No one could want to,' she said to the Admiral. 'You forget the way we behave now, and there's no other way. Civilized countries are polite to each other, just as you and I are to the people we know, and uncivilized countries are put down—but, if one thinks, there are beautifully few of those. Even savages really prefer wearing hats and coats. Once people wear hats and coats and can turn on electric light, they would no more want to be silly than you or I do. Or *do* you want to be silly?' she said to the Admiral.

He said: 'I did not mean to upset you.'

'You don't,' she said. 'I should not dream of suspecting *any* civilized country!'

'Which civilized country?' said Gavin. 'France?'

'For your information,' said the Admiral coldly, 'it is Germany we should be preparing to fight, for the reason that she is preparing to fight us.'

'I have never been happier anywhere,' said Mrs. Nicholson, more near definitely than usual. 'Why,' she added, turning to Gavin, 'if it were not for Germany, now I come to think of it, you would not be here!'

The Admiral, meanwhile, had become intent on spearing on the tip of his cane a straying fragment of paper, two inches torn off a letter, that was defiling the Promenade. Lips compressed, he crossed to a litter basket (which had till then stood empty, there being no litter) and knocked the fragment into it off his cane. He burst out: 'I should like to know what this place is coming to—we shall have trippers next!'

This concern his beautiful friend *could* share—and did so share that harmony was restored. Gavin, left to stare out to sea, reflected on one point in the conversation: he could never forget that the Admiral had called Mrs. Nicholson 'My dear'.

Also, under what provocation had the Admiral threatened Mrs. Nicholson with war?... Back at Gavin's home again, once more with his parents, nothing was, after all, so impossible: this was outside the zone of electric light. As late summer wore slowly over the Midlands, the elms in the Doddingtons' park casting lifeless slate-coloured shadows over sorrel, dung, thistles and tufted grass, it was borne in on Gavin that this existence belonged, by its nature, to *any* century. It was unprogressive. It had stayed as it was while, elsewhere, history jerked itself painfully off the spool; it could hardly be more depressed by the fateful passage of armies than by the flooding of tillage or the failure of crops; it was hardly capable, really, of being depressed further. It was an existence mortgaged to necessity; it was an inheritance of uneasiness, tension and suspicion. One could pre-assume the enmity of weather, prices, mankind, cattle. It was this dead weight of existence that had supplied to history not so much the violence or the futility that had been, as she said, apparent to Mrs. Nicholson, but its repetitive harshness and its power to scar. This existence had no volition, but could not stop; and its never stopping, because it could not, made history's ever stopping the less likely. No signs of, even, an agreeable pause were to be seen round Doddington Hall. Nor could one, at such a distance from Southstone, agree that time had laboured to make the world nice.

Gavin now saw his mother as Mrs. Nicholson's friend, Indeed, the best of the gowns in which Edith went out to dinner, when forced to go out to dinner, had been Lilian's once, and once or twice worn by her. Worn by Edith, they still had the exoticism of gifts, and dispelled from their folds not only the giver's sachets but the easy pitiful lovingness of the giver's mood. In them, Gavin's mother's thin figure assumed a grace whose pathos was lost to him at the time. While the brown-yellow upward light of the table oil lamp unkindly sharpened the hollows in Mrs. Doddington's face and throat, Gavin, thrown sideways out of his bed, fingered the mousseline or caressed the satin of the skirts with an adoring absorption that made his mother uneasy—for fetishism is, still, to be apprehended by those for whom it has never had any name. She would venture: 'You like, then, to see me in pretty clothes?' . . . It was, too, in the first of these intermissions between his visits to Southstone that he, for the first time, took stock of himself, of his assets—the evident pleasingness of his manner; his looks—he could take in better and better part his elder brother's jibes at his pretty-prettiness —his quickness of mind, which at times made even his father smile; and his masculinity, which, now he tried it out, gave him unexpected command of small situations. At home, nights were not a waste: he attached himself to his thoughts, which took him, by seven-league strides, onward to his next visit. He rehearsed, using his mother, all sorts of little gratuities of behaviour, till she exclaimed: 'Why, Lilian has made quite a little page of you!' At her heels round the garden or damp extensive offices of the Hall, at her elbow as she peered through her letters or resignedly settled to her accounts, he reiterated: 'Tell me about Germany.'

'Why Germany?'

'I mean, the year you were there.'

A gale tore the slates from the Hall stables, brought one tree down on to a fence and another to block the drive, the night before Gavin left for Southstone. This time he travelled alone. At Southstone, dull shingly roaring thumps from the beach travelled as far inland as the railway station; from the Promenade—on which, someone said, it was all but impossible to stand upright—there came a whistling strain down the avenues. It was early January. Rockham was kept to the house by a nasty cold; so it was Mrs. Nicholson who, with brilliantly heightened colour, holding her muff to the cheek on which the wind blew, was on the station platform to meet Gavin. A porter, tucking the two of them into the waiting carriage, replaced the footwarmer under the fur rug. She said: 'How different this is from when you were with me last. Or do you like winter?'

'I like anything, really.'

'I remember one thing you don't like: you said you didn't like thoughts.' As they drove past a lighted house from which music came to be torn about by the wind, she remembered: 'You've been invited to several parties.'

He was wary: 'Shall you be going to them?'

'Why, yes; I'm sure I *could* go,' she said.

Her house was hermetic against the storm: in the drawing-room, heat drew out the smell of violets. She dropped her muff on the sofa, and Gavin stroked it—'It's like a cat,' he said quickly, as she turned round. 'Shall I have a cat?' she said. 'Would you like me to have a cat?' All the other rooms, as they went upstairs, were tawny with fires that did not smoke.

Next morning, the wind had dropped; the sky reflected on

everything in its mild brightness; trees, houses and pavements glistened like washed glass. Rockham, puffy and with a glazed upper lip, said: 'Baster Gavid, you've brought us better weather.' Having blown her nose with what she seemed to hope was exhaustive thoroughness, she concealed her handkerchief in her bosom as guiltily as though it had been a dagger. 'Badam,' she said, 'doesn't like be to have a cold. Poor Bisses Cod-cadded,' she added, 'has been laid up agaid'.

Mrs. Concannon's recovery must be timed for the little dinner party that they were giving. Her friends agreed that she ought to reserve her strength. On the morning of what was to be the day it was, therefore, the Admiral whom one met out shopping: Gavin and Mrs. Nicholson came on him moodily selecting flowers and fruit. Delayed late autumn and forced early spring flowers blazed, under artificial light, against the milder daylight outside the florist's plate glass. 'For tonight, for the party?' exclaimed Mrs. Nicholson. 'Oh, let us have carnations, scarlet carnations!'

The Admiral hesitated. 'I think Constance spoke of chrysanthemums, white chrysanthemums.'

'Oh, but these are so washy, so like funerals. They will do poor Constance no good, if she still feels ill.'

Gavin, who had examined the prices closely, in parentheses said: 'Carnations are more expensive.'

'No, wait!' cried Mrs. Nicholson, gathering from their buckets all the scarlet carnations that were in reach, and gaily shaking the water from their stems. 'You must let me send these to Constance, because I am so much looking forward to tonight. It will be delightful.'

'I hope so,' the Admiral said. 'But I'm sorry to say we shall be an uneven number: we have just heard that poor Massing-ham has dropped out. Influenza.'

'Bachelors shouldn't have influenza, should they? But then, why not ask somebody else?'

'So very much at the last moment, that might seem a bit —informal.'

'Dear me,' she teased, 'have you really got *no* old friend?'

'Constance does not feel . . .'

Mrs. Nicholson's eyebrows rose: she looked at the Admiral over the carnations. This was one of the moments when the Admiral could be heard to click his finger and thumb. 'What a pity,' she said. 'I don't care for lopsided parties. *I* have one friend who is not touchy—invite Gavin!'

To a suggestion so completely outrageous, who was to think of any reply? It was a *coup*. She completed, swiftly: 'Tonight, then? We shall be with you at about eight.'

Gavin's squiring of Mrs. Nicholson to the Concannons' party symptomized this phase of their intimacy; without being, necessarily, its highest point. Rockham's cold had imperilled Rockham's prestige: as intervener or arbiter she could be counted out. There being no more talk of these odious drops to the beach, Gavin exercised over Mrs. Nicholson's mornings what seemed a conqueror's rights to a terrain; while with regard to her afternoons she showed a flattering indecision as to what might not please him or what he could not share. At her tea table, his position was made subtly manifest to her guests. His bedtime was becoming later and later; in vain did Rockham stand and cough in the hall; more than once or twice he had dined downstairs. When the curtains were drawn, it was he who lit the piano candles, then stood beside her as she played—ostensibly to turn over the music, but forgetting the score to watch her hands. At the same time, he envisaged their two figures as they would appear to someone—his other self—standing out there in the cold dark of the avenue, looking between the curtains into the glowing room. One evening, she sang, 'Two eyes of grey that used to be so bright'.

At the end, he said: 'But that's supposed to be a song sung by a man to a woman.'

Turning on the piano stool, she said: 'Then you must learn it.'

He objected: 'But your eyes are not grey.'

Indeed they were never neutral eyes. Their sapphire darkness, with that of the sapphire pendant she was wearing, was struck into by the Concannons' electric light. That round fitment on pulleys, with a red silk frill, had been so adjusted above the dinner table as to cast down a vivid circle, in which the guests sat. The stare and sheen of the cloth directly under the light appeared supernatural. The centrepiece was a silver or plated pheasant, around whose base the carnations—slightly but strikingly 'off' the red of the shade, but pre-eminently flattering in their contrast to Mrs. Nicholson's orchid *glacé* gown—were bunched in four silver cornets. This was a party of eight: if the Concannons had insisted on stressing its 'littleness', it was, still, the largest that they could hope to give. The evident choiceness of the guests, the glitter and the mathematical placing of the silver and glass, the prompt, meticulous service of the dishes by maids whose suspended breath could be heard—all, all bespoke art and care. Gavin and Mrs. Nicholson were so placed as to face one another across the table: her glance contained him, from time to time, in its leisurely, not quite attentive play. He wondered whether she felt, and supposed she must, how great had been the effrontery of their entrance.

For this dinner party lost all point if it were not *de rigueur*. The Concannon daughters, even (big girls, but with hair still down their backs) had, as not qualified for it, been sent out for the evening. It, the party, had been balanced up and up on itself like a house of cards: built, it remained as precarious. Now the structure trembled, down to its base, from one contemptuous flip at its top story—Mrs. Nicholson's caprice of bringing a little boy. Gavin perceived that night what he was not to forget: the helplessness, in the last resort, of society—which he was never, later, to be able to think of as a force. The pianola-like play of the conversation did not drown the nervousness round the table.

At the head of the table the Admiral leaned just forward, as though pedalling the pianola. At the far end, an irrepressible cough from time to time shook Mrs. Concannon's decoltage and the crystal *pince-nez* which, balanced high on her face, gave her a sensitive blankness. She had the *devote* air of some sailors' wives, and was heroic in pale blue without a wrap—arguably, nothing could make her iller. The Admiral's pride in his wife's courage passed a current over the silver pheasant. For Mrs. Concannon, joy in sustaining all this for his sake, and confidence in him, provided a light armour: she possibly did not feel what was felt for her. To Gavin she could not have been kinder; to Mrs. Nicholson she had only and mildly said: 'He will not be shy, I hope, if he does not sit beside you?'

Rearrangement of the table at the last moment could not but have disappointed one or other of the two gentlemen who had expected to sit, and were now sitting, at Mrs. Nicholson's right and left hand. More and more, as course followed course, these two showed how highly they rated their good fortune—indeed, the censure around the rest of the table only acted for them, like heat drawing out scent, to heighten the headiness of her immediate aura. Like the quick stuff of her dress her delinquency, even, gave out a sort of shimmer: while she, neither arch nor indolent, turned from one to the other her look—if you like, melting; for it dissolved her pupils, which had never been so dilated, dark, as tonight. In this look, as dinner proceeded, the two flies, ceasing to struggle, drowned.

The reckoning would be on the way home. Silent between the flies' wives, hypnotized by the rise and fall of Mrs. Nicholson's pendant, Gavin ate on and on. The ladies' move to the drawing-room sucked him along with it in the wake of the last skirt. It was without a word that, at the end of the evening, the Admiral saw Mrs. Nicholson to her carriage—Gavin, like an afterthought or a monkey, nipping in under his host's arm extended to hold open the carriage door. Light from the porch, as they drove off, fell for a moment longer on that erect form and implacable hatchet face. Mrs. Nicholson seemed to be occupied in gathering up her skirts to make room for Gavin. She then leaned back in her corner, and he in his: not a word broke the tension of the short dark drive home. Not till she had dropped her cloak in front of her drawing-room fire did she remark: 'The Admiral's angry with me.'

'Because of me?'

'Oh dear no; because of her. If I did not think to be angry was very silly, I could almost be a little angry with him.'

'But you meant to make him angry, didn't you?' Gavin said.

'Only because he's silly,' said Mrs. Nicholson. 'If he were not so silly, that poor unfortunate creature would stop coughing: she would either get better or die.' Still standing before her mantelpiece, she studied some freesias in a vase—dispassionately, she pinched off one fading bloom, rolled it into a wax pill between her thumb and finger, then flicked it away to sizzle in the heart of the fire. 'If people,' she said, 'give a party for no other reason but to show off their marriage, what kind of evening can one expect? However, I quite enjoyed myself. I hope you did.'

Gavin said: 'Mrs. Concannon's quite old. But then, so's the Admiral.'

'He quite soon will be, at this rate,' said Mrs. Nicholson. 'That's why he's so anxious to have that war. One would have thought a man could just be a man. What's the matter, Gavin; what are you staring at?'

'That is your most beautiful dress.'

'Yes; that's why I put it on.' Mrs. Nicholson sat down on a low blue velvet chair and drew the chair to the fire: she shivered slightly. 'You say such sweet things, Gavin: what fun we have!' Then, as though the seconds of silence ticked off over her head by the little Dresden clock or her own words had taken effect with her, she turned and, with an impulsive movement, invited him closer to her side. Her arm stayed round him; her short puffed sleeve, disturbed by the movement, rustled down into silence. In the fire a coal fell apart, releasing a seam of gas from which spurted a pale tense quivering flame. 'Aren't you glad we are back?' she said, 'that we are only you and me? Oh, why endure such people when all the time there is the whole world! Why do I stay on and on here; what am I doing? Why don't we go right away somewhere, Gavin; you and I? To Germany, or into the sun? Would that make you happy?'

'That—that flame's so funny,' he said, not shifting his eyes from it.

She dropped her arm and cried, in despair: 'After all, what a child you are!'

'I am not.'

'Anyhow, it's late; you must go to bed.'

She transmuted the rise of another shiver into a slight yawn.

Overcharged and trembling, he gripped his way, flight by flight, up the polished bannister rail, on which his palms left patches of mist; pulling himself away from her up the staircase as he had pulled himself towards her up the face of the cliff.

After that midwinter visit there were two changes: Mrs. Nicholson went abroad, Gavin went to school. He overheard his mother say to his father that Lilian found Southstone this winter really too cold to stay in. 'Or, has made it too hot to stay in?' said Mr. Doddington, from whose disapproval the story of Gavin and the Concannons' party had not been able to be kept. Edith Doddington coloured, loyal, and said no more. During his first term, Gavin received at school one bright picture postcard of Mentone. The carefully chosen small preparatory school confronted him, after all, with fewer trials than his parents had feared and his brother hoped. His protective adaptability worked quickly; he took enough colour, or colourlessness, from where he was to pass among the others, and along with them—a civil and indifferent little boy. His improved but never quite certain health got him out of some things and secured others—rests from time to time in the sick-room, teas by the matron's fire. This spectacled woman was not quite unlike Rockham; also, she was the most approachable edge of the grown-up ambience that connected him, however remotely, with Mrs. Nicholson. At school, his assets of feeling remained, one would now say, frozen.

His Easter holidays had to be spent at home; his summer holidays exhausted their greater part in the same concession to a supposed attachment. Not until September was he despatched to Southstone, for a week, to be set up before his return to school.

That September was an extension of summer. An admirable company continued its season of light opera at the theatre, in whose gardens salvias blazed. The lawns, shorn to the roots after weeks of mowing, were faintly blond after weeks of heat. Visitors were still many; and residents, after the fastidious retreat of August, were returning—along the Promenade, all day long, parasols, boater hats and light dresses flickered against the dense blue gauze backdrop that seldom let France be seen. In the evenings the head of the pier was a lighted musical box above the not yet cooling sea. Rare was the blade of chill, the too crystal morning or breathlike blur on the distance that announced autumn. Down the avenues the dark green trees hardened but did not change: if a leaf did fall, it was brushed away before anyone woke.

If Rockham remarked that Gavin was now quite a little man, her mistress made no reference to his schoolboy state. She did once ask whether the Norfolk jacket that had succeeded his sailor blouse were not, in this weather, a little hot; but that he might be expected to be more gruff, mum, standoffish or awkward than formerly did not appear to strike her. The change, if any, was in her. He failed to connect—why should he?—her new languor, her more marked contrarieties and her odd little periods of askance musing with the illness that was to be her death. She only said the summer had been too long. Until the evenings she and Gavin were less alone; for she rose late; and, on their afternoon drives through the country, inland along the coast or towards the downs, they were as often as not accompanied by, of all persons, Mrs. Concannon. On occasions when Mrs. Concannon returned to Mrs. Nicholson's house for tea, the Admiral made it his practice to call for her. The Concannons were very much occupied with preparations for another social event: a Southstone branch of the Awaken Britannia League was to be inaugurated by a drawing-room meeting at their house. The daughters were busy folding and posting leaflets. Mrs. Nicholson, so far, could be pinned down to nothing more than a promise to send cakes from her own, or rather her cook's kitchen.

'But at least,' pleaded Mrs. Concannon, at tea one afternoon, 'you should come if only to hear what it is about.'

By five o'clock, in September, Mrs. Nicholson's house cast its shadow across the avenue on to the houses opposite, which

should otherwise have received the descending sun. In
revenge, they cast a shadow back through her bow window:
everything in the drawing-room seemed to exist in copper-
mauve glass, or as though reflected into a tarnished mirror.
At this hour, Gavin saw the pale' walls, the silver lamp-stems,
the transparent frills of the cushions with a prophetic feeling
of their impermanence. At her friend's words, Mrs. Nicholson's hand, extended, paused for a moment over the cream-
jug. Turning her head she said: 'But I know what it is about;
and I don't approve.'

With so little reference to the Admiral were these words
spoken that he might not have been there. There, however,
he was, standing drawn up above the low tea-table, cup and
saucer in hand. For a moment, not speaking, he weighed
his cup with a frown that seemed to ponder its exact weight.
He then said: 'Then, logically, you should not be sending
cakes.'

'Lilian,' said Constance Concannon fondly, 'is never logical
with regard to her friends.'

'Aren't I?' said Mrs. Nicholson. 'But cake, don't you think,
makes everything so much nicer? You can't offer people
nothing but disagreeable ideas.'

'You are too naughty, Lilian. All the League wants is that
we should be alert and thoughtful. Perhaps Gavin would like
to come?'

Mrs. Nicholson turned on Gavin a considering look from
which complicity seemed to be quite absent; she appeared, if
anything, to be trying to envisage him as alert and thoughtful.
And the Admiral, at the same moment, fixed the candidate
with a measuring eye. 'What may come,' he said, 'is bound,
before it is done, to be his affair.' Gavin made no reply to the
proposition—and it was found, a minute or two later, that the
day fixed for the drawing-room meeting was the day fixed for
his return home. School began again after that. 'Well, what
a pity,' Mrs. Concannon said.

The day approached. The evenings were wholly theirs, for
Mrs. Nicholson dined out less. Always, from after tea, when
any guests had gone, he began to reign. The apartnesses and

frustrations of the preceding hours, and, most of all, the occasional dissonances that those could but produce between him
and her, sent him pitching towards the twilight in a fever that
rose as the week went on. This fever, every time, was confounded
by the sweet pointlessness of the actual hour when it came.
The warmth that lingered in the exhausted daylight made it
possible for Mrs. Nicholson to extend herself on the *chaise
longue* in the bow window. Seated on a stool at the foot of the
chaise longue, leaning back against the frame of the window,
Gavin could see, through the side pane of the glass projection
in which they sat, the salvias smouldering in the theatre
gardens. As it was towards these that her chair faced, in
looking at them he was looking away from her. On the other
hand, they were looking at the same thing. So they were on
the evening that was his last. At the end of a minute or two
of silence she exclaimed: 'No, I don't care, really, for scarlet
flowers. You do?'

'Except carnations?'

'I don't care for public flowers. And you look and look at
them till I feel quite lonely.'

'I was only thinking, *they* will be here tomorrow.'

'Have you been happy this time, Gavin? I haven't sometimes thought you've been quite so happy. Has it been my
fault?'

He turned, but only to finger the fringe of the Kashmir shawl
that had been spread by Rockham across her feet. Not looking
up, he said, 'I have not seen you so much.'

'There are times,' she said, 'when one seems to be at the
other side of a glass. One sees what is going on, but one cannot
help it. It may be what one does not like, but one cannot
feel.'

'Here, I always feel.'

'Always feel what?' she remotely and idly asked.

'I just mean, here, I feel. I don't feel, anywhere else.'

'And what is "here"?' she said, with tender mocking
obtuseness. 'Southstone? What do you mean by "here"?'

'Near you.'

Mrs. Nicholson's attitude, her repose, had not been come

at carelessly. Apparently, relaxed, but not supine, she was supported by six or seven cushions—behind her head, at the nape of her neck, between her shoulders, under her elbows and in the small of her back. The slipperiness of this architecture of comfort enjoined stillness—her repose depended on each cushion's staying just where it was. Up to now, she had lain with her wrists crossed on her dress: a random turn of the wrist or flexing of fingers were the nearest things to gestures she permitted herself—and, indeed, these had been enough. *Now*, her beginning to say, 'I wonder if they were right . . .' must, though it sounded nothing more than reflective, have been accompanied by an incautious movement, for a cushion fell with a plump to the ground. Gavin went round, recovered the cushion and stood beside her; they eyed one another with communicative amazement, as though a third person had spoken and they were uncertain if they had heard aright. She arched her waist up and Gavin replaced the cushion. He said: 'If who were right?'

'Rockham . . . The Admiral. She's always hinting, he's always saying, that I'm in some way thoughtless and wrong with you.'

'Oh, him.'

'I know,' she said. 'But you'll say good-bye to him nicely?'

He shrugged. 'I shan't see him again—this time.'

She hesitated. She was about to bring out something that, though slight, must be unacceptable. 'He *is* coming in,' she said 'for a moment, just after dinner, to fetch the cakes.'

'Which cakes?'

'The cakes for tomorrow. I had arranged to send them round in the morning, but that would not do; no, that would not be soon enough. Everything is for the Admiral's meeting to make us ready, so everything must be ready in good time."

When, at nine o'clock, the Admiral's ring was heard, Mrs. Nicholson, indecisively, put down her coffee cup. A wood fire, lit while they were at dinner, was blazing languidly in the already warm air: it was necessary to sit at a distance from it. While the bell still rang. Gavin rose, as though he had forgotten something, and left the drawing-room. Passing the maid on her way to open the front door, he made a bolt upstairs. In his bedroom, Rockham was in possession: his trunk waited, open, bottom layer packed; her mending basket was on the bureau; she was taking a final look through his things—his departure was to be early tomorrow morning. 'Time flies,' she said. 'You're no sooner come than you're gone.' She continued to count handkerchiefs, to stack up shirts. 'I'd have thought,' she said, 'you'd have wanted to bring your school cap.'

'Why? Anyway, it's a silly beastly old colour.'

'You're too old-fashioned,' she said sharply. 'It was high time somebody went to school. Now you *have* come up, just run down again, there's a good boy, and ask Madam if there's anything for your mother. If it's books, they ought to go in here among your boots.'

'The Admiral's there.'

'Well, my goodness, you know the Admiral!'

Gavin played for time, on the way down, by looking into the rooms on every floor. Their still only partial familiarity, their fullness with objects that, in the half light coming in from the landing, he could only half perceive and did not dare touch, made him feel he was still only at the first chapter of the mystery of the house. He wondered how long it would be before he saw them again. Fear of Rockham's impatience, of her calling down to ask what he was up to, made him tread cautiously on the thickly carpeted stairs: he gained the hall without having made a sound. Here he smelled the fresh-baked cakes, waiting in a hamper on the hall table. The drawing-room door stood ajar, on, for a minute, dead silence. The Admiral must have gone, without the cakes.

But then the Admiral spoke. 'You must see, there is nothing more to be said, I am only sorry I came. I did not expect you to be alone.'

'For once, that is not my fault,' replied Mrs. Nicholson, unsteadily. 'I do not even know where the child is.' In a voice that hardly seemed to be hers she cried out softly: 'Then this is to go on always? What more do you ask? What else am I to be or do?'

'There's nothing more you can do. And all you must be is, happy.'

'How easy,' Mrs. Nicholson said.

'You have always said that that was easy, for you. For my own part, I have never considered happiness. There you misunderstood me, quite from the first.'

'Not quite. Was I wrong in thinking you were a man?'

'I'm a man, yes. But I'm not that sort.'

'That is too subtle for me,' said Mrs. Nicholson.

'On the contrary, it is too simple for you. You ignore the greater part of my life. You cannot be blamed, perhaps; you have only known me since I was cursed with too much time on my hands. Your—your looks, charm and gaiety, my dear Lilian, I'd have been a fool not to salute at their full worth. Beyond that, I'm not such a fool as I may have seemed. Fool? —all things considered, I could not have been simply that without being something a good deal viler.'

'I have been nice to Constance,' said Mrs. Nicholson.

'Vile in my own eyes.'

'I know, that is all you think of.'

'I see, now, where you are in your element. You know as well as I do what your element is; which is why there's nothing more to be said. Flirtation's always been off my beat—so far off my beat, as a matter of fact, that I didn't know what it was when I first saw it. There, no doubt, I was wrong. If you can't live without it, you cannot, and that is that. If you have to be dangled after, you no doubt will be. But don't, my dear girl, go for that to the wrong shop. It would have been enough, where I am concerned, to watch you making a ninny of that unfortunate boy.'

'Who, poor little funny Gavin?' said Mrs. Nicholson. 'Must I have nothing?—I have no little dog. You would not like it, even, if I had a real little dog. And you expect me to think that you do not care . . .'

The two voices, which intensity more than caution kept pitched low, ceased. Gavin pushed open the drawing-room door.

The room, as can happen, had elongated. Like figures at the

end of a telescope the Admiral and Mrs. Nicholson were to be seen standing before the fire. Of this, not a glint had room to appear between the figures of the antagonists. Mrs. Nicholson, head bent as though to examine the setting of the diamond, was twisting round a ring on her raised left hand—a lace-edged handkerchief, like an abandoned piece of stage property, had been dropped and lay on the hearthrug near the hem of her skirts. She gave the impression of having not moved: if they had not, throughout, been speaking from this distance, the Admiral must have taken a step forward. But this, on his part, must have been, and must be, all—his head was averted from her, his shoulders were braced back, and behind his back he imprisoned one of his own wrists in a handcuff grip that shifted only to tighten. The heat from the fire must have made necessary, probably for the Admiral when he came, the opening of a window behind the curtains; for, as Gavin advanced into the drawing-room, a burst of applause entered from the theatre, and continued, drowning the music which had begun again.

Not a tremor recorded the moment when Mrs. Nicholson knew Gavin was in the room. Obliquely and vaguely turning her bowed head she extended to him, in an unchanged look, what might have been no more than an invitation to listen, also, to the music. 'Why, Gavin,' she said at last, 'we were wondering where you were.'

Here he was. From outside the theatre, stink still travelled to him from the lorry whose engine was being run. Nothing had changed in the colourless afternoon. Without knowing, he had plucked a leaf of the ivy which now bred and fed upon her house. A soldier, passing behind him to join the others, must have noticed his immobility all the way down the avenue: for the soldier said, out of the side of his mouth: 'Annie doesn't live here any more.' Gavin Doddington, humiliated, affected to study the ivy leaf, whose veins were like arbitrary, vulgar fatelines. He thought he remembered hearing of metal ivy; he knew he had seen ivy carved round monuments to signify fidelity, regret, or the tomb-defying tenaciousness of memory—what you liked. Watched by the soldiers, he did not care to make the gesture that would be involved by throwing the leaf away: instead, he shut his hand on it, as he turned from the house. Should he go straight to the station, straight back to London? Not while the impression remained so strong. On the other hand, it would be a long time before the bars opened.

Another walk round Southstone, this afternoon, was necessary: there must be a decrescendo. From his tour of annihilation, nothing out of the story was to be missed. He walked as though he were carrying a guide-book.

Once or twice he caught sight of the immune downs, on the ascent to whose contours war had halted the villas. The most open view was, still, from the gates of the cemetery, past which he and she had so often driven without a thought. Through those gates, the extended dulling white marble vista said to him, only, that the multiplicity of the new graves, in thirty years, was enough in itself to make the position of hers indifferent—she might, once more, be lying beside her husband. On the return through the town towards the lip of the plateau overhanging the sea, the voidness and the air of concluded meaning about the plan of Southstone seemed to confirm her theory: history, after this last galvanized movement forward, had come, as she expected, to a full stop. It had only not stopped where, or as, she foresaw. Crossing the Promenade obliquely, he made, between wire entanglements, for the railings; to become one more of the spaced-out people who leaned along them, willing to see a convoy or gazing with indifference towards liberated France. The path and steps up the cliff face had been destroyed; the hand rail hung out rotting into the air.

Back into the shopping centre, he turned a quickening step, past the shuttered, boarded or concave windows, towards the corner florists' where Mrs. Nicholson had insisted on the carnations. But this had received a direct hit: the entire corner was gone. When time takes our revenges out of our hands it is, usually, to execute them more slowly: her vindictiveness, more thorough than ours, might satisfy us, if, in the course of her slowness, we did not forget. In this case, however, she had worked in the less than a second of detonation. Gavin Doddington paused where there was no florist—was he not, none the less, entitled to draw a line through this?

Not until after some time back in the bar did it strike him—there had been one omission. He had not yet been to the Concannons'. He pushed his way out: it was about seven o'clock; twenty minutes or so before the black-out. They had lived in a crescent set just back from a less expensive reach of the Promenade. On his way, he passed houses and former hotels occupied by soldiers or A.T.S. who had not yet gone. These, from top to basement, were in a state of naked, hard, lemon-yellow illumination. Interposing dark hulks gave you the feeling of nothing more than their recent military occupation. The front door of the Concannons' crescent opened, on the inland side, into a curved street, which, for some military reason now probably out of date, had been blocked at the near end: Gavin had to go round. Along the pavements under the front door steps there was so much wire that he was thrust out into the road—opposite only one house was there an inviting gap in the loops. Admiral Concannon, having died in the last war, could not have obtained this as a concession—all the same this *was* as the number faintly confirmed, his house. Nobody now but Gavin recognized its identity or its importance. Here had dwelled, and here continued to dwell, the genius of Southstone that now was. Twice over had there been realized the Admiral's alternative to love.

The Concannons' dining-room window, with its high triple sashes, was raised some distance above the street. Gavin, standing opposite it, looked in at an A.T.S. girl seated at a table. She faced the window, the dusk and him. From above her head, a naked electric light bulb, on a flex shortened by being knotted, glared on the stripped, whitish walls of the room and emphasized the fact that she was alone. In her khaki shirt, sleeves rolled up, she sat leaning her bare elbows on the bare table. Her face was abrupt with youth. She turned one wrist, glanced at the watch on it, then resumed her steady stare through the window, downwards, at the dusk in which Gavin stood.

It was thus that, for the second time in his life, he saw straight up into eyes that did not see him. The intervening years had given him words for trouble: a phrase, '*l'horreur de mon néant*,' darted across his mind.

At any minute, the girl would have to approach the window to do the black-out—for that, along this coast, was still strictly enforced. It was worth waiting. He lighted a cigarette: she looked at her watch again. When she did rise it was, first, to unhook from a peg beside the dining-room door not only her tunic but her cap. Her being dressed for the street, when she did reach up, and, with a succession of movements he liked to watch, begin to twitch the black stuff across the window, made it his object *not* to be seen—just yet. Light staggered, a moment longer, on the desiccated pods of the wallflowers that, seeded from the front garden, had sprung up between the cracks of the pavement, and on the continuous regular loops or hoops of barbed wire, through all of which, by a sufficiently long leap, one *could* have projected oneself head foremost, unhurt. At last she had stopped the last crack of light. She had now nothing to do but come out.

Coming smartly down the Concannons' steps, she may just have seen the outline of the civilian waiting, smoking a cigarette. She swerved impassively, if at all. He said: 'A penny for your thoughts'. She might not have heard. He fell into step beside her. Next, appearing to hear what he had not said, she replied: 'No, I'm *not* going your way.'

'Too bad. But there's only one way out—can't get out, you know, at the other end. What have *I* got to do, then—stay here all night?'

'*I* don't know, I'm sure.' Unconcernedly humming, she did not even quicken her light but ringing tramp on the curved street. If he kept abreast with her, it was casually, and at an unpressing distance: this, and the widening sky that announced the open end of the crescent, must have been reassuring. He called across to her: 'That house you came out of, I used to know people who lived there. I was just looking round.'

She turned, for the first time—she could not help it. 'People

lived there?' she said. 'Just fancy. I know I'd sooner live in
a tomb. And that goes for all this place. Imagine anyone
coming here on a holiday!'

'I'm on a holiday.'

'Goodness. What do you do with yourself?'

'Just look round.'

'Well, I wonder how long you stick it out. Here's where we
go different ways. Good night.'

'I've got nobody to talk to,' Gavin said, suddenly standing
still in the dark. A leaf fluttered by. She was woman enough
to halt, to listen, because this had not been said to her. If her,
'Oh yes, we girls have heard that before,' was automatic, it
was, still more, wavering. He cast away the end of one cigarette and started lighting another: the flame of the lighter,
cupped inside his hands, jumped for a moment over his
features. Her first thought was: yes, he's quite old—that went
along with his desperate jauntiness. Civilian, yes: too young
for the last war, too old for this. A gentleman—they were the
clever ones. But he had, she perceived, forgotten about her
thoughts—what she saw, in that moment before he snapped
down the lighter, stayed on the darkness, puzzling her somewhere outside the compass of her own youth. She had seen
the face of somebody dead who was still there—'old' because
of the presence, under an icy screen, of a whole stopped
mechanism for feeling. Those features had been framed, long
ago, for hope. The dints above the nostrils, the lines extend-
ing the eyes, the lips' grimacing grip on the cigarette—all completed the picture of someone wolfish. A preyer. But who
had said, preyers are preyed upon?

His lower lip came out, thrusting the cigarette up at a
debonair angle towards his eyes. 'Not a soul,' he added—this
time with calculation, and to her.

'Anyway,' she said sharply, 'I've got a date. Anyway, what
made you pick on this dead place? Why not pick on some
place where you know someone?'

JOYCE CARY

A Good Investment

OLD Mrs. Bill of Hunter's Green had three daughters, Daisy, Letty, and Francie, the youngest. Daisy is a spinster of fifty who travels round the world from one friend's house to another on cargo boats, buses, hitchhikes, and has, she says, a gorgeous time. She drinks a good deal when she can get it free, eats enormously, and loves a noise. Letty is married to a lawyer called Gordon Todd with a taste for archaeology which, it is said, has damaged his practice. They have two children, boy and girl, and Letty complains very much of their wildness, of all her housekeeping troubles and expenses. She spends much of her time in bed, and whenever the children or the husband are too much for her nerves, she telephones to her mother for Francie, who duly rushes over and takes charge of house, husband, and children for as long as Letty can keep her, that is, as long as her mother is ready to spare her. This is usually four days at the most.

Letty complains bitterly of her mother's selfishness when she recalls Francie even after a week. 'What does she want with Francie—she has Mrs. Jones, and there's only herself to look after. And after all Mother is a good deal stronger than I am.'

Mrs. Bill says that Letty is a poor spoiled lily and that she preys on Francie. But she does not excuse Francie for deserting her because she blames Francie for having spoiled Letty at the beginning. 'There's no need for Francie to rush away at a word from Letty and it's very bad for Letty. But it's Francie's affair. I never interfere.'

Francie says nothing. She has no time between her various duties of keeping Mrs. Jones the housekeeper in a good temper, managing her mother's parties; and she knows too that anything she said would only irritate Letty and bring from her mother the remark, 'But why all the fuss? I never fuss, life is too short.'

Francie Bill is a very small woman, about thirty-five years of age, with a big round forehead, deeply lined, small grey eyes, and a rather prominent round chin. Her mouth is good and it has a very serious expression, except when she laughs. She laughs with her whole face, causing her eyes to disappear and her wrinkles to deepen.

Some time ago Francie had a love affair, but for months no one even realized it except the lover. He was a widower with a daughter of nine. His name was Catto, aged forty-eight, partner in a printing firm, moderately well off, and, as he considered, good at life. That is to say, he knew how to make a success of most things. His marriage had been successful, but he was not at all afraid, like so many prudent citizens who have had lucky marriages, of taking another chance. He realized very well how much luck had gone to his first choice —his wife, actually on the honeymoon, had changed into a different woman with exceedingly strong views on such delicate questions as where to live, how to decorate and manage a house, and which of her husband's friends were worth keeping up with. It was pure luck that he had agreed with her.

But he considered that a man of his age and experience would have more foresight in a second choice. He began to look round almost as soon as his wife was buried. He wanted above all a good housekeeper and a companion for his daughter—he was accustomed to good housekeeping and he distrusted nurses, even the most expensive. And he told himself that even from a financial point of view, the plan was justified. 'With wages at their highest and service at its worst, a competent wife is actually a first-class investment.'

And one day, by good luck, as he said afterwards, he met Daisy Bill at Wimbledon. He had barely settled himself on his stool in the morning queue, when a tall brown girl in a man's shirt, about three yards further down the row, called out loudly, 'Bill, Bill,' and then, 'Daisy.'

Catto as a small boy had known the Bill family very well. For three summers running they had shared the same lodgings at the seaside, and he had got on very well with Daisy especially, nearest to him in age. He had even fallen a good deal in love with Daisy at fifteen, during their last holiday together.

He thought, even before he identified the girl, 'Daisy Bill, could it be the old Daisy, and not married? If Daisy really isn't married, then what about her? The right age, too old for babies, I don't want a rival to poor little Jean, and Daisy was really a very nice girl in a very nice way—good-natured, healthy, and she would probably have money too. As far as I can remember all the Bill girls had something coming from the aunt who married into toothpaste.'

He looked round him, half stood up, and after a moment recognized Daisy. 'She must be that huge red-faced woman with the cigarette-holder shaped like a pipe. She couldn't be anyone else with that nose and those eyes. Yes, there she is waving to her friend.'

He excused himself to the neighbours and edged past them to present himself. Daisy knew him at once. She cried out in a voice to be heard ten yards away, 'Good Lord, Tommy, Tom Cat!' and wrung his fingers in a powerful clasp. 'But how wonderful, you haven't changed a bit. How extraordinary. What a bit of luck. You must join us.' The neighbours in the queue, discreetly interested and pleased, with that almost family feeling which belongs to the Wimbledon queue, made way for his stool, and he joined the Bill party. It consisted now of Daisy, a little thin, sharp woman who turned out to be a celebrated authoress, and the brown girl in the man's shirt who was a tennis star, a county champion.

Catto had been shocked by the change in Daisy's looks, but her greeting reassured him. He was reminded again of his old love, her easy good nature, her freedom from all those airs which in a girl of sixteen he most detested, touchiness and sudden changes of mood. He had told himself then that, with all her charm, she was as reliable a friend as any of the boys at school.

'Good heavens,' Daisy said, breathing tobacco in his face, 'do you remember those walks along the shore? And how you hated the kids for trailing after us?' She gave a loud laugh and then, dropping his hand, turned to the champion and exclaimed in a serious tone, as one who takes up again the more important affairs of life, 'So you don't think much of Seixas' service?'

And the pair continued their tennis gossip with enthusiasm. Catto might not have existed for either of them.

The authoress, having glared at the champion for some time, dismissed Catto with a single glance, and then, with a twist of her little pursed mouth and a droop of her eyelids, fell into a gloomy meditation which made her all at once ten years older and gave her a sad but distinguished beauty.

Catto had no recollection of his jealousy; Daisy seemed to have a more accurate memory of their affair. But he was already sorry that he had so impulsively presented himself. He observed his old friend with a rueful amusement. 'Yes, steady as a boy and now a regular fellow.' He recoiled from this bluff Daisy. It was obvious why she had never married. And neither of her sisters, even if they were unmarried, had ever attracted him. The languid, fragile, lovely Letty, always being rescued from crabs and wrapped up from the cold; the rat-tailed Francie, at six, with her red button of a nose, hurling herself into the seas and making love to the very fishermen.

But just before the party, having obtained its tickets, dispersed for lunch, Daisy recalled her manners and became even more hearty, asked after his family, expressed a manly sympathy for his loss, and told of her own father's death. But her mother was still at the old place, she would so like to see him again. Why not come out next week-end? There was to be quite an amusing party to dinner.

Catto accepted these attentions in their own spirit and resolved not to go to dinner on any account. Why waste time on the Bills if Daisy was not a suitable prospect? He was put out when Mrs. Bill wrote to him. She also expressed her sympathy, a cheerful sympathy: 'These things must happen, one has to take them,' and she pressed him to come to dinner. 'You remember Hunter's? It's just the same, and Daisy tells me so are you. Isn't that nice? It's quite encouraging in these days when everything else seems to get worse and worse, including the people. But poor things, I suppose they can't be blamed for being so flat when the newspapers are so full of bombs. Though I can't imagine why everyone should go off so terribly before the bombs even tick, or whatever they do when they drop.'

And in a postscript she wrote, 'Quite a small party, about eight, don't dress. Mrs. Mair is coming, who lost her husband last year in that plane crash, and the Offer girl who used to be so fond of you.'

Catto seemed to hear a voice, a rattling little voice like a cracked dinner bell. He had not heard it for thirty years, in fact since his last holiday with the Bills, before he had gone to the university and they had gone to Switzerland for Letty's health. He had not paid much attention to it then. Mrs. Bill had not talked much with boys of his age, nor, indeed, with her own children. She had been preoccupied with her handsome husband and the half-dozen other men, much older than herself, who frequented the house. Even at the seaside her life had been a series of parties, chiefly on yachts. The Bills had taken rooms at Clarksfoot, small and remote, unfashionable and even uncouth, with its mining workers, its Welsh Bethels singing hymns on the beach, because of her friend, Lord S., who kept his big yacht there.

S. asked her to his parties in harbour, but did not expect her to go cruising. Mrs. Bill was a very bad sailor. Her stories of her own feelings on the sea were among her most amusing. The voice tinkled with laughter in the background of Catto's mind. But now that it came back to him in the cadences of the note, so neatly written in a minute, precise hand, he found, to his surprise, that he liked his memory of Mrs. Bill, as of someone always gay, lively, good-tempered, and tolerant. 'Perhaps she did not trouble much with us children, but she never worried us either. She understood how to make things pleasant and comfortable. And then this widow, Mrs. Mair? I know Mrs. Bill was a bit of a match-maker. But why not—a widow might be the answer for me. She'd know the ropes and wouldn't have fantastic expectations, and yet she would appreciate the solid advantages of a husband and being on good terms with him. And this Offer girl too, she must be somewhere near my age if she was fond of me thirty years ago.'

He accepted Mrs. Bill's invitation; and it was true that the house had not changed. But the neighbourhood had. The place had been a farm, and Theodore Bill had even kept it as a farm, without a bailiff, losing money every year. Now the farm house with its garden stood incongruously in a vast new suburb which was actually named after it, Hunter's Green.

Catto, opening the old wooden gate, a farm gate still, had the sense of one who finds an unexpected treasure and, at the same moment sees it fall into the dust, as the bodies of the old saints are said to do when you dig them up. He had loved Hunter's Green where he had ridden his first pony, and had his first passionate love, with the slim, lovely girl who had put him over the jumps. With Daisy, in short. And where was that Daisy now? She was less than an existence, for the actual Daisy was already making faint and unreliable even that sweet memory that had been a vivid existence. And now Hunter's Green, the old Hunter's Green, the solid bricks, the immense elms, the coach-house with its dovecot, mysteriously disintegrated before his very eyes.

Hunter's Green had never pretended to beauty. It had always been a plain house—square, three-storied, with a slate roof a little too small, and a long lean-to conservatory.

In the farm among its trees, with the cows grazing opposite the windows, this plainness had been a charm. It seemed to say, 'I am the unpretending home of plain country people.' True, Theodore and Tottie Bill were anything but plain country people. But for that very reason, they had appreciated Hunter's Green, and carefully preserved its honest want of make-up.

But now the rough five-bar gate, the coarse grass in the lawn which was much too small for a paddock, a minute haycock in one corner of it, and the rusty pump at the angle of the wall, looked false, stagy. They had indeed become false by being preserved into a different age.

Catto went in expecting more disappointment of the same kind, relics of the past that spoiled and obscured the past by their meretricious survival. He was delighted, therefore, by Mrs. Bill. The little woman seemed no older. She was the same—pretty, vivacious, with her fine thin nose, her dead white skin, her black eyes that sparkled all the more for the contrast of her cheeks, her cracked voice, her high Edwardian handshake.

'Ah, but this is an occasion—don't you feel the sand between your toes? Don't you smell the stairs on the *Naiad*? I have never been able to use rubber since poor S. died. It makes me cry and it makes me seasick, and those are two things that simply can't go together. Some people drink claret with oysters, yes I know, I met such a man and he wasn't a character part. In fact, it was old Roger Kent.' And turning to another guest, 'Do you remember Roger in *Mrs. Tanqueray*?'

She had turned from Catto, as Daisy had turned from him, to a more responsive audience, and seeing her white curly head from behind, he reflected, 'But she was dark then—she must be seventy. I think she hasn't changed because I've been getting old too. And certainly she's kept her features.'

The dinner was quite good, the company distinguished, if not of the first distinction. A well-known Shakesperian actor, scholarly and earnest like all those who have never been stars; an ugly, amusing old critic with a broken nose, like a boxer's nose; and the vicar, a big red-faced man, full of good stories, and, Catto would have said, old port, a type that he had not met for years, and enjoyed. 'A sensible stout fellow,' he thought, 'and probably a fine preacher. I wish we had more of them in the Church. Good fellows with their feet on the ground.'

Mrs. Mair, a well-known women's editor under her maiden name, arrived late with a new husband, and the Offer girl, a thin pale creature of about seventeen, enthusiastic about ballet, had never even heard of Catto. He remembered that Mrs. Bill was celebrated for her inconsequence. It had been one of her charms and, because it had been a charm, he enjoyed it again.

Francie was the eighth at the table. That is to say, she did not appear till after the soup, when, flushed, hot, with damp hair and red shiny nose, she slipped into her place between the young bridegroom and the critic's wife.

As the vicar sat opposite Mrs. Bill it was impossible to alternate the sexes, and Catto, on her left, sat next to the critic. No one explained Francie, or her sudden appearance. Catto was left to infer, after some reflection, that this thick-set woman, with grey streaks in her hair, must be the youngest Bill daughter, Frank, Frankie, Francie. He could not recognize her at all. But when she disappeared again with the chickens, and came in soon after the ice pudding, he perceived that she was acting as cook. The maid who waited was no doubt a daily woman, possibly a waiter hired only for the party. And when the party moved to the veranda, overlooking the bogus paddock and the decorator's haycock, he noticed that Francie not only arranged her mother's cushions but mixed the vicar's whisky and fetched the actor's pipe from his room.

The actor, Maxton, was staying in the house. He seemed like an old family friend, and when Francie, noticing that he fumbled in his pocket, silently disappeared and brought the pipe, he did not interrupt his description of Bernhardt's absurd masterpiece in *L'Aiglon*, he received the pipe with his fingers as a man at table who has dropped a fork takes a new one from the waiter.

'Or a father from a daughter,' Catto thought. 'But she calls him Mr. Maxton. He can't be so familiar. Yet she knew what he wanted and where to find it.'

And suddenly he had a new recollection of the old Francie, the child of six who had always been so dirty, noisy, always falling into the water, tearing her frocks, so often in the way when he had wanted to be alone with the lovely, so friendly Daisy. He recalled a general cry of 'Frankie, Frankie,' and the small girl with flying tangled hair tearing madly along the corridor; his brain lighted up a snapshot of Mrs. Bill at her prettiest in a white serge frock, standing on the stairs above a group of men and saying with a charming bend of her head,

'But don't bother, I'm absolutely fated to lose things. Frankie will find it for me,' and then again, 'Frankie is the practical one, aren't you, Frankie?'

And again he saw, at forty-eight, an angle of his old friends that, at eighteen, had made only an impression on his memory, none on his observation. Daisy had been so easy, so friendly, yes, and Mrs. Bill's tinkling voice had usually been heard by the children in these cheerful laments. She was always needing something fetched or found. Her good-humour confessed, 'I'm a nuisance, I know, but you'll forgive me because I forgive everyone else.'

And Frankie had been the practical one. Had they given her the character and made her a family slave, was she really fit for nothing else? And looking at the girl's face as she sat, silent as usual, half hidden behind her mother's chair, listening to the actor and the critic discussing Bernhardt, he thought, amused by the recollection, 'Yes, how she trailed after me—after anything in trousers. How she would throw herself into my arms and say, "But Tom, you haven't kissed me good night." And I should think she's a real woman still—rather shy and dull perhaps but the tomboy has quite disappeared.' And suddenly he thought, 'Why not Francie, could I do better? A kind soul, modest, simple, pretty capable too if she cooked that dinner. Of course, she's a bit young—she can't be more than thirty-six. There could be a baby, and that's a complication I particularly wanted to avoid. Of course, one could make a bargain—babies barred. It's common enough in second marriages.'

He reflected a moment on this tricky point. But like many steady, careful fellows who look for a fair deal in life, he had also a strong sense of what is fair in dealing with others. 'No,' he thought, 'if she wanted a baby I should have to give her one. On the other hand, youth does have some advantages. She'd stand up better to the job.'

He looked again at Francie, and caught her at a plainer moment. The lamp shine on her nose and the prominent forehead, a strand of damp hair, well steamed from the kitchen, was lying limp against her cheek. But Catto rallied.

'Damn it, I'm not a boy. What do looks matter? What I need is a good home-maker—someone to take an interest in Jean—domestic competence and peace.'

He sought some private talk with her, but this was difficult to manage. Rain was falling in thick heavy lines and the cars could not come down to the door because, at Hunter's Green, as in a proper farmhouse, there was a little front garden full of old-fashioned flowers, with a narrow brick path to the front porch. The party stood crowded in the hall, looking out disgustedly, while Francie was busy with hats and coats.

When she brought him his coat he turned smiling and said, 'Frances, Frankie, do you remember Clarksfoot?'

But Mrs. Bill interrupted with a remark to the world, 'Dear me, there used to be a carriage umbrella in the hall. But it seems to have lost itself. Everything in this house gets itself lost.'

Francie, still silent, ran for the carriage umbrella in the back passage and escorted the guests to their cars.

Catto, who had come by train and taxi, had a lift in the critic's car. He made one more attempt to speak to Francie from the back window. 'Thank you, Francie, do you remember how you used to go round at bedtime and wish us all good night?'

The girl had turned away at a call from the house. Someone had dropped a scarf. She did not even hear him. But Catto was a determined man. He wrote to Mrs. Bill, thanking her for a delightful evening, and asked her to the theatre 'with my old friend Francie'.

And when Mrs. Bill refused on account of an engagement, he took the train again to Hunter's Green and called.

He was lucky. Mrs. Bill was out, and Frances was weeding the garden. In an old pair of trousers, gardening boots, a plaid shirt, and a handkerchief tied over her hair, she looked like a picture of slave labour in a Soviet camp. But she received Catto with something of Daisy's frankness. 'I'm sorry Mother's out, but she'll be in at six. Do wait. She'll be so upset to miss you.'

'Thanks, I should like to. And how are you, Francie? I didn't really see you last week.'

'Do you mind if I finish this border—I've got so behind with the weeds.'

'No—let me help you.'

'Oh you couldn't—you'll get filthy.'

'I can wash.'

'Are you sure you know which are weeds?'

'I see you're still practical.'

The woman looked at him in surprise. He explained his point, as a joke, but she did not smile. She reflected and said at last, 'I wonder——'

'You were a quaint little thing at six.'

But she was weeding again, he saw only the short broad back.

'You don't remember me at all.'

'Not really.' She stood up again and looked at him intently. She was obviously curious, she felt that his visit had some purpose beyond a mere call.

She shook her head, 'Mother says that you were Daisy's great friend.'

'I liked to think I was yours too. You never let me leave the house without a kiss.'

'Oh well, at six.' She dismissed this carelessly. She was not at all embarrassed, as Catto had expected. She showed no shyness. Indeed now that he had been able to talk to her, he felt that she had grown up with something of the Bill poise. She asked him abruptly, 'What do you do, Mr. Catto? Tell me about yourself.'

'That's a very dull story. I'm a printer, a widower, with a young daughter—forty-eight years old. Really there's nothing more to tell.'

'Is it long since you——' she hesitated.

'Lost my wife? No, eighteen months. But it seems a very long time indeed. We were very happy—I am a lonely man, Francie—a very lonely man. Men like me who have been happily married and then widowed, suffer a very special kind of loneliness.'

The woman looked at him and the wrinkles in her forehead were very noticeable. 'Yes, I can imagine it. I'm sorry. But then you did have all that happiness.'

'It's a danger.'

'Yes, it's a danger. But worth it. Or don't you think so? Perhaps now——'

'Oh yes, tremendously worth it.'

'In fact, in spite of everything, you've been——'

'Yes, I've been lucky. I was always rather lucky. I was lucky to know you when I was a boy.'

'Me——'

'I mean the family as a whole. Yes, you too. You were rather an important part of the experience.'

The woman looked at him and her expression was critical. She was taking a new view of this middle-aged man who made such rapid advances. Then she said that she must really get the weeding done, and set to work. No word was said for twenty minutes and the silence itself was expressive. It said plainly that there was a situation.

'I've been too sudden,' Catto said to himself. 'She doesn't seem shy—at thirty-six, she knows how to manage her feelings. But she's timid and wary.'

The bed finished, they straightened up together face to face, and the girl smiled in a broad and frank manner. Her whole face expressed a personal interest. She had settled something with herself. 'Come Mr. Catto, you need tea, or a drink.'

'Why Mr. Catto?'

'Well, what did I call you?'

'I was Tom to you all.'

'Come, Tom, we'll have tea.' She blushed as she spoke and stooped to gather her basket.

For the moment, Catto was afraid that he had been too enterprising. He did not want to commit himself to the girl before he knew her better. He had, as we have seen, as well as prudence, a strong sense of responsibility.

But the woman at once recovered her practical air. She had placed Catto to her satisfaction as a nice middle-aged man eager to renew his childhood memories. They talked of the days at Clarksfoot, they exchanged news. She told how Mrs. Bill after her husband's death had lost most of her money and sold the land, how Daisy loved travelling and seldom appeared at home, how Letty needed special treatment and how much it cost.

He told her about his marriage, about Jean, and how hard he thought it for a girl of nine to lose her mother. That he had seriously considered marrying again, on her account alone.

'I'm sure you're right,' Francie said, 'if you can find the right person.'

'That's the problem.'

'A widow perhaps, without children, who wanted a child to care for.'

'I'm not so sure. A younger woman might be a better companion.'

'A widow could be quite young. There are lots of young widows. What about war widows?'

'It's the person that matters. I don't see why she need be a widow.'

'Oh no, of course.'

'Or why I shouldn't have another baby if she were young enough.'

There was a pause, and Catto again thought that he had been indiscreet. But the woman was only reflecting. 'You'd have to discuss that with the new wife.' In fact, it was not till three months later, when Catto actually proposed in so many words that Francie understood him.

'You really want to marry me?'

'Yes, yes. I've been trying to tell you so for the last fortnight.'

'Well, I did wonder sometimes but I didn't like to think——'

'But you haven't answered me yet.'

'But don't you see?'

'What?'

'Why I didn't like to think. Why Tom,' and she laughed that tomboyish broad laugh which brought all her wrinkles and made her little eyes disappear, 'of course I'll marry you.'

The laugh disappeared and she looked suddenly very serious. All at once Catto understood that the headlong Francie of thirty years before was still there. He was much startled. He had not expected so passionate a kiss, so eager an embrace.

Mrs. Bill was greatly amused by the news. She congratulated Catto and said, laughing, 'Sir Galahad to the rescue, or is it Perseus? But I'm not really a monster, you know, and Francie loves her chains. She adores a fuss.' Catto, taken by surprise, found himself turning red. He did not know what to answer. But Mrs. Bill had dashed on at once, 'Letty will hate you, but it won't do Letty any harm to take a little exercise.'

He received a most friendly letter from Daisy in Venezuela, who said how glad she was to see that her darling Francie was to get away from home at last and have some life of her own. She wanted Catto to 'keep mother at bay, for Francie's sake, or you'll have no peace'.

The wedding was quiet. Mrs. Bill forgot to provide linen and Francie bought her own wedding dress, but Catto presented his bride with the latest refrigerator, freezer, enamelled stove, and double sink in a completely remodelled kitchen, and all Mrs. Bill's old friends sent autographed copies of their works—published twenty or thirty years before, period sensations now wearing as strange a look as the hats and skirts of that ancient world in which they had achieved their distinction.

Catto had already arranged for a honeymoon in Paris. His first honeymoon had been in Paris. Francie had hoped for Italy, but she enjoyed Paris enormously as a bride. And she was deeply apologetic when the month they had planned was cut a week short because Daisy came back from Jamaica, in a banana boat, with a mysterious illness called Daisy's fever, and the Cattos had to hurry home to look after her. But Catto could not complain that Daisy looked upon his home as a refuge in time of trouble.

Francie nursed her for six weeks before Catto got a hint, from Mrs. Bill, that Daisy's fever came on only when she was broke. 'Don't let her kill Francie,' she wrote. 'Daisy has always treated Francie as her private and personal slave. Have you tried the gold cure for the fever? A cheque, I've found, is far the best prescription.'

Daisy had been complaining every day of all the wonderful holidays she was missing by this unlucky illness, and Catto now offered her a loan of twenty pounds to take advantage of an invitation to Finland. She left the next morning by milk-float to catch a trawler whose captain was an old Bombay friend. Catto, relieved, told himself that Daisy would not come very often. But he protested when Francie confessed that she had engaged herself to stay three days at Hunter's Green in order to cook for her mother's traditional Easter party. He wrote to Mrs. Bill suggesting that he should advertise for a temporary cook. But she answered none was required.

'Francie seems to think she ought to come, but it's quite unnecessary—Mrs. Jones is quite lazy enough as it is. She does just as little as she dares.' She addressed the note to Galahad Catto, Esq., and signed herself 'the monster'.

Catto took it to Francie and said, 'You see, your mother doesn't even want you.'

'But it was Mummie told me that Mrs. Jones threatened to give notice if she asked five people to stay. And now she's asked seven people. And you know if we lose Mrs. Jones we'll never get another up to Mummie's standards.'

'Then she'll have to change her standards—like other people.'

Francie was silent, as usual in these arguments. But a certain obstinate desperation in her forehead and chin seemed to ask, 'How? It's easy to say, but how do you do it?' And she went to the work—Mrs. Bill's celebrated party was again a great success, for which she received much praise, even a graceful notice in a Sunday newspaper. And for three months afterwards she did not send for Francie; either she did not need her or she had been offended by Catto's note.

Francie believed that she was offended, and it worried her.

'Mummie is so sensitive about being a nuisance,' she said. 'And of course she'll never tell you when she's hurt.'

'She's no right to be hurt.'

Francie's wrinkles deepened. 'It's not very nice for her, living alone. I should hate it.'

Catto did not answer that Francie was off the point. He told himself that women have their own methods of argument and that, above all, he must not start a quarrel with Francie about her mother. That situation was too foolish as well as too vulgar. How easy for a sensible man to avoid it. And it seemed that Mrs. Bill, hurt or not, meant to leave Francie alone.

Francie's first baby was born in December, a very cold December; and on the day before she got up there was a note from Letty asking if she could take the elder girl to school, she herself had a migraine; and on the day after she got up, Mrs. Bill telephoned. She did not ask for help. Mrs. Bill's claim that she never sought Francie's help, was perfectly justified. Her method was to send news of trouble, as a joke, or to ask advice. This time she did both.

'I've got three people for the week-end and of course Mrs. Jones has sprained her ankle. You can rely on Mrs. Jones's ankle, it's never failed her yet when there's some real work to do. But meanwhile I have to find an experienced daily. Should I advertise? I'm so bad at these things. And I simply must get someone by this evening.'

Catto, running in from the works in the mid-morning, to have a glimpse of his wife, finds her up and dressed. She is at the telephone, nursing the baby through her opened coat and arguing with Letty about school clothes. Jean, with an expression of reserved disapproval which comically reproduces her father's look in the same kind of crisis, stands looking on. Jean, a sensible Catto, is already devoted, in her sensible way, to her stepmother. She knows how to value her practical good nature, and quite agrees with her father about the Bill relations.

'But Letty,' Francie's voice implores her sister to be reasonable. 'She simply must have four face towels. It may be ridiculous but you know there was trouble last time when she went with only two, and it upsets a child so much to be different.'

Catto, furious, tries to take the telephone out of Francie's hands. Startled, she turns crimson and fights him.

'No—what are you doing?'

And he, equally surprised by this strong resistance, gives way. She says hastily to Letty, 'It's all right, darling. Nothing. I'll be round in ten minutes,' and hangs up. She smiles nervously at Catto and says, 'I can do Letty on the way to Mother's. How lucky that I was going anyhow.'

'You're not going to do Letty, or your mother either. This is where we stop. You're not fit.' And seeing the obstinate look in her face, he begins to storm. Her mother and Letty are two of the most selfish people on earth. And has she no consideration for her baby, not to speak of her husband?

Francie, flustered, tries to interrupt. Suddenly she bursts into tears. Catto, alarmed by her violent agitation, sits down beside her and puts an arm around her.

'My darling, you see how it is. Someone has to make a stand. Let me do it for you if you're afraid.'

'But you can't, you can't. No one can.'

'But that's nonsense.'

'You don't understand. Letty would simply let that poor child go off again with all the wrong things, and of course Mother won't get a daily in time for dinner this evening. There isn't a hope. She'll leave everything to settle itself, and Mrs. Jones will limp about and get up a grievance till she gives notice. She loves a real grievance. And if Mother loses Mrs. Jones I'd have to go every day. Either that or Mother would have to live with us. And you'd hate that. Oh dear, there's Gordon in the car.' And still nursing, while her brother-in-law, chattering about Letty's headache, gathers her bag, she hurries out.

Six months later Mrs. Bill did lose Mrs. Jones, and she has failed to keep another housekeeper. She is very cheerful and says that on the whole she prefers to manage without Mrs. Jones, who had no humour.

Francie has her second baby, and she lives a still more distracted life, dashing over three times a week to manage her mother's household. It has been proposed that Mrs. Bill should live with the Cattos, but she absolutely refuses to give up her dear old house, with its glorious memories of William Archer, E. F. Benson, and George Alexander. And as for the proposal that the Cattos should live with her, taking half the house for their separate apartment, which is Mrs. Bill's solution to the problem, Catto can't bring himself to leave his home He points out that the kitchen was especially designed for Francie's convenience.

So that he too lives a distracted life. See him now at ten o'clock at night waiting at Hunter's Green to take Francie home. It is raining, but he is so angry that he won't leave the car to go into the house. This, of course, is stupid, for Mrs. Bill is always good-natured with him and says, 'My dear Tom, I don't ask Francie to run my show; it's Francie who insists on it. She's so practical—she hates a muddle. Now I don't mind muddle a bit.'

For Mrs. Bill has never suffered from a muddle—Francie sees to that. And Catto thinks bitterly, 'Practical and affectionate—how true that was—and is.'

Suddenly the house door opens and Francie comes running through the rain. He starts the engine, before he realizes that she has neither hat nor coat. She comes to the driver's side, pulls open the door, and puts her arms round his neck. 'Darling, only ten more minutes, I swear.'

'But you're getting wet.'

'Yes, I saw the car from the window and I knew how you were feeling. Only ten more minutes. And then we'll be off. And I am so longing——'

She kisses him again and again, there is a cry from the house, 'Francie,' and she runs.

Catto falls back in his seat. He is excited, his heart is beating fast, there are tears in his eyes. For he adores his wife, it is an agony for him to see Francie used, worn out by people that, to him, are worthless beside her. And it seems that there is

no cure. He suffers, he grumbles, he quarrels with the amused
Mrs. Bill, he makes a fool of himself, he does not know if he is
more happy or more wretched. All he knows is this passionate
love, a thing he has never imagined before—that devours him
with anxiety, with anger, with despair.

JOYCE CARY

Umaru

Iᴛ had been raining for two days, the drizzling mountain
rain of the Cameroons. The detachment, on special duty
behind the German lines, was under strict orders not to be
noticed. That was its duty as well as its only security. Fires
could not be lit except in brightest day. No tents were carried.
But the subaltern in charge, young Corner, had brought a
tent-fly with him; an old fly looted from some German camp.
Camouflage had not yet reached these remote parts, except
in practice, but this big oblong of canvas, once green, had
withered to shades of dun and olive which matched perfectly
the sparse northern bush.

At sundown the drizzle only became more varied in texture.
The wind was rising and the sky, till that moment one weeping
bank of water-grey mist, so low that at a little distance it could
be seen tangled in the thorns, began to break into enormous
clouds, or not yet clouds, shapeless drifts. Corner looking at
his men, huddled in their cloaks while they ate their cold
porridge, and feeling the rain trickle down his own back,
thought that no creature in the world could be more miserable
than a wet soldier. He called the old Sergeant. 'We'll sleep
under the fly, Sergeant. There's room for all of us with our
feet in the middle.'

Sergeant Umaru, thirty-year veteran, called often Father
Umaru by the men, heard with customary wooden disdain;
and answered only with a sketchy war-salute. But the men
were shy. When the party went to bed, in a well-drained sandy
hollow among low scrub, Corner and the Sergeant found
themselves alone at one edge, while the men's heads, pretty
close together, stuck out on the other three sides.

The arrangement, no doubt, would have looked comic to an
observer in a balloon; it would have seemed like a vast family
bed with one white and nineteen black faces sticking out all

round a large patchwork quilt. But it did not strike the family
as comic. The clouds, as they were lifted higher on the strong
wind and rolled into thicker lumps, let fall a much thicker
rain, in splashes as if from buckets carelessly tipped about.
The family was glad of its cover.

The men murmured together in their high voices, very like
sleepy children. Corner, with his head on a rolled macintosh,
tried to sleep, but he kept on being waked by some bit of talk
in a familiar voice, as a man, even asleep, catches anything
said by one of his own household. A certain Salé, a thin
gangling lad with a balky eye, remarked that for his part he'd
rather be a horseboy. And Corner's ear noted, That was
meant for me. So Salé has ambitions—he wants to be in the
horselines, and I thought he was hostile. That eye probably
meant only that he was wondering how to make an approach.
A moment later he was brought awake again by the deeper
voice of one Adamu, a tall and powerful river pagan, renowned
for his savage temper, who was talking about his village. 'A
good place—good land—plenty of water. You never saw
such onions. And the fish—aiee! Women too. Now up here
women are no good. The north is bad for women. In the sun
they burn up and go hard. You want to come down our way
for women. But it's what they always say. Women and fish,
if good you would wish, seek where shady groves by rivers
flourish. Yes, a moist folk.' All this in a soft chant like a man
repeating someone else's poem. 'Yes, a good land in all ways—
we have a lovely place—aiee!'

'A rotten place. I know it well.' This was from a little
bandy-legged hill pagan, called officially Moma Gombe, and
unofficially Shoot-Monkey. 'Now Kano—that is the place—
a real city.'

'No, it isn't very good, perhaps,' Adamu agreed unexpectedly in the same dreamy voice. 'Yes, it has its faults—too
many floods—too far from the big markets——'

One of the others suddenly uttered a loud yawn and
exclaimed, 'Ow, my bottom,' and the young Corporal at the
top left-hand corner reproved him, 'Shut up. You'll wake
Three-Eyes.'

Three-Eyes was Corner, who was therefore obliged to lie still and try to sleep. In a few minutes he was actually going to sleep, but at the last moment of half-consciousness, just as he was congratulating himself, I really am nearly asleep, he came so instantly and feverishly awake that it was hopeless even to think of sleeping. His legs ached, every nerve twitched, lights jumped in front of his shut eyes, and all the cells in his brain seemed to be darting about and banging together like bubbles in soda water.

The men were already asleep. There were snores and grunts. One of them muttered a few words, 'But it's so high—I don't——'

Corner gave it up; he could no longer stand the commotion inside. The rain had stopped some time before, abruptly, after five minutes' quick fire; he turned on his back and opened his eyes, to be startled by a commotion overhead even more wild and much more grand. There were now at least three levels of cloud all moving in different directions. The old round clouds, now once more joined in masses, but masses of enormous size and sharp outline, moved slowly with a vast piled dignity almost due east; a second layer much lower, was made up of fantastic torn shapes, swimming fast like the debris of a flood. One saw something like a drowned bullock, swollen and limp, with twisted body and its legs pointing opposite ways, and a haycock just breaking up into wafts of straw. Or it was more like the ruins of some immense jigsaw map—Germany, France, Italy, England, Scotland, with their jagged coastlines and frontiers, caught up in some furious gale of time, and being stretched, squeezed, joined and divided in the process; not by sudden jerks, but by a smooth, continuous deformation, which was much more expressive of the powers at work.

And below all, moving faster still, as fast as a horse could gallop, and in a third direction, white fragments, wisps trailing their filmy skirts not much higher than the trees, seemed like ghosts of clouds, lost benighted creatures rushing through the dark transparent space below the tumult in the desperate anxious hurry of all lost creatures trying to find out where they are, and what they are, and where they ought to be.

A sudden movement beside him made Corner turn his head.
Old Umaru, also on his back, with open eyes, had just
scratched the calf of one leg with the toe-nails of the other.
Corner spoke without meditation. It was as if the vivacity of
his nerves was glad to find tongue, 'How would you like to
be back in Bauchi, Sargy, in a nice warm house?'

Umaru said in his driest tone, 'I don't live in Bauchi.'

'Then why are you called Umaru Bauchi?'

'That's just a Company name.'

'Where do you come from, then?'

'Nowhere. I don't belong anywhere.'

'But where were you born?'

'On war.' He used the word used by the old Emirs to mean
an army in being, on the move. 'I go where the Company
goes,' and he added severely, as if instructing a small boy,
'that's the best way.'

'But the Company has a home; it was stationed at Bauchi.
That's where it has its wives and its friends.'

'Friends. I don't have friends. Friends are no good.'

Corner was now quite content to lie awake and to enjoy the
sky and the talk. He was extremely awake, but the commotion inside had suddenly vanished, as if drawn out of him by
that of the sky, that was, the lower sky. For in the upper layer,
that region of cold majestic forms, the moon, which had for a
long time, itself out of sight, been throwing a brilliant greenish
light on the precipices of the top clouds, as on a range of
Himalayas, was now very slowly projecting one edge of itself
into a small triangle of blue already so full of white glitter
that it was scarcely blue at all.

Suddenly in a different tone, abrupt and reluctant, but
undoubtedly curious, such as Corner had never before heard
from the old man, he asked, 'In your country, Caftin, among
the water, do you keep friends?'

'Of course, plenty.'

The Sergeant pondered. At last he exclaimed, 'Plenty. I
have friends too—like that.' His tone abolished this promiscuous relation as something casual and frivolous. But his

voice ended on a high note; it seemed that he was about to make further confidences. The young man waited with an expectation which seemed to have occupied all the place of those restless cells, a feeling not only of curiosity but discovery. He had taken the Sergeant for a good stolid Hausa, a sun-dried old soldier without an idea beyond his trade, and now it seemed that he had reflections of his own. He had always liked Umaru for his honesty and his courage, but now he felt, especially at the point where his elbow touched the old man's back, a warmth of sympathy.

The moon, but half disclosed, was cut off as by a shutter. A vast black cloud below, a ragged tormented thing shaped like Greece, but with an immensely stretched-out isthmus at Corinth, had come rushing across the middle darkness. It was hustled by in a few minutes, but as its distorted Peloponnese was dragged away by the neck, a volley of big rain, cold heavy drops, widely spaced, came smacking down as out of clear space. They made a quite surprisingly loud report on the hollow canvas and stung the face. But the young man did not pull in his head. He was still preoccupied with Umaru's last remark.

'But Umaru, it isn't good for a man to be lonely.'

'Yes, it is, very good.' This was with great conviction. Umaru was lying rigid with his little grey beard aimed truculently at the moon, now once more in sight, and with her full face. She had proceeded at least another half-inch upon her way during that interruption. 'Very, very good. That's the way to live—like a Haji.' A Haji is a pilgrim.

'Ah then, God is your friend.'

'No—no, no—no,' with all the explosive violence of the Hausa negative. 'God is——' he paused, trying to find an adequate word. Then he said in a mild tone, 'He is our great One.'

'Yes, that's true.' The young man certainly felt the great-ness at that moment, but not with any reverence, only elation. Simply because he began to admire the scene as beauty, it seemed to him more extraordinary. He said to Umaru, carrying on the conversation, 'it's a grand night now—look at those clouds.'

'A bad night,' Umaru said. 'Very bad. More storms coming. A bad, bad night. God help us.'

'But good to look at.'

'To look at.' Umaru said this with wondering contempt. Again there was a long silence. Then suddenly he muttered in a grumbling tone, 'Time for sleep—God bless you with it.'

'And you, Father.'

'And health.'

'And much health.'

'God prolong us,' in a growl. He turned on his side. But the young man lay on his back for another hour, and still at the place where his elbow touched Umaru's back he was aware of a certain activity of feeling at work as if by itself; an affectionate concern which did not stop. At least, it was still there when he noticed it some time later. It was laughing, too, by itself, but not at Umaru. It was quite independent, a serene enjoyment.

WALTER DE LA MARE

Seaton's Aunt

I HAD heard rumours of Seaton's aunt long before I actually encountered her. Seaton, in the hush of confidence,
or at any little show of toleration on our part, would remark,
'My aunt', or 'My old aunt, you know', as if his relative might
be a kind of cement to an *entente cordiale*.

He had an unusual quantity of pocket-money; or, at any
rate, it was bestowed on him in unusually large amounts; and
he spent it freely, though none of us would have described him
as an 'awfully generous chap'. 'Hullo, Seaton,' we would say,
'the old Begum?' At the beginning of term, too, he used to
bring back surprising and exotic dainties in a box with a trick
padlock that accompanied him from his first appearance at
Gummidge's in a billycock hat to the rather abrupt conclusion
of his schooldays.

From a boy's point of view he looked distastefully foreign
with his yellowish skin, slow chocolate-coloured eyes, and
lean weak figure. Merely for his looks, he was treated by
most of us true-blue Englishmen with condescension, hostility,
or contempt. We used to call him 'Pongo', but without
any much better excuse for the nickname than his skin. He
was, that is, in one sense of the term what he assuredly was
not in the other sense, a sport.

Seaton and I, as I may say, were never in any sense intimate
at school; our orbits only intersected in class. I kept deliber-
ately aloof from him. I felt vaguely he was a sneak, and
remained quite unmollified by advances on his side, which, in
a boy's barbarous fashion, unless it suited me to be magnani-
mous, I haughtily ignored.

We were both of us quick-footed, and at Prisoner's Base used
occasionally to hide together. And so I best remember
Seaton—his narrow watchful face in the dusk of a summer
evening; his peculiar crouch, and his inarticulate whisperings

and mumblings. Otherwise he played all games slackly and limply; used to stand and feed at his locker with a crony or two until his 'tuck' gave out; or waste his money on some outlandish fancy or other. He bought, for instance, a silver bangle, which he wore above his left elbow, until some of the fellows showed their masterly contempt of the practice by dropping it nearly red-hot down his neck.

It needed, therefore, a rather peculiar taste, and a rather rare kind of schoolboy courage and indifference to criticism, to be much associated with him. And I had neither the taste, nor, probably, the courage. None the less, he did make advances, and on one memorable occasion went to the length of bestowing on me a whole pot of some outlandish mulberry-coloured jelly that had been duplicated in his term's supplies. In the exuberance of my gratitude, I promised to spend the next half-term holiday with him at his aunt's house.

I had clean forgotten my promise when, two or three days before the holiday, he came up and triumphantly reminded me of it.

'Well, to tell you the honest truth, Seaton, old chap——' I began graciously: but he cut me short.

'My aunt expects you,' he said; 'she is very glad you are coming. She's sure to be quite decent to *you*, Withers.'

I looked at him in sheer astonishment; the emphasis was so uncalled for. It seemed to suggest an aunt not hitherto hinted at, and a friendly feeling on Seaton's side that was far more disconcerting than welcome.

We reached his aunt's house, partly by train, partly by a lift in an empty farm-cart, and partly by walking. It was a whole-day holiday, and we were to sleep the night; he lent me extraordinary night-gear, I remember. The village street was unusually wide, and was fed from a green by two converging roads, with an inn and a high green sign at the corner. About a hundred yards down the street was a chemist's shop—a Mr. Tanner's. We descended the two steps into his dusky and odorous interior to buy, I remember, some rat poison. A little beyond the chemist's was the forge. You then walked along a very narrow path, under a fairly high wall, nodding here and there with weeds and tufts of grass, and so came to the iron garden-gates, and saw the high flat house behind its huge sycamore. A coach-house stood on the left of the house, and on the right a gate led into a kind of rambling orchard. The lawn lay away over to the left again, and at the bottom (for the whole garden sloped gently to a sluggish and rushy pond-like stream) was a meadow.

We arrived at noon, and entered the gates out of the hot dust beneath the glitter of the dark-curtained windows. Seaton led me at once through the little garden-gate to show me his tadpole pond, swarming with what (being myself not in the least interested in low life) seemed to me the most horrible creatures—of all shapes, consistencies, and sizes, but with which Seaton was obviously on the most intimate of terms. I can see his absorbed face now as, squatting on his heels, he fished the slimy things out in his sallow palms. Wearying at last of these pets, we loitered about awhile in an aimless fashion. Seaton seemed to be listening, or at any rate waiting, for something to happen or for someone to come. But nothing did happen and no one came.

That was just like Seaton. Anyhow, the first view I got of his aunt was when, at the summons of a distant gong, we turned from the garden, very hungry and thirsty, to go into luncheon. We were approaching the house, when Seaton suddenly came to a standstill. Indeed, I have always had the impression that he plucked at my sleeve. Something, at least, seemed to catch me back, as it were, as he cried, 'Look out, there she is!'

She was standing at an upper window which opened wide on a hinge, and at first sight she looked an excessively tall and overwhelming figure. This, however, was mainly because the window reached all but to the floor of her bedroom. She was in reality rather an undersized woman, in spite of her long face and big head. She must have stood, I think, unusually still, with eyes fixed on us, though this impression may be due to Seaton's sudden warning and to my consciousness of the cautious and subdued air that had fallen on him at sight of her. I know that without the least reason in the world I felt a kind of guiltiness, as if I had been 'caught'. There was a silvery star pattern sprinkled on her black silk dress, and even from the ground I could see the immense coils of her hair and the rings on her left hand which was held fingering the small jet buttons of her bodice. She watched our united advance without stirring, until, imperceptibly, her eyes raised and lost themselves in the distance, so that it was out of an assumed reverie that she appeared suddenly to awaken to our presence beneath her when we drew close to the house.

'So this is your friend, Mr. Smithers, I suppose?' she said, bobbing to me.

'Withers, aunt,' said Seaton.

'It's much the same,' she said, with eyes fixed on me. 'Come in, Mr. Withers, and bring him along with you.'

She continued to gaze at me—at least, I think she did so. I know that the fixity of her scrutiny and her ironical 'Mr.' made me feel peculiarly uncomfortable. None the less she was extremely kind and attentive to me, though, no doubt, her kindness and attention showed up more vividly against her complete neglect of Seaton. Only one remark that I have any recollection of she made to him: 'When I look on my nephew, Mr. Smithers, I realize that dust we are, and dust shall become. You are hot, dirty, and incorrigible, Arthur.'

She sat at the head of the table, Seaton at the foot, and I, before a wide waste of damask tablecloth, between them. It was an old and rather close dining-room, with windows thrown wide to the green garden and a wonderful cascade of fading roses. Miss Seaton's great chair faced this window, so that its rose-reflected light shone full on her yellowish face, and on just such chocolate eyes as my schoolfellow's, except that hers were more than half covered by unusually long and heavy lids.

There she sat, steadily eating, with those sluggish eyes fixed for the most part on my face; above them stood the deep-lined fork between her eyebrows; and above that the wide expanse of a remarkable brow beneath its strange steep bank of hair. The lunch was copious, and consisted, I remember, of all such dishes as are generally considered too rich and too good for the schoolboy digestion—lobster mayonnaise, cold game sausages, an immense veal and ham pie farced with eggs, truffles, and numberless delicious flavours; besides kickshaws, creams and sweetmeats. We even had a wine, a half-glass of old darkish sherry each.

Miss Seaton enjoyed and indulged an enormous appetite. Her example and a natural schoolboy voracity soon overcame my nervousness of her, even to the extent of allowing me to enjoy to the best of my bent so rare a spread. Seaton was singularly modest; the greater part of his meal consisted of almonds and raisins, which he nibbled surreptitiously and as if he found difficulty in swallowing them.

I don't mean that Miss Seaton 'conversed' with me. She merely scattered trenchant remarks and now and then twinkled a baited question over my head. But her face was like a dense and involved accompaniment to her talk. She presently dropped the 'Mr.', to my intense relief, and called me now Withers, or Wither, now Smithers, and even once towards the end of the meal distinctly Johnson, though how on earth my name suggested it, or whose face mine had reanimated in memory, I cannot conceive.

'And is Arthur a good boy at school, Mr. Wither?' was one of her many questions. 'Does he please his masters? Is he first in his class? What does the reverend Dr. Gummidge think of him, eh?'

I knew she was jeering at him, but her face was adamant against the least flicker of sarcasm or facetiousness. I gazed fixedly at a blushing crescent of lobster.

'I think you're eighth, aren't you, Seaton?'

Seaton moved his small pupils towards his aunt. But she continued to gaze with a kind of concentrated detachment at me.

'Arthur will never make a brilliant scholar, I fear,' she said, lifting a dexterously burdened fork to her wide mouth. . . .

After luncheon she preceded me up to my bedroom. It was a jolly little bedroom, with a brass fender and rugs and a polished floor, on which it was possible, I afterwards found, to play 'snow-shoes'. Over the washstand was a little black-framed water-colour drawing, depicting a large eye with an extremely fishlike intensity in the spark of light on the dark pupil; and in 'illuminated' lettering beneath was printed very minutely, 'Thou God Seest ME', followed by a long looped monogram, 'S.S.', in the corner. The other pictures were all of the sea; brigs on blue water; a schooner overtopping chalk cliffs; a rocky island of prodigious steepness, with two tiny sailors dragging a monstrous boat up a shelf of beach.

'This is the room, Withers, my poor dear brother William died in when a boy. Admire the view!'

I looked out of the window across the tree-tops. It was a day hot with sunshine over the green fields, and the cattle were standing swishing their tails in the shallow water. But the view at the moment was no doubt made more vividly impressive by the apprehension that she would presently enquire after my luggage, and I had brought not even a toothbrush. I need have had no fear. Hers was not that highly civilized type of mind that is stuffed with sharp, material details. Nor could her ample presence be described as in the least motherly.

'I would never consent to question a schoolfellow behind my nephew's back,' she said, standing in the middle of the room, 'but tell me, Smithers, why is Arthur so unpopular? You, I understand, are his only close friend.' She stood in a dazzle of sun, and out of it her eyes regarded me with such leaden penetration beneath their thick lids that I doubt if my face concealed the least thought from her. 'But there, there,' she added very suavely, stooping her head a little, 'don't trouble to answer me. I never extort an answer. Boys are queer fish. Brains might perhaps have suggested his washing his hands before luncheon; but—not my choice, Smithers. God forbid! And now, perhaps, you would like to go into the garden again. I cannot actually see from here, but I should not be surprised if Arthur is now skulking behind that hedge.'

He was. I saw his head come out and take a rapid glance at the windows.

'Join him, Mr. Smithers; we shall meet again, I hope, at the tea-table. The afternoon I spend in retirement.'

Whether or not, Seaton and I had not been long engaged with the aid of two green switches in riding round and round a lumbering old grey horse we found in the meadow, before a rather bunched-up figure appeared, walking along the field-path on the other side of the water, with a magenta parasol studiously lowered in our direction throughout her slow progress, as if that were the magnetic needle and we the fixed Pole. Seaton at once lost all nerve and interest. At the next lurch of the old mare's heels he toppled over into the grass, and I slid off the sleek broad back to join him where he stood, rubbing his shoulder and sourly watching the rather pompous figure till it was out of sight.

'Was that your aunt, Seaton?' I enquired; but not till then. He nodded.

'Why didn't she take any notice of us, then?'

'She never does.'

'Why not?'

'Oh, she knows all right, without; that's the dam awful part of it.' Seaton was one of the very few fellows at Gummidge's who had the ostentation to use bad language. He had suffered for it too. But it wasn't, I think, bravado. I believe he really felt certain things more intensely than most of the other fellows, and they were generally things that fortunate and average people do not feel at all—the peculiar quality, for instance, of the British schoolboy's imagination.

'I tell you, Withers,' he went on moodily, slinking across the meadow with his hands covered up in his pockets, 'she sees everything. And what she doesn't see she knows without.'

'But how?' I said, not because I was much interested, but because the afternoon was so hot and tiresome and purpose-less, and it seemed more of a bore to remain silent. Seaton turned gloomily and spoke in a very low voice.

'Don't appear to be talking of her, if you wouldn't mind. It's—because she's in league with the Devil.' He nodded his head and stooped to pick up a round, flat pebble. 'I tell you,' he said, still stooping, 'you fellows don't realize what it is. I know I'm a bit close and all that. But so would you be if you had that old hag listening to every thought you think.'

I looked at him, then turned and surveyed one by one the windows of the house.

'Where's your *pater*?' I said awkwardly.

'Dead, ages and ages ago, and my mother too. She's not my aunt even by rights.'

'What is she, then?'

'I mean, she's not my mother's sister, because my grandmother married twice; and she's one of the first lot. I don't know what you call her, but anyhow she's not my real aunt.'

'She gives you plenty of pocket-money.'

Seaton looked steadfastly at me out of his flat eyes. 'She can't give me what's mine. When I come of age half of the whole lot will be mine; and what's more'—he turned his back on the house—'I'll make her hand over every blessed shilling of it.'

I put my hands in my pockets and stared at Seaton; 'Is it much?'

He nodded.

'Who told you?' He got suddenly very angry; a darkish red came into his cheeks, his eyes glistened, but he made no answer, and we loitered listlessly about the garden until it was time for tea. . . .

Seaton's aunt was wearing an extraordinary kind of lace jacket when we sidled sheepishly into the drawing-room together. She greeted me with a heavy and protracted smile, and bade me bring a chair close to the little table.

'I hope Arthur has made you feel at home,' she said as she handed me my cup in her crooked hand. 'He don't talk much to me; but then I'm an old woman. You must come again, Wither, and draw him out of his shell. You old snail!' She wagged her head at Seaton, who sat munching cake and watching her intently.

'And we must correspond, perhaps.' She nearly shut her eyes at me. 'You must write and tell me everything behind the creature's back.' I confess I found her rather disquieting company. The evening drew on. Lamps were brought in by a man with a nondescript face and very quiet footsteps.

Seaton was told to bring out the chess-men. And we played a game, she and I, with her big chin thrust over the board at every move as she gloated over the pieces and occasionally croaked 'Check!'—after which she would sit back inscrutably staring at me. But the game was never finished. She simply hemmed me in with a gathering cloud of pieces that held me impotent, and yet one and all refused to adminster to my poor flustered old king a merciful *coup de grâce*.

'There,' she said, as the clock struck ten—'a drawn game, Withers. We are very evenly matched. A very creditable defence, Withers. You know your room. There's supper on a tray in the dining-room. Don't let the creature over-eat himself. The gong will sound three-quarters of an hour *before* a punctual breakfast.' She held out her cheek to Seaton, and he kissed it with obvious perfunctoriness. With me she shook hands.

'An excellent game,' she said cordially, 'but my memory is poor, and'—she swept the pieces helter-skelter into the box—'the result will never be known.' She raised her great head far back. 'Eh?'

It was a kind of challenge, and I could only murmur: 'Oh, I was absolutely in a hole, you know!' when she burst out laughing and waved us both out of the room.

Seaton and I stood and ate our supper, with one candlestick to light us, in a corner of the dining-room. 'Well, and how would you like it?' he said very softly, after cautiously poking his head round the doorway.

'Like what?'

'Being spied on—every blessed thing you do and think?'

'I shouldn't like it at all,' I said, 'if she does.'

'And yet you let her smash you up at chess!'

'I didn't let her!' I said indignantly.

'Well, you funked it, then.'

'And I didn't funk it either,' I said; 'she's so jolly clever with her knights.' Seaton stared at the candle. 'Knights,' he said slowly. 'You wait, that's all.' And we went upstairs to bed.

I had not been long in bed, I think, when I was cautiously

awakened by a touch on my shoulder. And there was Seaton's face in the candlelight—and his eyes looking into mine.

'What's up?' I said, lurching on to my elbow.

'*Ssh!* Don't scurry,' he whispered. 'She'll hear. I'm sorry for waking you, but I didn't think you'd be asleep so soon.'

'Why, what's the time, then?' Seaton wore, what was then rather unusual, a night-suit, and he hauled his big silver watch out of the pocket in his jacket.

'It's a quarter to twelve. I never get to sleep before twelve —not here.'

'What do you do, then?'

'Oh, I read: and listen.'

'Listen?'

Seaton stared into his candle-flame as if he were listening even then. 'You can't guess what it is. All you read in ghost stories, that's all rot. You can't see much, Withers, but you know all the same.'

'Know what?'

'Why, that they're there.'

'Who's there?' I asked fretfully, glancing at the door.

'Why in the house. It swarms with 'em. Just you stand still and listen outside my bedroom door in the middle of the night. I have, dozens of times; they're all over the place.'

'Look here, Seaton,' I said, 'you asked me to come here, and I didn't mind chucking up a leave just to oblige you and because I'd promised; but don't get talking a lot of rot, that's all, or you'll know the difference when we get back.'

'Don't fret,' he said coldly, turning away. 'I shan't be at school long. And what's more, you're here now, and there isn't anybody else to talk to. I'll chance the other.'

'Look here, Seaton,' I said, 'you may think you're going to scare me with a lot of stuff about voices and all that. But I'll just thank you to clear out; and you may please yourself about pottering about all night.'

He made no answer; he was standing by the dressing table looking across his candle into the looking-glass; he turned and stared slowly round the walls.

'Even this room's nothing more than a coffin. I suppose she

told you—"It's all exactly the same as when my brother
William died"—trust her for that! And good luck to him, say
I. Look at that.' He raised his candle close to the little water-
colour I have mentioned. 'There's hundreds of eyes like that
in this house; and even if God does see you, He takes precious
good care you don't see Him. And it's just the same with
them. I tell you what, Withers, I'm getting sick of all this. I
shan't stand it much longer.'

The house was silent within and without, and even in the
yellowish radiance of the candle a faint silver showed through
the open window on my blind. I slipped off the bedclothes,
wide awake, and sat irresolute on the bedside.

'I know you're only guying me,' I said angrily, 'but why is
the house full of—what you say? Why do you hear—what
you *do* hear? Tell me that, you silly fool!'

Seaton sat down on a chair and rested his candlestick on his
knee. He blinked at me calmly. 'She brings them,' he said,
with lifted eyebrows.

'Who? Your aunt?'

He nodded.

'How?'

'I told you,' he answered pettishly. 'She's in league. You
don't know. She as good as killed my mother; I know that.
But it's not only her by a long chalk. She just sucks you dry.
I know. And that's what she'll do for me; because I'm like
her—like my mother I mean. She simply hates to see me
alive. I wouldn't be like that old she-wolf for a million pounds.
And so'—he broke off, with a comprehensive wave of his
candlestick—'they're always here. Ah, my boy, wait till
she's dead! She'll hear something then, I can tell you. It's
all very well now, but wait till then! I wouldn't be in her
shoes when she has to clear out—for something. Don't you
go and believe I care for ghosts, or whatever you like to call
them. We're all in the same box. We're all under her thumb.'

He was looking almost nonchalantly at the ceiling at the
moment, when I saw his face change, saw his eyes suddenly
drop like shot birds and fix themselves on the cranny of the
door he had left just ajar. Even from where I sat I could see

his cheek change colour; it went greenish. He crouched with-out stirring, like an animal. And I, scarcely daring to breathe, sat with creeping skin, sourly watching him. His hands relaxed, and he gave a kind of sigh.

'Was *that* one?' I whispered, with a timid show of jauntiness. He looked round, opened his mouth, and nodded. 'What?' I said. He jerked his thumb with meaningful eyes, and I knew that he meant that his aunt had been there listening at our door cranny.

'Look here, Seaton,' I said once more, wriggling to my feet. 'You may think I'm a jolly noodle; just as you please. But your aunt has been civil to me and all that, and I don't believe a word you say about her, that's all, and never did. Every fellow's a bit off his pluck at night, and you may think it a fine sport to try your rubbish on me. I heard your aunt come upstairs before I fell asleep. And I'll bet you a level tanner she's in bed now. What's more, you can keep your blessed ghosts to yourself. It's a guilty conscience, I should think.'

Seaton looked at me intently, without answering for a moment. 'I'm not a liar, Withers; but I'm not going to quarrel either. You're the only chap I care a button for; or, at any rate, you're the only chap that's ever come here; and it's something to tell a fellow what you feel. I don't care a fig for fifty thousand ghosts, although I swear on my solemn oath that I know they're here. But she'—he turned deliber-ately—'you laid a tanner she's in bed, Withers; well, I know different. She's never in bed much of the night, and I'll prove it too, just to show you I'm not such a nolly as you think I am. Come on!'

'Come on where?'

'Why, to see.'

I hesitated. He opened a large cupboard and took out a small dark dressing-gown and a kind of shawl-jacket. He threw the jacket on the bed and put on the gown. His dusky face was colourless, and I could see by the way he fumbled at the sleeves he was shivering. But it was no good showing the white feather now. So I threw the tasselled shawl over my shoulders and, leaving our candle brightly burning on the chair, we went out together and stood in the corridor.

'Now then, listen!' Seaton whispered.

We stood leaning over the staircase. It was like leaning over a well, so still and chill the air was all around us. But presently, as I suppose happens in most old houses, began to echo and answer in my ears a medley of infinite small stirrings and whisperings. Now out of the distance an old timber would relax its fibres, or a scurry die away behind the perishing wainscot. But amid and behind such sounds as these I seemed to begin to be conscious, as it were, of the lightest of footfalls, sounds as faint as the vanishing remembrance of voices in a dream. Seaton was all in obscurity except his face; out of that his eyes gleamed darkly, watching me.

'You'd hear, too, in time, my fine soldier,' he muttered. 'Come on!'

He descended the stairs, slipping his lean fingers lightly along the balusters. He turned to the right at the loop, and I followed him barefooted along a thickly-carpeted corridor. At the end stood a door ajar. And from here we very stealthily and in complete blackness ascended five narrow stairs. Seaton, with immense caution, slowly pushed open a door, and we stood together, looking into a great pool of duskiness, out of which, lit by the feeble clearness of a night-light, rose a vast bed. A heap of clothes lay on the floor; beside them two slippers dozed, with noses each to each, a foot or two apart. Somewhere a little clock ticked huskily. There was a close smell; lavender and eau-de-Cologne, mingled with the fragrance of ancient sachets, soap, and drugs. Yet it was a scent even more peculiarly compounded than that.

And the bed! I stared warily in; it was mounded gigantically, and it was empty.

Seaton turned a vague pale face, all shadows: 'What did I say?' he muttered. 'Who's—who's the fool now, I say? How are we going to get back without meeting her, I say? Answer me that! Oh, I wish to God you hadn't come here, Withers.'

He stood audibly shivering in his skimpy gown, and could hardly speak for his teeth chattering. And very distinctly, in the hush that followed his whisper, I heard approaching a faint unhurried voluminous rustle. Seaton clutched my arm, dragged me to the right across the room to a large cupboard, and drew the door close to on us. And, presently, as with bursting lungs I peeped out into the long, low, curtained bedroom, waddled in that wonderful great head and body. I can see her now, all patched and lined with shadow, her tied-up hair (she must have had enormous quantities of it for so old a woman), her heavy lids above those flat, slow, vigilant eyes. She just passed across my ken in the vague dusk; but the bed was out of sight.

We waited on and on, listening to the clock's muffled ticking. Not the ghost of a sound rose up from the great bed. Either she lay archly listening or slept a sleep serener than an infant's. And when, it seemed, we had been hours in hiding and were cramped, chilled, and half suffocated, we crept out on all fours, with terror knocking at our ribs, and so down the five narrow stairs and back to the little candle-lit blue-and-gold bedroom.

Once there, Seaton gave in. He sat livid on a chair with closed eyes.

'Here,' I said, shaking his arm, 'I'm going to bed; I've had enough of this foolery; I'm going to bed.' His lips quivered, but he made no answer. I poured out some water into my basin and, with that cold pictured azure eye fixed on us, bespattered Seaton's sallow face and forehead and dabbled his hair. He presently sighed and opened fish-like eyes.

'Come on!' I said. 'Don't get shamming, there's a good chap. Get on my back, if you like, and I'll carry you into your bedroom.'

He waved me away and stood up. So, with my candle in one hand, I took him under the arm and walked him along according to his direction down the corridor. His was a much dingier room than mine, and littered with boxes, paper, cages, and clothes. I huddled him into bed and turned to go. And suddenly, I can hardly explain it now, a kind of cold and deadly terror swept over me. I almost ran out of the room, with eyes fixed rigidly in front of me, blew out my candle, and buried my head under the bedclothes.

When I awoke, roused not by a gong, but by a long-continued tapping at my door, sunlight was raying in on cornice and bedpost, and birds were singing in the garden. I got up, ashamed of the night's folly, dressed quickly, and went downstairs. The breakfast room was sweet with flowers and fruit and honey. Seaton's aunt was standing in the garden beside the open french window, feeding a great flutter of birds. I watched her for a moment, unseen. Her face was set in a deep reverie beneath the shadow of a big loose sun-hat. It was deeply lined, crooked, and, in a way I can't describe, fixedly vacant and strange. I coughed politely, and she turned with a prodigious, smiling grimace to ask how I had slept. And in that mysterious fashion by which we learn each other's secret thoughts without a syllable said, I knew that she had followed every word and movement of the night before, and was triumphing over my affected innocence and ridiculing my friendly and too easy advances.

We returned to school, Seaton and I, lavishly laden, and by rail all the way. I made no reference to the obscure talk we had had, and resolutely refused to meet his eyes or to take up the hints he let fall. I was relieved—and yet I was sorry—to be going back, and strode on as fast as I could from the station, with Seaton almost trotting at my heels. But he insisted on buying more fruit and sweets—my share of which I accepted with a very bad grace. It was uncomfortably like a bribe; and, after all, I had no quarrel with his rum old aunt, and hadn't really believed half the stuff he had told me.

I saw as little of him as I could after that. He never referred to our visit or resumed his confidences, though in class I would sometimes catch his eye fixed on mine, full of a mute understanding, which I easily affected not to understand. He left Gummidge's, as I have said, rather abruptly, though I never heard of anything to his discredit. And I did not see him or have any news of him again till by chance we met one summer afternoon in the Strand.

He was dressed rather oddly in a coat too large for him and

a bright silky tie. But we instantly recognized one another under the awning of a cheap jeweller's shop. He immediately attached himself to me and dragged me off, not too cheerfully, to lunch with him at an Indian restaurant near by. He chattered about our old school, which he remembered only with dislike and disgust; told me cold-bloodedly of the disastrous fate of one or two of the older fellows who had been among his chief tormentors; insisted on an expensive wine and the whole gamut of the foreign menu; and finally informed me, with a good deal of niggling, that he had come up to town to buy an engagement-ring.

And of course: 'How is your aunt?' I enquired at last.

He seemed to have been awaiting the question. It fell like a stone into a deep pool, so many expressions flitted across his long, sad, sallow, un-English face.

'She's aged a good deal,' he said softly, and broke off.

'She's been very decent,' he continued presently after, and paused again. 'In a way.' He eyed me fleetingly. 'I dare say you heard that—she—that is, that we—had lost a good deal of money.'

'No,' I said.

'Oh, yes!' said Seaton, and paused again.

And somehow, poor fellow, I knew in the clink and clatter of glass and voices that he had lied to me; that he did not possess, and never had possessed, a penny beyond what his aunt had squandered on his too ample allowance of pocket-money.

'And the ghosts?' I enquired quizzically.

He grew instantly solemn, and, though it may have been my fancy, slightly yellowed. But 'You are making game of me, Withers,' was all he said.

He asked for my address, and I rather reluctantly gave him my card.

'Look here, Withers,' he said , as we stood together in the sunlight on the kerb, saying good-bye, 'here I am, and—and it's all very well. I'm not perhaps as fanciful as I was. But you are practically the only friend I have on earth—except Alice. . . . And there—to make a clean breast of it, I'm not sure that my aunt cares much about my getting married. She doesn't say so, of course. You know her well enough for that.' He looked sidelong at the rattling gaudy traffic.

'What I was going to say is this: Would you mind coming down? You needn't stay the night unless you please, though, of course, you know you would be awfully welcome. But I should like you to meet my—to meet Alice; and then, perhaps you might tell me your honest opinion of—of the other too.'

I vaguely demurred. He pressed me. And we parted with a half promise that I would come. He waved his ball-topped cane at me and ran off in his long jacket after a bus.

A letter arrived soon after, in his small weak handwriting, giving me full particulars regarding route and trains. And without the least curiosity, even perhaps with some little annoyance that chance should have thrown us together again, I accepted his invitation and arrived one hazy midday at his out-of-the-way station to find him sitting on a low seat under a clump of 'double' hollyhocks, awaiting me.

He looked preoccupied and singularly listless; but seemed, none the less, to be pleased to see me.

We walked up the village street, past the little dingy apothecary's and the empty forge, and, as on my first visit, skirted the house together, and, instead of entering by the front door, made our way down the green path into the garden at the back. A pale haze of cloud muffled the sun; the garden lay in a grey shimmer—its old trees, its snap-dragoned faintly glittering walls. But now there was an air of slovenliness where before all had been neat and methodical. In a patch of shallowly dug soil stood a worn-down spade leaning against a tree. There was an old decayed wheelbarrow. The roses had run to leaf and briar; the fruit-trees were unpruned. The goddess of neglect had made it her secret resort.

'You ain't much of a gardener, Seaton,' I said at last, with a sigh of relief.

'I think, do you know, I like it best like this,' said Seaton. 'We haven't any man now, of course. Can't afford it.' He stood staring at his little dark oblong of freshly turned earth. 'And it always seems to me,' he went on ruminatingly, 'that, after all, we are all nothing better than interlopers on the earth, disfiguring and staining wherever we go. It may sound shocking blasphemy to say so; but then it's different here, you see. We are further away.'

'To tell you the truth, Seaton, I *don't* quite see,' I said; 'but it isn't a new philosophy, is it? Anyhow it's a precious beastly one.'

'It's only what I think,' he replied, with all his odd old stubborn meekness. 'And one thinks as one *is*.'

We wandered on together, talking little, and still with that expression of uneasy vigilance on Seaton's face. He pulled out his watch as we stood gazing idly over the green meadows and the dark motionless bulrushes.

'I think, perhaps, it's nearly time for lunch,' he said. 'Would you like to come in?'

We turned and walked slowly towards the house, across whose windows I confess my own eyes, too, went restlessly meandering in search of its rather disconcerting inmate. There was a pathetic look of bedraggledness, of want of means and care, rust and overgrowth and faded paint. Seaton's aunt, a little to my relief, did not share our meal. So he carved the cold meat, and dispatched a heaped-up plate by an elderly servant for his aunt's private consumption. We talked little and in half-suppressed tones, and sipped some Madeira which Seaton after listening for a moment or two fetched out of the great mahogany sideboard.

I played him a dull and effortless game of chess, yawning between the moves he himself made almost at haphazard, and with attention elsewhere engaged. Towards five o'clock came the sound of a distant ring, and Seaton jumped up, overturning the board, and so ended a game that else might have fatuously continued to this day. He effusively excused himself, and after some little while returned with a slim, dark, pale-faced girl of about nineteen, in a white gown and hat, to whom I was presented with some little nervousness as his 'dear old friend and schoolfellow'.

We talked on in the golden afternoon light, still, as it seemed to me, and even in spite of our efforts to be lively and gay, in a half-suppressed, lack-lustre fashion. We all seemed, if it were not my fancy, to be expectant, to be almost anxiously awaiting an arrival, the appearance of someone whose image filled our collective consciousness. Seaton talked least of all, and in a restless interjectory way, as he continually fidgeted from chair to chair. At last he proposed a stroll in the garden before the sun should have quite gone down.

Alice walked between us. Her hair and eyes were conspicuously dark against the whiteness of her gown. She carried herself not ungracefully, and yet with peculiarly little movement of her arms and body, and answered us both without turning her head. There was a curious provocative reserve in that impassive melancholy face. It seemed to be haunted by some tragic influence of which she herself was unaware.

And yet somehow I knew—I believe we all knew—that this walk, this discussion of their future plans was a futility. I had nothing to base such scepticism on, except only a vague sense of oppression, a foreboding consciousness of some inert invincible power in the background, to whom optimistic plans and love-making and youth are as chaff and thistledown. We came back, silent, in the last light. Seaton's aunt was there— under an old brass lamp. Her hair was as barbarously massed and curled as ever. Her eyelids, I think, hung even a little heavier in age over their slow-moving, inscrutable pupils. We filed in softly out of the evening, and I made my bow.

'In this short interval, Mr. Withers,' she remarked amiably, 'you have put off youth, put on the man. Dear me, how sad it is to see the young days vanishing! Sit down. My nephew tells me you met by chance—or act of Providence, shall we call it?—and in my beloved Strand! You, I understand, are to be best man—yes, best man! Or am I divulging secrets?' She surveyed Arthur and Alice with overwhelming graciousness. They sat apart on two low chairs and smiled in return.

'And Arthur—how do you think Arthur is looking?'

'I think he looks very much in need of a change,' I said.

'A change! Indeed?' She all but shut her eyes at me and with an exaggerated sentimentality shook her head. 'My dear Mr. Withers! Are we not *all* in need of a change in this fleeting, fleeting world?' She mused over the remark like a connoisseur. 'And you,' she continued, turning abruptly to Alice, 'I hope you pointed out to Mr. Withers all my pretty bits?'

'We only walked round the garden,' the girl replied; then, glancing at Seaton, added almost inaudibly, 'it's a very beautiful evening.'

'*Is* it?' said the old lady, starting up violently. 'Then on this very beautiful evening we will go in to supper. Mr. Withers, your arm; Arthur, bring in your bride.'

We were a queer quartet, I thought to myself, as I solemnly led the way into the faded, chilly dining-room, with this indefinable old creature leaning wooingly on my arm—the large flat bracelet on the yellow-laced wrist. She fumed a little, breathing heavily, but as if with an effort of the mind rather than of the body; for she had grown much stouter and yet little more proportionate. And to talk into that great white face, so close to mine, was a queer experience in the dim light of the corridor, and even in the twinkling crystal of the candles. She was naïve—appallingly naïve; she was crafty and challenging; she was even arch; and all these in the brief, rather puffy passage from one room to the other, with these two tongue-tied children bringing up the rear. The meal was tremendous. I have never seen such a monstrous salad. But the dishes were greasy and over-spiced, and were indifferently cooked. One thing only was quite unchanged— my hostess's appetite was as Gargantuan as ever. The heavy candelabra that lighted us stood before her high-backed chair. Seaton sat a little removed, his plate almost in darkness.

And throughout this prodigious meal his aunt talked, mainly to me, mainly *at* him, but with an occasional satirical sally at Alice and muttered explosions of reprimand to the servant. She had aged, and yet, if it be not nonsense to say so, seemed no older. I suppose to the Pyramids a decade is but as the rustling down of a handful of dust. And she reminded me of some such unshakable prehistoricism. She certainly was an amazing talker—rapid, egregious, with a delivery that was perfectly overwhelming. As for Seaton—her flashes of silence

were for him. On her enormous volubility would suddenly
fall a hush: acid sarcasm would be left implied; and she would
sit softly moving her great head, with eyes fixed full in a
dreamy smile; but with her whole attention, one could see,
slowly, joyously absorbing his mute discomfiture.

She confided in us her views on a theme vaguely occupying
at the moment, I suppose, all our minds. 'We have barbarous
institutions, and so must put up, I suppose, with a never-
ending procession of fools—of fools *ad infinitum*. Marriage, Mr.
Withers, was instituted in the privacy of a garden; *sub rosa*, as
it were. Civilization flaunts it in the glare of day. The dull
marry the poor; the rich the effete; and so our New Jerusalem
is peopled with naturals, plain and coloured, at either end. I
detest folly; I detest still more (if I must be frank, dear
Arthur) mere cleverness. Mankind has simply become a tail-
less host of uninstinctive animals. We should never have taken
to Evolution, Mr. Withers. "Natural Selection!"—little gods
and fishes!—the deaf for the dumb. We should have used our
brains—intellectual pride, the ecclesiastics call it. And by
brains I mean—what do I mean, Alice?—I mean, my dear
child,' and she laid two gross fingers on Alice's narrow sleeve,
'I mean courage. Consider it, Arthur. I read that the scientific
world is once more beginning to be afraid of spiritual agencies.
Spiritual agencies that tap, and actually float, bless their
hearts! I think just one more of those mulberries—thank you.

'They talk about "blind Love",' she ran on derisively as she
helped herself, her eyes roving over the dish, 'but why blind?
I think, Mr. Withers from weeping over its rickets. After all,
it is we plain women that triumph, is it not so—beyond the
mockery of time. Alice, now! Fleeting, fleeting is youth, my
child. What's that you were confiding to your plate, Arthur.
Satirical boy. He laughs at his old aunt: nay, but thou didst
laugh. He detests all sentiment. He whispers the most acid
asides. Come, my love, we will leave these cynics; we will go
and commiserate with each other on our sex. The choice of
two evils, Mr. Smithers!' I opened the door, and she swept out
as if borne on a torrent of unintelligible indignation; and
Arthur and I were left in the clear four-flamed light alone.

For a while we sat in silence. He shook his head at my cigarette-case, and I lit a cigarette. Presently he fidgeted in his chair and poked his head forward into the light. He paused to rise, and shut again the shut door.

'How long will you be?' he asked me.

I laughed.

'Oh, it's not that!' he said, in some confusion. 'Of course, I like to be with her. But it's not that. The truth is, Withers, I don't care about leaving her too long with my aunt.'

I hesitated. He looked at me questioningly.

'Look here, Seaton,' I said, 'you know well enough that I don't want to interfere in your affairs, or to offer advice where it is not wanted. But don't you think perhaps you may not treat your aunt quite in the right way? As one gets old, you know, a little give and take. I have an old godmother, or something of the kind. She's a bit queer too. . . . A little allowance; it does no harm. But hang it all, I'm no preacher.'

He sat down with his hands in his pockets and still with his eyes fixed almost incredulously on mine. 'How?' he said.

'Well, my dear fellow, if I'm any judge—mind, I don't say that I am—but I can't help thinking she thinks you don't care for her; and perhaps takes your silence for—for bad temper. She has been very decent to you, hasn't she?'

' "Decent"? My God!' said Seaton.

I smoked on in silence; but he continued to look at me with that peculiar concentration I remembered of old.

'I don't think, perhaps, Withers,' he began presently, 'I don't think you quite understand. Perhaps you are not quite our kind. You always did, just like the other fellows, guy me at school. You laughed at me that night you came to stay here—about the voices and all that. But I don't mind being laughed at—because I know.'

'Know what?' It was the same old system of dull question and evasive answer.

'I mean I know that what we see and hear is only the smallest fraction of what is. I know she lives quite out of this. She *talks* to you; but it's all make-believe. It's all a "parlour game". She's not really with you; only pitting her outside wits against yours and enjoying the fooling. She's living on inside on what you're rotten without. That's what it is—a cannibal feast. She's a spider. It doesn't much matter what you call it. It means the same kind of thing. I tell you, Withers, she hates me; and you can scarcely dream what that hatred means. I used to think I had an inkling of the reason. It's oceans deeper than that. It just lies behind: herself against myself. Why, after all, how much do we really understand of anything? We don't even know our own histories, and not a tenth, not a tenth of the reasons. What has life been to me?— nothing but a trap. And when one sets oneself free for a while, it only begins again. I thought you might understand; but you are on a different level: that's all.'

'What on earth are you talking about?' I said contemptuously, in spite of myself.

'I mean what I say,' he said gutturally. 'All this outside's only make-believe—but there! what's the good of talking? So far as this is concerned I'm as good as done. You wait.'

Seaton blew out three of the candles and, leaving the vacant room in semi-darkness, we groped our way along the corridor to the drawing-room. There a full moon stood shining in at the long garden windows. Alice sat stooping at the door, with her hands clasped in her lap, looking out, alone.

'Where is she?' Seaton asked in a low tone.

She looked up; and their eyes met in a glance of instantaneous understanding, and the door immediately afterwards opened behind us.

'*Such* a moon!' said a voice, that once heard, remained unforgettably on the ear. 'A night for lovers, Mr. Withers, if ever there was one. Get a shawl, my dear Arthur, and take Alice for a little promenade. I dare say we old cronies will manage to keep awake. Hasten, hasten, Romeo! My poor, poor Alice, how laggard a lover!'

Seaton returned with a shawl. They drifted out into the moonlight. My companion gazed after them till they were out of hearing, turned to me gravely, and suddenly twisted her white face into such a convulsion of contemptuous amusement that I could only stare blankly in reply.

'Dear innocent children!' she said, with inimitable unctuousness. 'Well, well, Mr. Withers, we poor seasoned old creatures must move with the times. Do you sing?'

I scouted the idea.

'Then you must listen to my playing. Chess'—she clasped her forehead with both cramped hands—'chess is now completely beyond my poor wits.'

She sat down at the piano and ran her fingers in a flourish over the keys. 'What shall it be? How shall we capture them, those passionate hearts? That first fine careless rapture? Poetry itself.' She gazed softly into the garden a moment, and presently, with a shake of her body, began to play the opening bars of Beethoven's 'Moonlight' Sonata. The piano was old and woolly. She played without music. The lamplight was rather dim. The moonbeams from the window lay across the keys. Her head was in shadow. And whether it was simply due to her personality or to some really occult skill in her playing I cannot say; I only know that she gravely and deliberately set herself to satirize the beautiful music. It brooded on the air, disillusioned, charged with mockery and bitterness. I stood at the window; far down the path I could see the white figure glimmering in that pool of colourless light. A few faint stars shone, and still that amazing woman behind me dragged out of the unwilling keys her wonderful grotesquerie of youth and love and beauty. It came to an end. I knew the player was watching me. 'Please, please, go on!' I murmured, without turning. '*Please* go on playing, Miss Seaton.'

No answer was returned to this honeyed sarcasm, but I realized in some vague fashion that I was being acutely scrutinized, when suddenly there followed a procession of quiet, plaintive chords which broke at last softly into the hymn, 'A Few More Years Shall Roll.'

I confess it held me spellbound. There is a wistful, strained plangent pathos in the tune; but beneath those masterly old hands it cried softly and bitterly the solitude and desperate estrangement of the world. Arthur and his lady-love vanished from my thoughts. No one could put into so hackneyed an old hymn tune such an appeal who had never known the meaning of the words. Their meaning, anyhow, isn't commonplace.

I turned a fraction of an inch to glance at the musician. She was leaning forward a little over the keys, so that at the approach of my silent scrutiny she had but to turn her face into the thin flood of moonlight for every feature to become distinctly visible. And so, with the tune abruptly terminated, we steadfastly regarded one another; and she broke into a prolonged chuckle of laughter.

'Not quite so seasoned as I supposed, Mr. Withers. I see you are a real lover of music. To me it is too painful. It evokes too much thought. . . .'

I could scarcely see her little glittering eyes under their penthouse lids.

'And now,' she broke off crisply, 'tell me, as a man of the world, what do you think of my new niece?'

I was not a man of the world, nor was I much flattered in my stiff and dullish way of looking at things by being called one; and I could answer her without the least hesitation:

'I don't think, Miss Seaton, I'm much of a judge of character. She's very charming.'

'A brunette?'

'I think I prefer dark women.'

'And why? Consider, Mr. Withers; dark hair, dark eyes, dark cloud, dark night, dark vision, dark death, dark grave, dark DARK!'

Perhaps the climax would have rather thrilled Seaton, but I was too thick-skinned. 'I don't know much about all that,' I answered rather pompously. 'Broad daylight's difficult enough for most of us.'

'Ah,' she said with a sly, inward burst of satirical laughter.

'And I suppose,' I went on, perhaps a little nettled, 'it isn't the actual darkness one admires, it's the contrast of the skin, and the colour of the eyes, and—and their shining. Just as,' I went blundering on, too late to turn back, 'just as you only see the stars in the dark. It would be a long day without any evening. As for death and the grave, I don't suppose we shall much notice that.' Arthur and his sweetheart were slowly returning along the dewy path. 'I believe in making the best of things.'

'How very interesting!' came the smooth answer. 'I see you are a philosopher, Mr. Withers. H'm! "As for death and the grave, I don't suppose we shall much notice that." Very interesting. . . . And I'm sure,' she added in a particularly suave voice, 'I profoundly hope so.' She rose slowly from her stool. 'You will take pity on me again, I hope. You and I would get on famously—kindred spirits—elective affinities. And, of course, now that my nephew's going to leave me, now that his affections are centred on another, I shall be a very lonely old woman. . . . Shall I not, Arthur!'

Seaton blinked stupidly. 'I didn't hear what you said, aunt.'

'I was telling our old friend, Arthur, that when you are gone I shall be a very lonely old woman.'

'Oh, I don't think so;' he said in a strange voice.

'He means, Mr. Withers, he means, my dear child,' she said, sweeping her eyes over Alice, 'he means that I shall have memory for company—heavenly memory—the ghosts of other days. Sentimental boy! And did you enjoy our music, Alice? Did I really stir that youthful heart? . . . O, O, O,' continued the horrible old creature, 'you billers and cooers, I have been listening to such flatteries, such confessions! Beware, beware, Arthur, there's many a slip.' She rolled her little eyes at me, she shrugged her shoulders at Alice, and gazed an instant stonily into her nephew's face.

I held out my hand. 'Good night, good night!' she cried. 'He that fights and runs away. Ah, good night, Mr. Withers; come again soon!' She thrust out her cheek at Alice, and we all three filed slowly out of the room.

Black shadow darkened the porch and half the spreading sycamore. We walked without speaking up the dusty village street. Here and there a crimson window glowed. At the fork of the high-road I said good-bye. But I had taken hardly more than a dozen paces when a sudden impulse seized me.

'Seaton!' I called.

He turned in the cool stealth of the moonlight.

'You have my address; if by any chance, you know, you should care to spend a week or two in town between this and the—the Day, we should be delighted to see you.'

'Thank you, Withers, thank you,' he said in a low voice.

'I dare say'—I waved my stick gallantly at Alice—'I dare say you will be doing some shopping; we could all meet,' I added, laughing.

'Thank you, thank you Withers—immensely,' he repeated. And so we parted.

But they were out of the jog-trot of my prosaic life. And being of a stolid and incurious nature, I left Seaton and his marriage, and even his aunt, to themselves in my memory, and scarcely gave a thought to them until one day I was walking up the Strand again, and passed the flashing gloaming of the second-rate jeweller's shop where I had accidentally encountered my old schoolfellow in the summer. It was one of those stagnant autumnal days after a night of rain. I cannot say why, but a vivid recollection returned to my mind of our meeting and of how suppressed Seaton had seemed, and of how vainly he had endeavoured to appear assured and eager. He must be married by now, and had doubtless returned from his honeymoon. And I had clean forgotten my manners, had sent not a word of congratulation, nor—as I might very well have done, and as I knew he would have been pleased at my doing—even the ghost of a wedding present. It was just as of old.

On the other hand, I pleaded with myself, I had had no invitation. I paused at the corner of Trafalgar Square, and at the bidding of one of those caprices that seize occasionally on even an unimaginative mind, I found myself pelting after a green bus, and actually bound on a visit I had not in the least intended or foreseen.

The colours of autumn were over the village when I arrived. A beautiful late afternoon sunlight bathed thatch and meadow. But it was close and hot. A child, two dogs, a very old woman with a heavy basket I encountered. One or two incurious tradesmen looked idly up as I passed by. It was all so rural and remote, my whimsical impulse had so much flagged, that for a while I hesitated to venture under the shadow of the sycamore-tree to enquire after the happy pair. Indeed, I first passed by the faint-blue gates and continued my walk under the high, green and tufted wall. Hollyhocks had attained their topmost bud and seeded in the little cottage gardens beyond; the Michaelmas daisies were in flower; a sweet warm aromatic smell of fading leaves was in the air. Beyond the cottages lay a field where cattle were grazing, and beyond that I came to a little churchyard. Then the road wound on, pathless and houseless, among gorse and bracken. I turned impatiently and walked quickly back to the house and rang the bell.

The rather colourless elderly woman who answered my enquiry informed me that Miss Seaton was at home, as if only taciturnity forbade her adding, 'But she doesn't want to see *you.*'

'Might I, do you think, have Mr. Arthur's address?' I said.

She looked at me with quiet astonishment, as if waiting for an explanation. Not the faintest of smiles came into her thin face.

'I will tell Miss Seaton,' she said after a pause. 'Please walk in.'

She showed me into the dingy undusted drawing-room, filled with evening sunshine and with the green-dyed light that penetrated the leaves overhanging the long french windows. I sat down and waited on and on, occasionally aware of a creaking footfall overhead. At last the door opened a little, and the great face I had once known peered round at me. For it was enormously changed; mainly, I think, because the aged eyes had rather suddenly failed, and so a kind of stillness and darkness lay over its calm and wrinkled pallor.

'Who is it?' she asked.

I explained myself and told her the occasion of my visit.

She came in, shut the door carefully after her, and, though the fumbling was scarcely perceptible, groped her way to a chair. She had on an old dressing-gown, like a cassock, of a patterned cinnamon colour.

'What is it you want?' she said, seating herself and lifting her blank face to mine.

'Might I just have Arthur's address?' I said deferentially. 'I am so sorry to have disturbed you.'

'H'm. You have come to see my nephew?'

'Not necessarily to see him, only to hear how he is, and, of course, Mrs. Seaton, too. I am afraid my silence must have appeared . . .'

'He hasn't noticed your silence,' croaked the old voice out of the great mask; 'besides, there isn't any Mrs. Seaton.'

'Ah, then,' I answered, after a momentary pause, 'I have not seemed so black as I painted myself! And how is Miss Outram?'

'She's gone into Yorkshire,' answered Seaton's aunt.

'And Arthur too?'

She did not reply, but simply sat blinking at me with lifted chin, as if listening, but certainly not for what I might have to say. I began to feel rather at a loss.

'You were no close friend of my nephew's, Mr. Smithers?' she said presently.

'No,' I answered, welcoming the cue, 'and yet, do you know, Miss Seaton, he is one of the very few of my old school-fellows I have come across in the last few years, and I suppose as one gets older one begins to value old associations. . . .' My voice seemed to trail off into a vacuum. 'I thought Miss Outram', I hastily began again, 'a particularly charming girl. I hope they are both quite well.'

Still the old face solemnly blinked at me in silence.

'You must find it very lonely, Miss Seaton, with Arthur away?'

'I was never lonely in my life,' she said sourly. 'I don't look to flesh and blood for my company. When you've got to be my age, Mr. Smithers (which God forbid), you'll find life a very different affair from what you seem to think it is now. You won't seek company then, I'll be bound. It's thrust on you.' Her face edged round into the clear green light, and her eyes groped, as it were, over my vacant disconcerted face. 'I dare say, now,' she said, composing her mouth, 'I dare say my nephew told you a good many tarradiddles in his time. Oh, yes, a good many, eh? He was always a liar. What, now, did he say of me? Tell me, now.' She leant forward as far as she could, trembling, with an ingratiating smile.

'I think he is rather superstitious,' I said coldly, 'but, honestly, I have a very poor memory, Miss Seaton.'

'Why?' she said. '*I* haven't.'

'The engagement hasn't been broken off, I hope.'

'Well, between you and me,' she said, shrinking up and with an immensely confidential grimace, 'it has.'

'I'm sure I'm very sorry to hear it. And where is Arthur?'

'Eh?'

'Where is Arthur?'

We faced each other mutely among the dead old bygone furniture. Past all my analysis was that large, flat, grey, cryptic countenance. And then, suddenly, our eyes for the first time really met. In some indescribable way out of that thick-lidded obscurity a far small something stooped and looked out at me for a mere instant of time that seemed of almost intolerable protraction. Involuntarily I blinked and shook my head. She muttered something with great rapidity, but quite inarticulately; rose and hobbled to the door. I thought I heard, mingled in broken mutterings, something about tea.

'Please, please don't trouble,' I began, but could say no more, for the door was already shut between us. I stood and looked out on the long-neglected garden. I could just see the bright weedy greenness of Seaton's tadpole pond. I wandered about the room. Dusk began to gather, the last birds in that dense shadowiness of trees had ceased to sing. And not a sound was to be heard in the house. I waited on and on, vainly speculating. I even attempted to ring the bell; but the wire was broken, and only jangled loosely at my efforts.

I hesitated, unwilling to call or to venture out, and yet more unwilling to linger on, waiting for a tea that promised to be an exceedingly comfortless supper. And as darkness drew down, a feeling of the utmost unease and disquietude came over me. All my talks with Seaton returned on me with a suddenly enriched meaning. I recalled again his face as we had stood hanging over the staircase, listening in the small hours to the inexplicable stirrings of the night. There were no candles in the room; every minute the autumnal darkness deepened. I cautiously opened the door and listened, and with some little dismay withdrew, for I was uncertain of my way out. I even tried the garden, but was confronted under a veritable thicket of foliage by a padlocked gate. It would be a little too ignominious to be caught scaling a friend's garden fence!

Cautiously returning into the still and musty drawing-room, I took out my watch, and gave the incredible old woman ten minutes in which to reappear. And when that tedious ten minutes had ticked by I could scarcely distinguish its hands. I determined to wait no longer, drew open the door and, trusting to my sense of direction, groped my way through the corridor that I vaguely remembered led to the front of the house.

I mounted three or four stairs and, lifting a heavy curtain, found myself facing the starry fanlight of the porch. From here I glanced into the gloom of the dining-room. My fingers were on the latch of the outer door when I heard a faint stirring in the darkness above the hall. I looked up and became conscious of, rather than saw, the huddled old figure looking down on me.

There was an immense hushed pause. Then, 'Arthur, Arthur,' whispered an inexpressibly peevish rasping voice, 'is that you? Is that you, Arthur?'

I can scarcely say why, but the question horribly startled me. No conceivable answer occurred to me. With head craned back, hand clenched on my umbrella, I continued to stare up into the gloom, in this fatuous confrontation.

'Oh, oh,' the voice croaked. 'It is *you*, is it? *That* disgusting man! . . . Go away out. Go away out.'

At this dismissal, I wrenched open the door and, rudely slamming it behind me, ran out into the garden, under the gigantic old sycamore, and so out at the open gate.

I found myself half up the village street before I stopped running. The local butcher was sitting in his shop reading a piece of newspaper by the light of a small oil-lamp. I crossed the road and enquired the way to the station. And after he had with minute and needless care directed me, I asked casually if Mr. Arthur Seaton still lived with his aunt at the big house just beyond the village. He poked his head in at the little parlour door.

'Here's a gentleman enquiring after young Mr. Seaton, Millie,' he said. 'He's dead, ain't he?'

'Why, yes, bless you,' replied a cheerful voice from within. 'Dead and buried these three months or more—young Mr. Seaton. And just before he was to be married, don't you remember, Bob?'

I saw a fair young woman's face peer over the muslin of the little door at me.

'Thank you,' I replied, 'then I go straight on?'

'That's it, sir; past the pond, bear up the hill a bit to the left, and then there's the station lights before your eyes.'

We looked intelligently into each other's faces in the beam of the smoky lamp. But not one of the many questions in my mind could I put into words.

And again I paused irresolutely a few paces further on. It was not, I fancy, merely a foolish apprehension of what the raw-boned butcher might 'think' that prevented my going back to see if I could find Seaton's grave in the benighted churchyard. There was precious little use in pottering about in the muddy dark merely to discover where he was buried. And yet I felt a little uneasy. My rather horrible thought was that, so far as I was concerned—one of his extremely few friends—he had never been much better than 'buried' in my mind.

GRAHAM GREENE

When Greek meets Greek

I

WHEN the chemist had shut his shop for the night he went through a door at the back of the hall that served both him and the flats above, and then up two flights and a half of stairs, carrying an offering of a little box of pills. The box was stamped with his name and address: Priskett, 14 New End Street, Oxford. He was a middle-aged man with a thin moustache and scared, evasive eyes: he wore his long white coat even when he was off duty as if it had the power of protecting him like a King's uniform from his enemies. So long as he wore it he was free, as it were, from summary trial and execution.

On the top landing was a window: outside Oxford spread through the spring evening: the peevish noise of innumerable bicycles, the gasworks, the prison, and the grey spires, beyond the bakers and confectioners, like paper frills. A door was marked with a visiting card Mr. Nicholas Fennick, B.A.: the chemist rang three short times.

The man who opened the door was sixty years old at least, with snow-white hair and a pink babyish skin. He wore a mulberry velvet dinner jacket, and his glasses swung on the end of a wide black ribbon. He said with a kind of boisterousness, 'Ah, Priskett, step in, Priskett. I had just sported my oak for a moment. . . .'

'I brought you some more of my pills.'

'Invaluable Priskett. If only you had taken a degree—the Society of Apothecaries would have been enough—I would have appointed you resident medical officer of St. Ambrose's.'

'How's the college doing?'

'Give me your company for a moment in the common-room, and you shall know all.'

Mr. Fennick led the way down a little dark passage cluttered with mackintoshes: Mr. Priskett, feeling his way uneasily from mackintosh to mackintosh, kicked in front of him a pair of girl's shoes. 'One day,' Mr. Fennick said, 'we must build . . .' and he made a broad confident gesture with his glasses that seemed to press back the walls of the common-room: a small round table covered with a landlady's cloth, three or four shiny chairs and a glass-fronted bookcase containing a copy of *Every Man His Own Lawyer*. 'My niece Elisabeth,' Mr. Fennick said, 'my medical adviser.' A very young girl with a lean pretty face nodded perfunctorily from behind a typewriter. 'I am going to train Elisabeth,' Mr. Fennick said, 'to act as bursar. The strain of being both bursar and president of the college is upsetting my stomach. The pills . . . thank you.'

Mr. Priskett said humbly, 'And what do you think of the college, Miss Fennick?'

'My name's Cross,' the girl said. 'I think it's a good idea. I'm surprised my uncle thought of it.'

'In a way it was—partly—my idea.'

'I'm more surprised still,' the girl said firmly.

Mr. Priskett, folding his hands in front of his white coat as though he were pleading before a tribunal, went on: 'You see I said to your uncle that with all these colleges being taken over by the military and the tutors having nothing to do they ought to start teaching by correspondence.'

'A glass of audit ale, Priskett?' Mr. Fennick suggested. He took a bottle of brown ale out of a cupboard and poured out two gaseous glasses.

'Of course,' Mr. Priskett pleaded, 'I hadn't thought of all this—the common-room, I mean, and St. Ambrose's.'

'My niece,' Mr. Fennick said, 'knows very little of the set-up.' He began to move restlessly around the room, touching things with his hand. He was rather like an aged bird of prey inspecting the grim components of its nest.

The girl said briskly, 'As I see it, Uncle is running a swindle called St. Ambrose's College, Oxford.'

'Not a swindle, my dear. The advertisement was very carefully worded.' He knew it by heart: every phrase had been carefully checked with his copy of *Every Man His Own Lawyer* open on the table. He repeated it now in a voice full and husky with bottled brown ale. 'War conditions prevent you going up to Oxford. St. Ambrose's—Tom Brown's old college —has made an important break with tradition. For the period of the war only it will be possible to receive tuition by post wherever you may be, whether defending the Empire on the cold rocks of Iceland or on the burning sands of Libya, in the main street of an American town or a cottage in Devonshire. . . .'

'You've overdone it,' the girl said. 'You always do. That hasn't got a cultured ring. It won't catch anybody but saps.'

'There are plenty of saps,' Mr. Fennick said.

'Go on.'

'Well, I'll skip that bit. "Degree-diplomas will be granted at the end of three terms instead of the usual three years." ' He explained: 'That gives a quick turnover. One can't wait for money these days. "Gain a real Oxford education at Tom Brown's old college. For full particulars of tuition fees, battels, &c., write to the Bursar." '

'And do you mean to say the University can't stop that?'

'Anybody,' Mr. Fennick said with a kind of pride, 'can start a college anywhere. I've never said it was part of the University.'

'But battels—battels mean board and lodging.'

'In this case,' Mr. Fennick said, 'it's quite a nominal fee— to keep your name in perpetuity on the books of the old firm—I mean, the college.'

'And the tuition . . .'

'Priskett here is the science tutor. I take history and classics. I thought that you, my dear, might tackle— economics?'

'I don't know anything about them.'

'The examinations, of course, have to be rather simple— within the capacity of the tutors. (There is an excellent public library here.) And another thing—the fees are returnable if the diploma-degree is not granted.'

'You mean . . .'

'Nobody will ever fail,' Mr. Priskett brought breathlessly out with scared excitement.

'And are you really getting results?'

'I waited, my dear, until I could see the distinct possibility of at least six hundred a year for the three of us before I wired you. And today—beyond all my expectations—I have received a letter from Lord Driver. He is entering his son at St. Ambrose's.'

'But how can he come here?'

'In his absence, my dear, on his country's service. The Drivers have always been a military family. I looked them up in *Debrett*.'

'What do you think of it?' Mr. Priskett asked with anxiety and triumph.

'I think it's rich. Have you arranged a boat race?'

'There, Priskett,' Mr. Fennick said proudly, raising his glass of audit ale, 'I told you she was a girl of ideas.'

2

Directly he heard his landlady's feet upon the stairs, the elderly man with the grey shaven head began to lay his wet tea-leaves round the base of the aspidistra. When she opened the door he was dabbing the tea-leaves in tenderly with his fingers. 'A lovely plant, my dear.'

But she wasn't going to be softened at once: he could tell that: she waved a letter at him. 'Listen,' she said, 'what's this Lord Driver business?'

'My name, my dear: a good Christian name like Lord George Sanger had.'

'Then why don't they put Mr. Lord Driver on the letter?'

'Ignorance, just ignorance.'

'I don't want any hanky-panky from my house. It's always been honest.'

'Perhaps they didn't know if I was an esquire or just a plain mister, so they left it blank.'

'It's sent from St. Ambrose's College, Oxford: people like that ought to know.'

'It comes, my dear, of your having such a good address.

W.1. And all the gentry live in Mewses.' He made a half-hearted snatch at the letter, but the landlady held it out of reach.

'What are the likes of you writing to Oxford College about?'

'My dear,' he said with strained dignity, 'I may have been a little unfortunate: it may even be that I have spent a few years in chokey, but I have the rights of a free man.'

'And a son in quod.'

'Not in quod, my dear. Borstal is quite another institution. It is—a kind of college.'

'Like St. Ambrose's.'

'Perhaps not quite of the same rank.'

He was too much for her: he was usually in the end too much for her. Before his first stay at the Scrubs he had held a number of positions as manservant and even butler: the way he raised his eyebrows he had learned from Lord Charles Manville: he wore his clothes like an eccentric peer, and you might say that he had even learned the best way to pilfer from old Lord Bellew who had a penchant for silver spoons.

'And now, my dear, if you'd just let me have my letter?' He put his hand tentatively forward: he was as daunted by her as she was by him: they sparred endlessly and lost to each other: interminably the battle was never won—they were always afraid. This time it was his victory. She slammed the door. Suddenly, ferociously, when the door had closed, he made a little vulgar noise at the aspidistra. Then he put on his glasses and began to read.

His son had been accepted for St. Ambrose's, Oxford. The great fact stared up at him above the sprawling decorative signature of the President. Never had he been more thankful for the coincidence of his name. 'It will be my great pleasure,' the President wrote, 'to pay personal attention to your son's career at St. Ambrose's. In these days it is an honour to welcome a member of a great military family like yours.' Driver felt an odd mixture of amusement and of genuine pride. He'd put one over on them, but his breast swelled within his waistcoat at the idea that now he had a son at Oxford.

But there were two snags—minor snags when he considered how far he'd got already. It was apparently an old Oxford custom that fees should be paid in advance, and then there were the examinations. His son couldn't do them himself: Borstal would not allow it, and he wouldn't be out for another six months. Besides the whole beauty of the idea was that he should receive the gift of an Oxford degree as a kind of welcome home. Like a chess-player who is always several moves ahead he was already seeing his way around these difficulties.

The fees he felt sure in his case were only a matter of bluff: a peer could always get credit, and if there was any trouble after the degree had been awarded, he could just tell them to sue and be damned. No Oxford college would like to admit that they'd been imposed on by an old lag. But the examinations. A funny little knowing smile twitched the corners of his mouth: a memory of the Scrubs five years ago and the man they called Daddy, the Reverend Simon Milan. He was a short-time prisoner—they were all short-time prisoners at the Scrubs: no sentence of over three years was ever served there. He remembered the tall lean aristocratic parson with his iron-grey hair and his narrow face like a lawyer's which had gone somehow soft inside with too much love. A prison, when you came to think of it, contained as much knowledge as a University: there were doctors, financiers, clergy. He knew where he could find Mr. Milan: he was employed in a boarding-house near Euston Square, and for a few drinks he would do most things—he would certainly make out some fine examination papers. 'I can just hear him now,' Driver told himself ecstatically, 'talking Latin to the warders.'

3

It was autumn in Oxford: people coughed in the long queues for sweets and cakes: and the mists from the river seeped into the cinemas past the commissionaires on the look-out for people without gas-masks. A few undergraduates picked their way through the evacuated swarm: they always looked in a hurry: so much had to be got through in so little time before the army claimed them. There were lots of pickings for racketeers, Elisabeth Cross thought, but not much chance for a girl to find a husband: the oldest Oxford racket had been elbowed out by the black markets in Woodbines, toffees, tomatoes.

There had been a few days last spring when she had treated St. Ambrose's as a joke, but when she saw the money actually coming in, the whole thing seemed less amusing. Then for some weeks she was acutely unhappy—until she realized that of all the war-time rackets this was the most harmless. They were not reducing supplies like the Ministry of Food, or destroying confidence like the Ministry of Information: her uncle paid income tax, and they even to some extent educated people. The saps, when they took their diploma-degrees would know several things they hadn't known before.

But that didn't help a girl to find a husband.

She came moodily out of the matinée, carrying a bunch of papers she should have been correcting. There was only one 'student' who showed any intelligence at all, and that was Lord Driver's son. The papers were forwarded from 'somewhere in England' via London by his father: she had nearly found herself caught out several times on points of history, and her uncle she knew was straining his rusty Latin to the limit.

When she got home she knew that there was something in the air: Mr. Priskett was sitting in his white coat on the edge of a chair and her uncle was finishing a stale bottle of beer. When something went wrong he never opened a new bottle: he believed in happy drinking. They watched her come in in silence: Mr. Priskett's silence was gloomy, her uncle's preoccupied. Something had to be got round—it couldn't be the university authorities: they had stopped bothering him long ago—a lawyer's letter, an irascible interview, and their attempt to maintain 'a monopoly of local education'—as Mr. Fennick put it—had ceased.

'Good evening,' Elisabeth said: Mr. Priskett looked at Mr. Fennick and Mr. Fennick frowned.

'Has Mr. Priskett run out of pills?'

Mr. Priskett winced.

'I've been thinking,' Elisabeth said, 'that as we are now in the third term of the academic year, I should like a rise in salary.'

Mr. Priskett drew in his breath sharply, keeping his eyes on Mr. Fennick.

'I should like another three pounds a week.'

Mr. Fennick rose from the table; he glared ferociously into the top of his dark ale; his frown beetled. The chemist scraped his chair a little backward. And then Mr. Fennick spoke.

'We are such stuff as dreams are made on,' he said and hiccupped slightly.

'Kidneys,' Elisabeth said.

'Rounded by a sleep. And these our cloud-capped towers . . .'

'You are misquoting.'

'Vanished into air, into thin air.'

'You've been correcting the English papers.'

'Unless you allow me to think, to think rapidly and deeply, there won't be any more examination papers,' Mr. Fennick said.

'Trouble?'

'I've always been a Republican at heart. I don't see why we want a hereditary peerage.'

'*A la lanterne*,' Elisabeth said.

'This man, Lord Driver: why should a mere accident of birth . . .?'

'He refuses to pay?'

'It isn't that. A man like that expects credit: it's right that he should have credit. But he's written to say that he's coming down to-morrow to see his boy's college. The old fat-headed sentimental fool,' Mr. Fennick said.

'I knew you'd be in trouble sooner or later.'

'That's the sort of damn fool comfortless thing a girl would say.'

'It just needs brain.'

Mr. Fennick picked up a brass ash-tray—and then put it down again carefully.

'It's quite simple as soon as you begin to think.'

'Think.'

Mr. Priskett scraped a chair-leg.

'I'll meet him at the station with a taxi, and take him to—say Balliol. Lead him straight through into the inner quad, and there you'll be, just looking as if you'd come out of the Master's lodging.'

'He'll know it's Balliol.'

'He won't. Anybody who knew Oxford couldn't be sap enough to send his son to St. Ambrose's.'

'Of course it's true. These military families are a bit crass.'

'You'll be in an enormous hurry. Consecration or something. Whip him round the Hall, the Chapel, the Library, and hand him back to me outside the Master's. I'll take him out to lunch and see him into his train. It's simple.'

Mr. Fennick said broodingly, 'Sometimes I think you're a terrible girl, terrible. Is there nothing you wouldn't think up?'

'I believe,' Elisabeth said, 'that if you're going to play your own game in a world like this, you've got to play it properly. Of course,' she said, 'if you are going to play a different game you go to a nunnery or to the wall and like it. But I've only got one game to play.'

4

It really went off very smoothly. Driver found Elisabeth at the barrier: she didn't find him because she was expecting something different. Something about him worried her: it wasn't his clothes or the monocle he never seemed to use—it was something subtler than that. It was almost as though he were afraid of her, he was so ready to fall in with her plans. 'I don't want to be any trouble, my dear, any trouble at all. I know how busy the President must be.' When she explained that they would be lunching together in town, he even seemed relieved. 'It's just the bricks of the dear old place,' he said. 'You mustn't mind my being a sentimentalist, my dear.'

'Were you at Oxford?'

'No, no. The Drivers, I'm afraid, have neglected the things of the mind.'

'Well, I suppose a soldier needs brains?'

He took a sharp look at her, and then answered in quite a different sort of voice: 'We believed so in the Lancers.' Then he strolled beside her to the taxi, twirling his monocle, and all the way up from the station he was silent, taking little quiet sideways peeks at her, appraising, approving.

'So this is St. Ambrose's,' he said in a hearty voice just beside the porter's lodge and she pushed him quickly by, through the first quad towards the Master's house, where on the doorstep with a B.A. gown over his arm stood Mr. Fennick permanently posed like a piece of garden statuary. 'My uncle, the President,' Elisabeth said.

'A charming girl, your niece,' Driver said as soon as they were alone together: he had really only meant to make conversation, but as soon as he had spoken the old two crooked minds began to move in harmony.

'She's very home-loving,' Mr. Fennick said. 'Our famous elms,' he went on, waving his hand skywards. 'St. Ambrose's rooks.'

'Crooks?' Driver said with astonishment.

'Rooks. In the elms. One of our great modern poets wrote about them. "St. Ambrose elms, oh St. Ambrose elms", and about "St. Ambrose rooks calling in wind and rain".'

'Pretty. Very pretty.'

'Nicely turned, I think.'

'I mean your niece.'

'Ah, yes. This way to the Hall. Up these steps. So often trodden, you know, by Tom Brown.'

'Who was Tom Brown?'

'The great Tom Brown—one of Rugby's famous sons.' He added thoughtfully, 'She'll make a fine wife—and mother.'

'Young men are beginning to realise that the flighty ones are not what they want for a lifetime.'

They stopped by mutual consent on the top step: they nosed towards each other like two old blind sharks who each believes that what stirs the water close to him is tasty meat.

'Whoever wins her,' Mr. Fennick said, 'can feel proud.

She'll make a fine hostess . . .' as the future Lady Driver, he thought.

'I and my son,' Driver said, 'have talked seriously about marriage. He takes rather an old-fashioned view. He'll make a good husband. . . .'

They walked into the hall, and Mr. Fennick led the way round the portraits. 'Our founder,' he said, pointing at a full-bottomed wig. He chose it deliberately: he felt it smacked a little of himself. Before Swinburne's portrait he hesitated: then pride in St. Ambrose's conquered caution. 'The great poet Swinburne,' he said. 'We sent him down.'

'Expelled him?'

'Yes. Bad morals.'

'I'm glad you are strict about those.'

'Ah, your son is in safe hands at St. Ambrose's.'

'It makes me very happy,' Driver said. He began to scrutinise the portrait of a nineteenth-century divine. 'Fine brushwork,' he said. 'Now religion—I believe in religion. Basis of the family.' He said with a burst of confidence, 'You know our young people ought to meet.'

Mr. Fennick gleamed happily. 'I agree.'

'If he passes . . .'

'Oh, he'll certainly pass,' Mr. Fennick said.

'He'll be on leave in a week or two. Why shouldn't he take his degree in person?'

'Well, there'd be difficulties.'

'Isn't it the custom?'

'Not for postal graduates. The Vice-Chancellor likes to make a small distinction. . . . But, Lord Driver, in the case of so distinguished an alumnus I suggest that I should be deputed to present the degree to your son in London.'

'I'd like him to see his college.'

'And so he shall in happier days. So much of the college is shut now. I would like him to visit it for the first time when its glory is restored. Allow me and my niece to call on you.'

'We are living very quietly.'

'Not serious financial trouble, I hope?'

'Oh, no, no.'

'I'm so glad. And now let us rejoin the dear girl.'

5

It always seemed to be more convenient to meet at railway stations. The coincidence didn't strike Mr. Fennick who had fortified himself for the journey with a good deal of audit ale, but it struck Elisabeth. The college lately had not been fulfilling expectations, and that was partly due to the laziness of Mr. Fennick: from his conversation lately it almost seemed as though he had begun to regard the college as only a step to something else—what she couldn't quite make out. He was always talking about Lord Driver and his son Frederick and the responsibilites of the peerage. His Republican tendencies had quite lapsed. 'That dear boy,' was the way he referred to Frederick, and he marked him 100 per cent. for Classics. 'It's not often Latin and Greek go with military genius,' he said. 'A remarkable boy.'

'He's not so hot on economics,' Elisabeth said.

'We mustn't demand too much book-learning from a soldier.'

At Paddington Lord Driver waved anxiously to them through the crowd: he wore a very new suit—one shudders to think how many coupons had been gambled away for the occasion. A little behind him was a very young man with a sullen mouth and a scar on his cheek. Mr. Fennick bustled forward: he wore a black raincoat over his shoulders like a cape and carrying his hat in his hand he disclosed his white hair venerably among the porters.

'My son—Frederick,' Lord Driver said. The boy sullenly took off his hat and put it on again quickly: they wore their hair in the army very short.

'St. Ambrose's welcomes her new graduate,' Mr. Fennick said.

Frederick grunted.

The presentation of the degree was made in a private room at Mount Royal. Lord Driver explained that his house had been bombed—a time bomb, he added, a rather necessary explanation since there had been no raids recently. Mr. Fennick was satisfied if Lord Driver was: he had brought up a B.A. gown, a mortar-board and a Bible in his suitcase, and he made quite an imposing little ceremony between the book-table, the sofa and the radiator, reading out a Latin oration and tapping Frederick lightly on the head with the Bible. The degree-diploma had been expensively printed in two colours by an Anglo-Catholic firm. Elisabeth was the only uneasy person there. Could the world, she wondered, really contain two such saps? What was this painful feeling growing up in her that perhaps it contained four?

After a little light lunch with bottled brown beer—'almost as good, if I may say so, as our audit ale,' Mr. Fennick beamed—the President and Lord Driver made elaborate moves to drive the two young people out together. 'We've got to talk a little business,' Mr. Fennick said, and Lord Driver hinted, 'You've not been to the flickers for a year, Frederick.' They were driven out together into bombed shabby Oxford Street while the old men rang cheerfully down for whisky.

'What's the idea?' Elisabeth said.

He was good-looking: she liked his scar and his sullenness; there was almost too much intelligence and purpose in his eyes. Once he took off his hat and scratched his head: Elisabeth again noticed his short hair. He certainly didn't look a military type. And his suit, like his father's, looked new and ready-made. Hadn't he had any clothes to wear when he came on leave?

'I suppose,' she said, 'they are planning a wedding.'

His eyes lit gleefully up. 'I wouldn't mind,' he said.

'You'd have to get leave from your C.O., wouldn't you?'

'C.O.?' he asked in astonishment, flinching a little like a boy who has been caught out, who hasn't been prepared beforehand with that question. She watched him carefully, remembering all the things that had seemed to her since the beginning odd.

'So you haven't been to the movies for a year,' she said.

'I've been on service.'

'Not even an Ensa show?'

'Oh, I don't count those.'

'It must be awfully like being in prison.'

He grinned weakly, walking faster all the time, so that she might really have been pursuing him through the Hyde Park gates.

'Come clean,' she said. 'Your father's not Lord Driver.'

'Oh yes he is.'

'Any more than my uncle's President of a College.'

'What?' He began to laugh—it was an agreeable laugh, a laugh you couldn't trust but a laugh which made you laugh back and agree that in a crazy world like this all sorts of things didn't matter a hang. 'I'm just out of Borstal,' he said. 'What's yours?'

'Oh, I haven't been in prison yet.'

He said, 'You'll never believe me, but all that ceremony— it looked phoney to me. Of course the Dad swallowed it.'

'And my uncle swallowed you. . . . I couldn't quite.'

'Well, the wedding's off. In a way I'm sorry.'

'I'm still free.'

'Well,' he said, 'we might discuss it,' and there in the pale autumn sunlight of the park they did discuss it—from all sorts of angles. There were bigger frauds all round them; officials of the Ministries passed carrying little portfolios: controllers of this and that purred by in motor-cars, and men with the big blank faces of advertisement hoardings strode purposefully in khaki with scarlet tabs down Park Lane from the Dorchester. Their fraud was a small one by the world's standard, and a harmless one: the boy from Borstal and the girl from nowhere at all—from the draper's counter and the semi-detached villa. 'He's got a few hundred stowed away. I'm sure of that,' said Fred. 'He'd make a settlement if he thought he could get the President's niece.'

'I wouldn't be surprised if Uncle had five hundred. He'd put it all down for Lord Driver's son.'

'We'd take over this college business. With a bit of capital we could really make it go. It's just chicken-feed now.'

They fell in love for no reason at all, in the park, on a bench to save twopences, planning their fraud on the old frauds they knew they could outdo. Then they went back, and Elisabeth declared herself before she'd got properly inside the door. 'Frederick and I want to get married.' She almost felt sorry for the old fools as their faces lit suddenly simultaneously up because everything had been so easy, and then darkened with caution as they squinted at each other. 'This is very surprising,' Lord Driver said, and the President said, 'My goodness, young people work fast.'

All night the two old men planned their settlements, and the two young ones sat happily back in a corner, watching the elaborate fence, with the secret knowledge that the world is always open to the young.

L. P. HARTLEY

The Killing Bottle

UNLIKE the majority of men, Jimmy Rintoul enjoyed the hour or so's interval between being called and having breakfast; for it was the only part of the day upon which he imposed an order. From nine-fifteen onwards the day imposed its order upon him. The 'bus, the office, the hasty city luncheon; then the office, the 'bus, and the unsatisfactory interval before dinner: such a promising time and yet, do what he would with it, it always seemed to be wasted. If he was going to dine alone at his club, he felt disappointed and neglected; if, as seldom happened, in company, he felt vaguely apprehensive. He expected a good deal from his life, and he never went to bed without the sense of having missed it. Truth to tell, he needed a stimulus, the stimulus of outside interest and appreciation, to get the best out of himself. In a competitive society, with rewards dangled before his eyes, his nature fulfilled itself and throve. How well he had done at school, and even afterwards, while his parents lived to applaud his efforts. Now he was thirty-three; his parents were dead; there was no one close enough to him to care whether he made a success of his life or not. Nor did life hand out to grown-up men incontestable signs of merit and excellence, volumes bound in vellum or silver cups standing proudly on ebony pedestals. No, its awards were far less tangible, and Jimmy, from the shelter of his solicitors' office, sometimes felt glad that its more sensational prizes were passing out of his reach—that he need no longer feel obliged, as he had once felt, to climb the Matterhorn, play the 'Moonlight Sonata,' master the Spanish language, and read the *Critique of Pure Reason* before he died. His ambition was sensibly on the ebb.

But not in the mornings. The early mornings were still untouched by the torpors of middle age. Dressing was for

Jimmy a ritual, and like all rituals it looked forward to a culmination. Act followed act in a recognised sequence, each
stage contributing its peculiar thrill, opening his mind to a
train of stimulating and agreeable thoughts, releasing it,
encouraging it. And the culmination: what was it? Only his
morning's letters and the newspaper! Not very exciting. But
the newspaper might contain one of those helpful, sympathetic
articles about marriage, articles that warned the reader not to
rush into matrimony, but to await the wisdom that came with
the early and still more with the late thirties; articles which,
with a few tricks of emphasis, of skipping here and reading
between the lines there, demonstrated that Jimmy Rintoul's
career, without any effort of his own, was shaping itself on
sound, safe lines. The newspaper, then, for reassurance; the
letters for surprise! And this morning an interesting letter
would be particularly welcome. It would distract his mind
from a vexing topic that even the routine of dressing had not
quite banished—the question of his holiday, due in a fortnight's time.

Must it be Swannick Fen again? Partly for lack of finding
others to take their place, he had cherished the interests of his
boyhood, of which butterfly-collecting was the chief. He was
solitary and competitive, and the hobby ministered to both
these traits. But alas! he had not the patience of the true
collector; his interest fell short of the lesser breeds, the irritating
varieties of Wainscots and Footmen and whatnots. It embraced
only the more sensational insects—the large, the beautiful,
and the rare. His desire had fastened itself on the Swallow-
tail butterfly as representing all these qualities. So he went to
Swannick, found the butterfly, bred it, and presently had a
whole hutch-full of splendid green caterpillars. Their mere
number, the question of what to do with them when they
came out, whether to keep them all in their satiating similarity,
to give them away, or to sell them; to let them go free so that
the species might multiply, to the benefit of all collectors; to
kill all but a few, thus enhancing the value of his own—these
problems vexed his youthful, ambitious, conscientious mind.
Finally he killed them all. But the sight of four setting-boards

plastered with forty identical insects destroyed by a surfeit his passion for the Swallow-tail butterfly. He had coaxed it with other baits: the Pine Hawk moth, the Clifden Nonpareil; but it would not respond, would accept no substitute, being, like many passions, monogamous and constant. Every year, in piety, in conservatism, in hope, he still went to Swannick Fen; but with each visit the emotional satisfaction diminished. Soon it would be gone.

However, there on his dressing-table (for some reason) stood the killing bottle—mutely demanding prey. Almost without thinking he released the stopper and snuffed up the almond-breathing fumes. A safe, pleasant smell; he could never understand how anything died of it, or why cyanide of potassium should figure in the chemists' book of poisons. But it did; he had had to put his name against it. Now, since the stuff was reputed to be so deadly, he must add a frail attic to the edifice of dressing and once more wash his hands. In a fortnight's time, he thought, I shall be doing this a dozen times a day.

On the breakfast-table lay a large, shiny blue envelope. He did not recognise the handwriting, nor, when he examined the post-mark, did it convey anything to him. The flap, gummed to the top and very strong, resisted his fingers. He opened it with a knife and read:

                                        'VERDEW CASTLE.

MY DEAR RINTOUL,
    How did you feel after our little dinner on Saturday? None the worse, I hope. However, I'm not writing to inquire about your health, which seems pretty good, but about your happiness, or what I should like to think would be your happiness. Didn't I hear you mutter (the second time we met, I think it was, at Smallhouse's) something about going for a holiday in the near future? Well, then, couldn't you spend it here with us, at Verdew? Us being my brother Randolph, my wife, and your humble servant. I'm afraid there won't be a party for you; but we could get through the day somehow, and play

bridge in the evenings. Randolph and you would make perfect partners, you would be so kind to each other. And didn't you say you collected bugs? Then by all means bring your butterfly-net and your killing bottle and your other engines of destruction and park them here; there are myriads of greenflies, bluebottle-flies, may-flies, dragon-flies, and kindred pests which would be all the better for your attentions. Now don't say no. It would be a pleasure to us, and I'm sure it would amuse you to see ye olde castle and us living in our medieval seclusion. I await the favour of a favourable reply, and will then tell you the best way of reaching the Schloss, as we sometimes call it in our German fashion.

Yours,
ROLLO VERDEW.'

Jimmy stared at this facetious epistle until its purport faded from his mind, leaving only a blurred impression of redundant loops and twirls. Verdew's handwriting was like himself, bold and dashing and unruly. At least, this was the estimate Jimmy had formed of him, on the strength of three meetings. He had been rather taken by the man's bluff, hearty manner, but he did not expect Verdew to like him: they were birds of a different feather. He hadn't felt very well after the dinner, having drunk more than was good for him in the effort to fall in with his host's mood; but apparently he had succeeded better than he thought. Perhaps swashbucklers like Verdew welcomed mildness in others. If not, why the invitation? He considered it. The district might be entomologically rich. Where exactly was Verdew Castle? He had, of course, a general idea of its locality, correct to three counties; he knew it was somewhere near the coast. Further than that, nothing; and directly he began to sift his knowledge he found it to be even less helpful than he imagined. The notepaper gave a choice of stations: wayside stations they must be, they were both unknown to him. The postal, telegraphic, and telephonic addresses all confidently cited different towns—Kirton Tracy, Shrivecross, and Pawlingham—names which seemed to stir memories but never fully awakened recollection.

Still, what did it matter? Verdew had promised to tell him the best route, and it was only a question of getting there, after all. He could find his own way back.

Soon his thoughts, exploring the future, encountered an obstacle and stopped short. He was looking ahead as though he had made up his mind to go. Well, hadn't he? The invitation solved his immediate difficulty: the uncertainty as to where he should take his holiday. The charm of Swannick had failed to hold him. And yet, perversely enough, his old hunting-ground chose this very moment to trouble him with its lures: its willows, its alders, the silent clumps of grey rushes with the black water in between. The conservatism of his nature, an almost superstitious loyalty to the preferences of his early life, protested against the abandonment of Swannick— Swannick, where he had always done exactly as he liked, where bridge never intruded, and the politenesses of society were unknown. For Jimmy's mind had run forward again, and envisaged existence at Verdew Castle as divided between holding open the door for Mrs. Rollo Verdew and exchanging compliments and forbearances and commiseration with Rollo's elder (or perhaps younger, he hadn't said) brother Randolph across the bridge-table, with a lot of spare time that wasn't really spare and a lot of being left to himself that really meant being left to everybody.

Jimmy looked at the clock: it was time to go. If it amused his imagination to fashion a mythical Verdew Castle, he neither authorised nor forbade it. He still thought himself free to choose. But when he reached his office his first act was to write his friend a letter of acceptance.

Four days later a second blue envelope appeared on his breakfast-table. It was evidently a two-days' post to Verdew Castle, for Rollo explained that he had that moment received Jimmy's welcome communication. There followed a few references, necessarily brief, to matters of interest to them both. The letter closed with the promised itinerary:

'So we shall hope to see you in ten days' time, complete with lethal chamber and big-game apparatus. I forget whether you have a car; but if you have, I strongly advise you to leave it at home. The road bridge across the estuary has been dicky for a long time. They may close it any day now, since it was felt to wobble the last time the Lord-Lieutenant crossed by it. You would be in a mess if you found it shut and had to go trailing thirty miles to Amplesford (a hellish road, since it's no one's interest to keep it up). If the bridge carried the Lord-Lieutenant it would probably bear you, but I shouldn't like to have your blood on my head! Come, then, by train to Verdew Grove. I recommend the four o'clock; it doesn't get here till after dark, but you can dine on it, and it's almost express part of the way. The morning train is too bloody for anything: you would die of boredom before you arrived, and I should hate that to happen to any of my guests. I'm sorry to present you with such ghastly alternatives, but the Castle was built here to be out of everyone's reach, and by Heaven, it is! Come prepared for a long stay. You must. I'm sure the old office can get on very well without you. You're lucky to be able to go away as a matter of course, like a gentleman. Let us have a line and we'll send to meet you, not my little tin kettle but Randolph's majestic Daimler. Good-bye.

Yours,

ROLLO.'

It was indeed a troublesome, tedious journey, involving changes of train and even of station. More than once the train, having entered a terminus head first, steamed out tail first, with the result that Rintoul lost his sense of direction and had a slight sensation of vertigo whenever, in thought, he tried to recapture it. It was half-past nine and the sun was setting when they crossed the estuary. As always in such places the tide was low, and the sun's level beams illuminated the too rotund and luscious curves of a series of mud-flats. The railway-line approached the estuary from its marshy side, by a steep embankment. Near by, and considerably below, ran the road bridge—an antiquated affair of many arches, but apparently still in use, though there seemed to be no traffic on it. The line curved inwards, and by straining his neck

Rintoul could see the train bent like a bow, and the engine approaching a hole, from which a few wisps of smoke still issued, in the ledge of rock that crowned the farther shore. The hole rushed upon him; Rintoul pulled in his head and was at once in darkness. The world never seemed to get light again. After the long tunnel they were among hills that shut out the light that would have come in, and stifled the little that was left behind. It was by the help of the station lantern that he read the name, Verdew Grove, and when they were putting his luggage on the motor he could scarcely distinguish between the porter and the chauffeur. One of them said:

'Did you say it was a rabbit?'

And the other: 'Well, there was a bit of fur stuck to the wheel.'

'You'd better not let the boss see it,' said the first speaker.

'Not likely.' And so saying, the chauffeur, who seemed to be referring to an accident, climbed into the car. As Rollo had said, it was a very comfortable one. Jimmy gave up counting the turns and trying to catch glimpses of the sky over the high hedges, and abandoned himself to drowsiness. He must have dozed, for he did not know whether it was five minutes or fifty before the opening door let in a gust of cool air and warned him that he had arrived.

For a moment he had the hall to himself. It did not seem very large, but to gauge its true extent was difficult, because of the arches and the shadows. Shaded lamps on the tables gave a diffused but very subdued glow; while a few unshaded lights, stuck about in the groining of the vault, consuming their energy in small patches of great brilliancy, dazzled rather than assisted the eye. The fact that the spaces between the vaulting-ribs were white-washed seemed to increase the glare. It was curious and not altogether happy, the contrast between the brilliance above and the murk below. No trophies of the chase adorned the walls; no stags' heads or antlers, no rifles, javelins, tomahawks, assegais, or krisses. Clearly the Verdews were not a family of sportsmen. In what did Randolph Verdew's interests lie? Rintoul wondered, and he was walking across to the open grate, in whose large recess a log-fire flickered, when the sound of a footfall startled him. It came close, then died away completely, then still in the same rhythm began again. It was Rollo.

Rollo with his black moustaches, his swaggering gait, his large expansive air, his noisy benevolence. He grasped Jimmy's hand.

But before he could say more than 'Damned glad,' a footman appeared. He came so close to Jimmy and Rollo that the flow of the latter's eloquence was checked.

'Mr. Rintoul is in the Pink Room,' announced the footman.

Rollo put his little finger in his mouth and gently bit it.

'Oh, but I thought I said——'

'Yes, sir,' interrupted the footman. 'But Mr. Verdew thought he might disturb Mr. Rintoul in the Onyx Room, because sometimes when he lies awake at night he has to move about, as you know, sir. And he thought the Pink Room had a better view. So he gave orders for him to be put there, sir.'

The footman finished on a tranquil note and turned to go. But Rollo flushed faintly and seemed put out.

'I thought it would have been company for you having my brother next door,' he said. 'But he's arranged otherwise, so it can't be helped. Shall I take you to the room now, or will you have a drink first? That is, if I can find it,' he muttered. 'They have a monstrous habit of sometimes taking the drinks away when Randolph has gone to bed. And by the way, he asked me to make his excuses to you. He was feeling rather tired. My wife's gone, too. She always turns in early here; she says there's nothing to do at Verdew. But, my God, there's a lot that wants doing, as I often tell her. This way.'

Though they found the whisky and soda in the drawing-room, Rollo still seemed a little crestfallen and depressed; but Jimmy's spirits, which sometimes suffered from the excessive buoyancy of his neighbour's, began to rise. The chair was comfortable; the room, though glimpses of stone showed alongside the tapestries, was more habitable and less ecclesiastical than the hall. In front of him was an uncurtained window through which he could see, swaying their heads as though

bent on some ghostly conference, a cluster of white roses. I'm
going to enjoy myself here, he thought.

Whatever the charms of the Onyx Room, whatever virtue
resided in the proximity of Mr. Randolph Verdew, one thing
was certain: the Pink Room had a splendid view. Leaning out
of his window the next morning Jimmy feasted his eyes on it.
Directly below him was the moat, clear and apparently deep.
Below that again was the steep conical hill on which the castle
stood, its side intersected by corkscrew paths and level terraces.
Below and beyond, undulating ground led the eye onwards
and upwards to where, almost on the horizon, glittered and
shone the silver of the estuary. Of the castle were visible only
the round wall of Jimmy's tower, and a wing of the Tudor
period, the gables of which rose to the level of his bedroom
window. It was half-past eight and he dressed quickly, meaning to make a little tour of the castle precincts before his hosts
appeared.

His intention, however, was only partially fulfilled, for on
arriving in the hall he found the great door still shut, and fastened with a variety of locks and bolts, of antique design and
as hard to open, it seemed, from within as from without. He
had better fortune with a smaller door and found himself on
a level oblong stretch of grass, an island of green, bounded by
the moat on the east and on the other side by the castle walls.
There was a fountain in the middle. The sun shone down
through the open end of the quadrangle, making the whole
place a cave of light, flushing the warm stone of the Eliza-
bethan wing to orange, and gilding the cold, pale, mediaeval
stonework of the rest. Jimmy walked to the moat and tried to
find, to right or left, a path leading to other parts of the building. But there was none. He turned round and saw Rollo
standing in the doorway.

'Good-morning,' called his host. 'Already thinking out a
plan of escape?'

Jimmy coloured slightly. The thought had been present
in his mind, though not in the sense that Rollo seemed to
mean it.

'You wouldn't find it very easy from here,' remarked Rollo,

whose cheerful humour the night seemed to have restored. 'Because even if you swam the moat you couldn't get up the bank: it's too steep and too high.'

Jimmy examined the farther strand and realised that this was true.

'It would be prettier,' Rollo continued, 'and less canal-like, if the water came up to the top; but Randolph prefers it as it used to be. He likes to imagine we're living in a state of siege.'

'He doesn't seem to keep any weapons for our defence,' commented Jimmy. 'No arquebuses or bows and arrows; no vats of molten lead.'

'Oh, he wouldn't hurt anyone for the world,' said Rollo. 'That's one of his little fads. But it amuses him to look across to the river like one of the first Verdews and feel that no one can get in without his leave.'

'Or out either, I suppose,' suggested Jimmy.

'Well,' remarked Rollo, 'some day I'll show you a way of getting out. But now come along and look at the view from the other side; we have to go through the house to see it.'

They walked across the hall, where the servants were laying the breakfast-table, to a door at the end of a long narrow passage. But it was locked. 'Hodgson!' shouted Rollo.

A footman came up.

'Will you open this door, please?' said Rollo. Jimmy expected him to be angry, but there was only a muffled irritation in his voice. At his leisure the footman produced the key and let them through.

'That's what comes of living in someone else's house,' fumed Rollo, once they were out of earshot. 'These lazy devils want waking up. Randolph's a damned sight too easy-going.'

'Shall I see him at breakfast?' Jimmy inquired.

'I doubt it.' Rollo picked up a stone, looked round, for some reason, at the castle, and threw the pebble at a thrush, narrowly missing it. 'He doesn't usually appear till lunch-time. He's interested in all sorts of philanthropical societies. He's always helping them to prevent something. He hasn't prevented you, though, you naughty fellow,' he went on,

stooping down and picking up from a stone several fragments
of snails' shells. 'This seems to be the thrushes' Tower Hill.'

'He's fond of animals, then?' asked Jimmy.

'Fond, my boy?' repeated Rollo. 'Fond is not the word.
But we aren't vegetarians. Some day I'll explain all that.
Come and have some bacon and eggs.'

That evening, in his bath, a large wooden structure like a
giant's coffin, Jimmy reviewed the day, a delightful day. In
the morning he had been taken round the castle; it was not
so large as it seemed from outside—it had to be smaller, the
walls were so thick. And there were, of course, a great many
rooms he wasn't shown, attics, cellars, and dungeons. One
dungeon he had seen: but he felt sure that in a fortress of such
pretentions there must be more than one. He couldn't quite
get the 'lie' of the place at present; he had his own way of
finding his room, but he knew it wasn't the shortest way. The
hall, which was like a Clapham Junction to the castle's topo-
graphical system, still confused him. He knew the way out,
because there was only one way, across a modernised drawbridge, and that made it simpler. He had crossed it to get at
the woods below the castle, where he had spent the afternoon,
hunting for caterpillars. 'They' had really left him alone—
even severely alone! Neither of Rollo's wife nor of his brother
was there yet any sign. But I shall see them at dinner, he
thought, wrapping himself in an immense bath-towel.

The moment he saw Randolph Verdew, standing pensive
in the drawing-room, he knew he would like him. He was an
etherealized version of Rollo, taller and slighter. His hair was
sprinkled with grey and he stooped a little. His cloudy blue
eyes met Jimmy's with extraordinary frankness as he held out
his hand and apologized for his previous non-appearance.

'It is delightful to have you here,' he added. 'You are a
naturalist, I believe?'

His manner was formal but charming, infinitely reassuring.

'I am an entomologist,' said Jimmy, smiling.

'Ah, I love to watch the butterflies fluttering about the
flowers—and the moths, too, those big heavy fellows that
come in of an evening and knock themselves about against

the lights. I have often had to put as many as ten out of the windows, and back they come—the deluded creatures. What a pity that their larvae are harmful and in some cases have to be destroyed! But I expect you prefer to observe the rarer insects?'

'If I can find them,' said Jimmy.

'I'm sure I hope you will,' said Randolph, with much feeling. 'You must get Rollo to help you.'

'Oh,' said Jimmy, 'Rollo——'

'I hope you don't think Rollo indifferent to nature?' asked his brother, with distress in his voice and an engaging simplicity of manner. 'He has had rather a difficult life, as I expect you know. His affairs have kept him a great deal in towns, and he has had little leisure—very little leisure.'

'He must find it restful here,' remarked Jimmy, again with the sense of being more tactful than truthful.

'I'm sure I hope he does. Rollo is a dear fellow; I wish he came here oftener. Unfortunately his wife does not care for the country, and Rollo himself is very much tied by his new employment—the motor business.'

'Hasn't he been with Scorcher and Speedwell long?'

'Oh no; poor Rollo, he is always trying his hand at something new. He ought to have been born a rich man instead of me.' Randolph spread his hands out with a gesture of helplessness. 'He could have done so much, whereas I—ah, here he comes. We were talking about you, Rollo.'

'No scandal, I hope; no hitting a man when he's down?'

'Indeed no. We were saying we hoped you would soon come into a fortune.'

'Where do you think it's coming from?' demanded Rollo, screwing up his eyes as though the smoke from his cigarette had made them smart.

'Perhaps Vera could tell us,' rejoined Randolph mildly, making his way to the table, though his brother's cigarette was still unfinished. 'How is she, Rollo? I hoped she would feel sufficiently restored to make a fourth with us this evening.'

'Still moping,' said her husband. 'Don't waste your pity on her. She'll be all right tomorrow.'

They sat down to dinner.

The next day, or it might have been the day after, Jimmy
was coming home to tea from the woods below the castle.
On either side of the path was a hayfield. They were mowing
the hay. The mower was a new one, painted bright blue; the
horse tossed its head up and down; the placid afternoon air
was alive with country sounds, whirring, shouts, and clump-
ing footfalls. The scene was full of an energy and gentleness
that refreshed the heart. Jimmy reached the white iron fence
that divided the plain from the castle mound, and, with a
sigh, set his feet upon the zigzag path. For though the hill
was only a couple of hundred feet high at most, the climb
called for an effort he was never quite prepared to make. He
was tramping with lowered head, conscious of each step,
when a voice hailed him.

'Mr. Rintoul!'

It was a foreign voice, the i's pronounced like e's. He
looked up and saw a woman, rather short and dark, watching
him from the path above.

'You see I have come down to meet you,' she said, advanc-
ing with short, brisk, but careful and unpractised steps. And
she added, as he still continued to stare at her: 'Don't you
know? I am Mrs. Verdew.'

By this time she was at his side.

'How could I know?' he asked, laughing and shaking the
hand she was already holding out to him. All her gestures
seemed to be quick and unpremeditated.

'Let us sit here,' she said, and almost before she had spoken
she was sitting, and had made him sit, on the wooden bench
beside them. 'I am tired from walking downhill; you will be
tired by walking uphill; therefore we both need a rest.'

She decided it all so quickly that Jimmy, whose nature had a
streak of obstinacy, wondered if he was really so tired after all.

'And who should I have been, who could I have been, but
Mrs. Verdew?' she demanded challengingly.

Jimmy saw that an answer was expected, but couldn't
think of anyone who Mrs. Verdew might have been.

'I don't know,' he said feebly.

'Of course you don't, silly,' said Mrs. Verdew. 'How long have you been here?'

'I can't remember. Two or three days, I think,' said Jimmy, who disliked being nailed down to a definite fact.

'Two or three days? Listen to the man, how vague he is!' commented Mrs. Verdew, with a gesture of impatience apostrophizing the horizon. 'Well, whether it's three days or only two, you must have learnt one thing—that no one enters these premises without leave.'

'Premises?' murmured Jimmy.

'Hillside, garden, grounds, premises,' repeated Mrs. Verdew. 'How slow you are! But so are all Englishmen.'

'I don't think Rollo is slow,' remarked Jimmy, hoping to carry the war into her country.

'Sometimes too slow, sometimes too fast, never the right pace,' pronounced his wife. 'Rollo misdirects his life.'

'He married you,' said Jimmy gently.

Mrs. Verdew gave him a quick look. 'That was partly because I wanted him to. But only just now, for instance, he has been foolish.'

'Do you mean he was foolish to come here?'

'I didn't mean that. Though I hate the place, and he does no good here.'

'What good could he do?' asked Jimmy, who was staring vacantly at the sky. 'Except, perhaps, help his brother to look after—to look after——'

'That's just it,' said Mrs. Verdew. 'Randolph doesn't need any help, and if he did he wouldn't let Rollo help him. He wouldn't even have him made a director of the coal-mine!'

'What coal-mine?' Jimmy asked.

'Randolph's. You don't mean to say you didn't know he had a coal-mine? One has to tell you everything!'

'I like you to tell me things!' protested Jimmy.

'As you don't seem to find out anything for yourself, I suppose I must. Well, then: Randolph has a coal-mine, he is very rich, and he spends his money on nothing but charitable societies for contradicting the laws of nature. And he won't give Rollo a penny—not a penny though he is his only brother, his one near relation in the world! He won't even help him to get a job!'

'I thought he had a job,' said Jimmy, in perplexity.

'You thought that! You'd think anything!' exclaimed Mrs. Verdew, her voice rising in exasperation.

'No, but he told me he came here for a holiday,' said Jimmy pacifically.

'Holiday, indeed! A long holiday. I can't think why Rollo told you that. Nor can I think why I bore you with all our private troubles. A man can talk to a woman about anything; but a woman can only talk to a man about what interests him.'

'But who is to decide that?'

'The woman, of course; and I see you're getting restless.'

'No, no. I was so interested. Please go on.'

'Certainly not. I am a Russian, and I often know when a man is bored sooner than he knows himself. Come along,' pulling him from the bench much as a gardener uproots a weed; 'and I will tell you something very interesting. Ah, how fast you walk! Don't you know it's less fatiguing to walk uphill slowly—and you with all those fishing-nets and pill-boxes. And what on earth is that great bottle for?'

'I try to catch butterflies in these,' Jimmy explained. 'And this is my killing bottle.'

'What a horrible name. What is it for?'

'I'm afraid I kill the butterflies with it.'

'Ah, what a barbarian! Give it to me a moment. Yes, there are their corpses, poor darlings. Is that Randolph coming towards us? No, don't take it away. I can carry it quite easily under my shawl. What was I going to tell you when you interrupted me? I remember—it was about the terrace. When I first came here I used to feel frightfully depressed—it was winter and the sun set so early, sometimes before lunch! In the afternoons I used to go down the mound, where I met you, and wait for the sun to dip below that bare hill on the left. And I would begin to walk quite slowly towards the castle, and all the while the sun was balanced on the hilltop like a ball! And the shadow covered the valley and kept lapping my feet, like the oncoming tide! And I would wait till it reached my ankles, and then run up into the light, and be safe for a moment. It was such fun, but I don't expect you'd enjoy it, you're too sophisticated. Ah, here's Randolph. Randolph, I've been showing Mr. Rintoul the way home; he didn't know it—he doesn't know anything! Do you know what he does with this amusing net? He uses it to catch tiny little moths, like the ones that get into your furs. He puts it over them and looks at them, and they're so frightened, they think they can't get out; then they notice the little holes, and out they creep and fly away! Isn't it charming?'

'Charming,' said Randolph, glancing away from the net and towards the ground.

'Now we must go on. We want our tea terribly!' And Mrs. Verdew swept Jimmy up the hill.

With good fortune the morning newspaper arrived at Verdew Castle in time for tea, already a little out of date. Jimmy accorded it, as a rule, the tepid interest with which, when abroad, one contemplates the English journals of two days ago. They seem to emphasize one's remoteness, not lessen it. Never did Jimmy seem farther from London, indeed, farther from civilization, than when he picked up the familiar sheet of *The Times*. It was like a faint rumour of the world that had somehow found its way down hundreds of miles of railway, changed trains and stations, rumbled across the estuary, and threaded the labyrinth of lanes and turnings between Verdew Grove and the castle. Each day its news seemed to grow less important, or at any rate less important to Jimmy. He began to turn over the leaves. Mrs. Verdew had gone to her room, absent-mindedly taking the killing bottle with her. He was alone; there was no sound save the crackle of the sheets. Unusually insipid the news seemed. He turned more rapidly. What was this? In the middle of page fourteen, a hole? No, not a mere hole: a deliberate excision, the result of an operation performed with scissors. What item of news could anyone have found worth reading, much less worth cutting out? To

Jimmy's idle mind, the centre of page fourteen assumed a tremendous importance, it became the sun of his curiosity's universe. He rose; with quick cautious fingers he searched about, shifting papers, delving under blotters, even fumbling in the more public-looking pigeon-holes.

Suddenly he heard the click of a door opening, and with a bound he was in the middle of the room. It was only Rollo, whom business of some kind had kept all day away from home.

'Enter the tired bread-winner,' he remarked. 'Like to see the paper? I haven't had time to read it.' He threw something at Jimmy and walked off.

It was *The Times*. With feverish haste Jimmy turned to page fourteen and seemed to have read the paragraph even before he set eyes on it. It was headed: *Mysterious Outbreak at Verdew*.

'The sequestered, little-known village of Verdew-le-Dale has again been the scene of a mysterious outrage, recalling the murders of John Didwell and Thomas Presland in 1910 and 1912, and the occasional killing of animals which has occurred since. In this instance, as in the others, the perpetrator of the crime seems to have been actuated by some vague motive of retributive justice. The victim was a shepherd dog, the property of Mr. J. R. Cross. The dog, which was known to worry cats, had lately killed two belonging to an old woman of the parish. The Bench, of which Mr. Randolph Verdew is chairman, fined Cross and told him to keep the dog under proper control, but did not order its destruction. Two days ago the animal was found dead in a ditch, with its throat cut. The police have no doubt that the wound was made by the same weapon that killed Didwell and Presland, who, it will be remembered, had both been prosecuted by the R.S.P.C.A. for cruelty and negligence resulting in the deaths of domestic animals. At present no evidence has come to light that might lead to the detection of the criminal, though the police are still making investigations.'

'And I don't imagine it will ever come to light,' Jimmy muttered.

'What do you suppose won't come to light?' inquired a

voice at his elbow. He looked up. Randolph Verdew was standing by his chair and looking over his shoulder at the newspaper.

Jimmy pointed to the paragraph.

'Any clue to the identity of the man who did this?'

'No,' said Randolph after a perceptible pause. 'I don't suppose there will be.' He hesitated a moment and then added:

'But it would interest me much to know how that paragraph found its way back into the paper.'

Jimmy explained.

'You see,' observed Randolph, 'I always cut out, and paste into a book, any item of news that concerns the neighbourhood, and especially Verdew. In this way I have made an interesting collection.'

'There seem to have been similar occurrences here before,' remarked Jimmy.

'There have, there have,' Randolph Verdew said.

'It's very strange that no one has even been suspected.'

Randoph Verdew answered obliquely:

'Blood calls for blood. The workings of justice are secret and incalculable.'

'Then you sympathize a little with the murderer?' Jimmy inquired.

'I?' muttered Randolph. 'I think I hate cruelty more than anything in the world.'

'But wasn't the murderer cruel?' persisted Jimmy.

'No,' said Randolph Verdew with great decision. 'At least,' he added in a different tone, 'the victims appear to have died with the minimum of suffering. But here comes Vera. We must find a more cheerful topic of conversation. Vera, my dear, you won't disappoint us of our bridge to-night?'

Several days elapsed, days rendered slightly unsatisfactory for Jimmy from a trivial cause. He could not get back his killing bottle from Mrs. Verdew. She had promised it, she had even gone upstairs to fetch it; but she never brought it down. Meanwhile, several fine specimens (in particular a large female Emperor moth) languished in match-boxes and other narrow receptacles, damaging their wings and even having to be set at liberty. It was very trying. He began to feel that the retention of the killing bottle was deliberate. In questions of conduct he was often at sea. But in the domain of manners, though he sometimes went astray, he considered that he knew very well which road to take, and the knowledge was a matter of pride to him. The thought of asking Mrs. Verdew a third time to restore his property irked him exceedingly. At last he screwed up his courage. They were walking down the hill together after tea.

'Mrs. Verdew,' he began.

'Don't go on,' she exclaimed. 'I know exactly what you're going to say. Poor darling, he wants to have his killing bottle back. Well, you can't. I need it myself for those horrible hairy moths that come in at night.'

'But Mrs. Verdew——!' he protested.

'And please don't call me Mrs. Verdew. How long have we known each other? Ten days! And soon you've got to go! Surely you could call me Vera!'

Jimmy flushed. He knew that he must go soon, but didn't realise that a term had been set to his stay.

'Listen,' she continued, beginning to lead him down the hill. 'When you're in London I hope you'll often come to see us.'

'I certainly will,' said he.

'Well, then, let's make a date. Will you dine with us on the tenth? That's to-morrow week.'

'I'm not quite sure——' began Jimmy unhappily, looking down on to the rolling plain and feeling that he loved it.

'How long you're going to stay?' broke in Mrs. Verdew, who seemed to be able to read his thoughts. 'Why do you want to stay? There's nothing to do here: think what fun we might have in London. You can't like this place and I don't believe it's good for you; you don't look half as well as you did when you came.'

'But you didn't see me when I came, and I feel very well,' said Jimmy.

'Feeling is nothing,' said Mrs. Verdew. 'Look at me. Do I look well?' She turned up to him her face: it was too large, he thought, and dull and pallid with powder; the features were too marked; but undeniably it had beauty. 'I suppose I do: I feel well. But in this place I believe my life might stop any moment of its own accord! Do you never feel that?'

'No,' said Jimmy, smiling.

'Sit down,' she said suddenly, taking him to a seat as she had done on the occasion of their first meeting, 'and let me have your hand—not because I love you, but because I'm happier holding something, and it's a pretty hand.' Jimmy did not resist: he was slightly stupefied, but somehow not surprised by her behaviour. She held up his drooping hand by the wrist, level with her eyes, and surveyed it with a smile, then she laid it, palm upward, in her lap. The smile vanished from her face: she knitted her brows.

'I don't like it,' she said, a sudden energy in her voice.

'I thought you said it was a pretty hand,' murmured Jimmy.

'I did; you know I don't mean that. It is pretty: but you don't deserve to have it, nor your eyes, nor your hair; you are idle and complacent and unresponsive and ease-loving— you only think of your butterflies and your killing bottle!' She looked at him fondly; and Jimmy for some reason was rather pleased to hear all this. 'No, I meant that I see danger in your hand, in the lines.'

'Danger to me?'

'Ah, the conceit of men! Yes, to you.'

'What sort of danger—physical danger?' inquired Jimmy, only moderately interested.

'*Danger de mort*,' pronounced Mrs. Verdew.

'Come, come,' said Jimmy, bending forward and looking into Mrs. Verdew's face to see if she was pretending to be serious. 'When does the danger threaten?'

'Now,' said Mrs. Verdew.

Oh, thought Jimmy, what a tiresome woman! So you think I'm in danger, do you, Mrs. Verdew, of losing my head at this moment? God, the conceit of women! He stole a glance at her; she was looking straight ahead, her lips pursed up and trembling a little as though she wanted him to kiss her. Shall I? he thought, for compliance was in his blood and he always wanted to do what was expected of him. But at that very moment a wave of irritability flooded his mind and changed it: she had taken his killing bottle, spoilt and stultified several precious days, and all to gratify her caprice. He turned away.

'Oh, I'm tougher than you think,' he said.

'Tougher?' she said. 'Do you mean your skin? All Englishmen have thick skins.' She spoke resentfully; then her voice softened. 'I was going to tell you——' She uttered the words with difficulty, and as though against her will. But Jimmy, not noticing her changed tone and still ridden by his irritation, interrupted her.

'That you'd restore my killing bottle?'

'No, no,' she cried in exasperation, leaping to her feet. 'How you do harp on that wretched old poison bottle! I wish I'd broken it!' She caught her breath, and Jimmy rose too, facing her with distress and contrition in his eyes. But she was too angry to heed his change of mood. 'It was something I wanted you to know—but you make things so difficult for me! I'll fetch you your bottle,' she continued wildly, 'since you're such a child as to want it! No, don't follow me; I'll have it sent to your room.'

He looked up; she was gone, but a faint sound of sobbing disturbed the air behind her.

It was evening, several days later, and they were sitting at dinner. How Jimmy would miss these meals when he got back to London! For a night or two, after the scene with Mrs. Verdew, he had been uneasy under the enforced proximity which the dining-table brought; she looked at him reproachfully, spoke little, and when he sought occasions to apologise to her, she eluded them. She had never been alone with him since. She had, he knew, little control over her emotions, and perhaps her pride suffered. But her pique, or whatever it was, now seemed to have passed away. She looked lovely to-night, and he realised he would miss her. Rollo's voice, when he began to speak, was like a commentary on his thoughts.

'Jimmy says he's got to leave us, Randolph,' he said. 'Back to the jolly old office.'

'That is a great pity,' said Randolph in his soft voice. 'We shall miss him, shan't we, Vera?'

Mrs. Verdew said they would.

'All the same, these unpleasant facts have to be faced,' remarked Rollo. 'That's why we were born. I'm afraid you've had a dull time, Jimmy, though you must have made the local flora and fauna sit up. Have you annexed any prize specimens from your raids upon the countryside?'

'I have got one or two good ones,' said Jimmy with a reluctance that he attributed partially to modesty.

'By the way,' said Rollo, pouring himself out a glass of port, for the servants had left the room, 'I would like you to show Randolph that infernal machine of yours, Jimmy. Anything on the lines of a humane killer bucks the old chap up no end.' He looked across at his brother, the ferocious cast of his features softened into an expression of fraternal solicitude.

After a moment's pause Randolph said: 'I should be much interested to be shown Mr. Rintoul's invention.'

'Oh, it's not my invention,' said Jimmy a little awkwardly.

'You'll forgive me disagreeing with you, Rollo,' Mrs. Verdew, who had not spoken for some minutes, suddenly remarked. 'I don't think it's worth Randolph's while looking at it. I don't think it would interest him a bit.'

'How often have I told you, my darling,' said Rollo, leaning across the corner of the table towards his wife, 'not to contradict me? I keep a record of the times you agree with me. December, 1919, was the last.'

'Sometimes I think that was a mistake,' said Mrs. Verdew, rising in evident agitation, 'for it was then I promised to marry you.' She reached the door before Jimmy could open it for her.

'Ah, these ladies!' moralised Rollo, leaning back and closing his eyes. 'What a dance the dear things lead us, with their temperaments.' And he proceeded to enumerate examples of feminine caprice, until his brother proposed that they should adjourn to the bridge table.

The next morning Jimmy was surprised to find a note accompany his early morning tea.

'DEAR MR. RINTOUL (it began), since I mustn't say "Dear Jimmy." ('I never said she mustn't' Jimmy thought.) I know it isn't easy for any man, most of all an Englishman, to understand moods, but I do beg you to forgive my foolish outburst of a few days ago. I think it must have been the air or the lime in the water that made me *un po' nervosa*, as the Italians say. I know you prefer a life utterly flat and dull and even—it would kill me, but there! I am sorry. You can't expect me to change, *à mon âge*! But anyhow try to forgive me.
Yours,
VERA VERDEW.
PS.—I wouldn't trouble to show that bottle to Randolph. He has quite enough silly ideas in his head as it is.'

What a nice letter, thought Jimmy drowsily. He had forgotten the killing bottle. I won't show it to Randolph, Jimmy thought, unless he asks me.

But soon after breakfast a footman brought him a message: Mr. Verdew was in his room and would be glad to see the invention (the man's voice seemed to put the word into inverted commas) at Mr. Rintoul's convenience. 'Well,' reflected Jimmy, 'if he's to see it working it must have something to work on.' Aimlessly he strolled over the drawbridge and made his way, past blocks of crumbling wall, past grassy hummocks and hollows, to the terraces. They were gay with flowers; and looked at from above, the lateral stripes and bunches of colour, succeeding each other to the bottom of the hill, had a peculiarly brilliant effect. What should he catch? A dozen white butterflies presented themselves for the honour of exhibiting their death-agony to Mr. Randolph Verdew, but Jimmy passed them by. His collector's pride demanded a nobler sacrifice. After twenty minutes' search he was rewarded; his net fell over a slightly battered but still recognisable specimen of the Large Tortoiseshell butterfly. He put it in a pill-box and bore it away to the house. But as he went he was visited by a reluctance, never experienced by him before, to take the butterfly's life in such a public and cold-blooded fashion; it was not a good specimen, one that he could add to his collection; it was just cannon-fodder. The heat of the day, flickering visibly upwards from the turf and flowers, bemused his mind; all around was a buzzing and humming that seemed to liberate his thoughts from contact with the world and give them the intensity of sensations. So vivid was his vision, so flawless the inner quiet from which it sprang, that he came up with a start against his own bedroom door. The substance of his day-dream had been forgotten; but it had left its ambassador behind it—something that whether apprehended by the mind as a colour, a taste, or a local inflammation, spoke with an insistent voice and always to the same purpose: 'Don't show Randolph Verdew the butterfly; let it go, here, out of the window, and send him an apology.'

For a few minutes, such was the force of this inward monitor, Jimmy did contemplate setting the butterfly at liberty. He was prone to sudden irrational scruples and impulses, and if there was nothing definite urging him the other way he often gave in to them. But in this case there was. Manners demanded that he should accede to his host's request; the rules of manners, of all rules in life, were the easiest to recognise and the most satisfactory to act upon. Not to go would clearly be a breach of manners.

'How kind of you,' said Randolph, coming forward and shaking Jimmy's hand, a greeting that, between two members of the same household, struck him as odd. 'You have brought your invention with you?'

Jimmy saw that it was useless to disclaim the honour of its discovery. He unwrapped the bottle and handed it to Randolph.

Randolph carried it straight away to a high window, the sill of which was level with his eyes and above the top of Jimmy's head. He held the bottle up to the light. Oblong in shape and about the size of an ordinary jam jar, it had a deep whitish pavement of plaster, pitted with brown furry holes like an overripe cheese. Resting on the plaster, billowing and coiling up to the glass stopper, stood a fat column of cotton-wool. The most striking thing about the bottle was the word *poison* printed in large, loving characters on a label stuck to the outside.

'May I release the stopper?' asked Randolph at length.

'You may,' said Jimmy, 'but a whiff of the stuff is all you want.'

Randolph stared meditatively into the depths of the bottle. 'A rather agreeable odour,' he said. 'But how small the bottle is. I had figured it to myself as something very much larger.'

'Larger?' echoed Jimmy. 'Oh, no, this is quite big enough for me. I don't need a mausoleum.'

'But I was under the impression,' Randolph Verdew remarked, still fingering the bottle, 'that you used it to destroy pests.'

'If you call butterflies pests,' said Jimmy, smiling.

'I am afraid that some of them must undeniably be included in that category,' pronounced Mr. Verdew, his voice edged with a melancholy decisiveness. 'The cabbage butterfly, for instance. And it is, of course, only the admittedly noxious insects that need to be destroyed.'

'All insects are more or less harmful,' Jimmy said.

Randolph Verdew passed his hand over his brow. The shadow of a painful thought crossed his face, and he murmured uncertainly:

'I think that's a quibble. There are categories . . . I have been at some pains to draw them up. . . . The list of destructive lepidoptera is large, too large. . . . That is why I imagined your lethal chamber would be a vessel of considerable extent, possibly large enough to admit a man, and its use attended by some danger to an unpractised exponent.'

'Well,' said Jimmy, 'there's enough poison here to account for half a town. But let me show you how it works.' And he took the pill-box from his pocket. Shabby, battered and cowed, the butterfly stood motionless, its wings closed and upright.

'Now,' said Jimmy, 'you'll see.'

The butterfly was already between the fingers and halfway

to the bottle, when he heard, faint but clear, the sound of a cry. It was two-syllabled, like the interval of the cuckoo's call inverted, and might have been his own name.

'Listen!' he exclaimed. 'What was that? It sounded like Mrs. Verdew's voice.' His swiftly turning head almost collided with his host's chin, so near had the latter drawn to watch the operation, and chased the tail-end of a curious look from Randolph Verdew's face.

'It's nothing,' he said. 'Go on.'

Alas, alas, for the experiment in humane slaughter! The butterfly must have been stronger than it looked; the power of the killing bottle had no doubt declined with frequent usage. Up and down, round and round flew the butterfly; frantic flutterings could be heard through the thick walls of its glass prison. It clung to the cotton-wool, pressed itself into corners, its straining, delicate tongue coiling and uncoiling in the effort to suck in a breath of living air. Now it was weakening. It fell from the cotton-wool and lay with its back on the plaster slab. It jolted itself up and down and, when strength for this movement failed, it clawed the air with its thin legs as though pedalling an imaginary bicycle. Suddenly, with a violent spasm, it gave birth to a thick cluster of yellowish eggs. Its body twitched once or twice and at last lay still.

Jimmy shrugged his shoulders in annoyance and turned to his host. The look of horrified excitement whose vanishing vestige he had seen a moment before, lay full and undisguised upon Randolph Verdew's face. He only said:

'Of what flower or vegetable is that dead butterfly the parasite?'

'Oh, poor thing,' said Jimmy carelessly, 'it's rather a rarity. Its caterpillar may have eaten an elm-leaf or two—nothing more. It's too scarce to be a pest. It's fond of gardens and frequented places, the book says—rather sociable, like a robin.'

'It could not be described as injurious to human life?'

'Oh, no. It's a collector's specimen really. Only this is too damaged to be any good.'

'Thank you for letting me see the invention in operation,'

said Randolph Verdew, going to his desk and sitting down. Jimmy found his silence a little embarrassing. He packed up the bottle and made a rather awkward, self-conscious exit.

The four bedroom candles always stood, their silver flashing agreeably, cheek by jowl with the whisky decanter and the hot-water kettle and the soda. Now, the others having retired, there were only two, one of which (somewhat waste-fully, for he still had a half-empty glass in his left hand) Rollo was lighting.

'My dear fellow,' he was saying to Jimmy, 'I'm sorry you think the new model insecticide fell a bit flat. But Randolph's like that, you know: damned undemonstrative cove, I must say, though he's my own brother.'

'He wasn't exactly undemonstrative,' answered Jimmy, perplexity written on his face.

'No, rather like an iceberg hitting you amidships,' said his friend. 'Doesn't make a fuss, but you feel it all the same. But don't you worry, Jimmy; I happen to know that he enjoyed your show. Fact is, he told me so.' He gulped down some whisky.

'I'm relieved,' said Jimmy, and he obviously spoke the truth. 'I've only one more whole day here, and I should be sorry if I'd hurt his feelings.'

'Yes, and I'm afraid you'll have to spend it with him alone,' said Rollo, compunction colouring his voice. 'I was coming to that. Fact is, Vera and I have unexpectedly got to go away tomorrow for the day.' He paused; a footman entered and began walking uncertainly about the room. 'Now, Jimmy,' he went on, 'be a good chap and stay on a couple of days more. You do keep us from the blues so. That's all right, William, we don't want anything,' he remarked parenthetically to the footman's retreating figure. 'I haven't mentioned it to Randolph, but he'd be absolutely charmed if you'd grace our humble dwelling a little longer. You needn't tell anyone any-thing: just stay and we shall be back the day after tomorrow. It's hellish that we've got to go, but you know this bread-winning business: it's the early bird that catches the worm.

And talking of that, we have to depart at cock-crow. I may not see you again—that is, unless you stay, as I hope you will. Just send a wire to the old blighter who works with you and tell him to go to blazes.'

'Well,' said Jimmy, delighted by the prospect, 'you certainly do tempt me.'

'Then fall, my lad,' said Rollo, catching him a heavy blow between the shoulder-blades. 'I shan't say goodbye, but *au revoir*. Don't go to bed sober; have another drink.'

But Jimmy declined. The flickering candles lighted them across the hall and up the stone stairs.

And it's lucky I have a candle, Jimmy thought, trying in vain the third and last switch, the one on the reading-lamp by the bed. The familiar room seemed to have changed, to be closing hungrily, with a vast black embrace, upon the nimbus of thin clear dusk that shone about the candle. He walked uneasily up and down, drew a curtain and let in a ray of moonlight. But the silver gleam crippled the candlelight without adding any radiance of its own, so he shut it out. This window must be closed, thought Jimmy, that opens on to the parapet, for I really couldn't deal with a stray cat in this localised twilight. He opened instead a window that gave on to the sheer wall. Even after the ritual of tooth-cleaning he was still restless and dissatisfied, so after a turn or two he knelt by the bed and said his prayers—whether from devotion or superstition he couldn't tell: he only knew that he wanted to say them.

'Come in!' he called next morning, in answer to the footman's knock.

'I can't come in, sir,' said a muffled voice. 'The door's locked.'

How on earth had that happened? Then Jimmy remembered. As a child he always locked the door because he didn't like to be surprised saying his prayers. He must have done so last night, unconsciously. How queer! He felt full of self-congratulation—he didn't know why. 'And—oh, William!' he called after the departing footman.

'Yes, sir?'

'The light's fused, or something. It wouldn't go on last night.'

'Very good, sir.'

Jimmy addressed himself to the tea. But what was this? Another note from Mrs. Verdew!

'DEAR JIMMY (he read),

'You will forgive this impertinence, for I've got a piece of good news for you. In future, you won't be able to say that women never help a man in his career! (Jimmy was unaware of having said so.) As you know, Rollo and I have to leave tomorrow morning. I don't suppose he told you why, because it's rather private. But he's embarking on a big undertaking that will mean an enormous amount of litigation and lawyer's fees! Think of that! (Though I don't suppose you think of anything else.) I know he wants you to act for him: but to do so you positively *must* leave Verdew tomorrow. Make any excuse to Randolph; send yourself a telegram if you want to be specially polite: but you must catch the night train to London. It's the chance of a life. You can get through to Rollo on the telephone next morning. Perhaps we could lunch together— or dine? *A bientôt*, therefore.

VERA VERDEW.

'PS.—I shall be furious if you don't come.'

Jimmy pondered Mrs. Verdew's note, trying to read between its lines. One thing was clear: she had fallen in love with him. Jimmy smiled at the ceiling. She wanted to see him again, so soon, so soon! Jimmy smiled once more. She couldn't bear to wait an unnecessary day. How urgent women were! He smiled more indulgently. And, also, how exacting. Here was this cock-and-bull story, all about Rollo's 'undertaking' which would give him, Jimmy, the chance of a lifetime! And because she was so impatient she expected him to believe it! Luncheon, indeed! Dinner! How could they meet for dinner, when Rollo was to be back at Verdew that same evening? In her haste she had not even troubled to make her date credible. And then: 'I shall be furious if you don't come.' What an argument! What confidence in her own powers did not that sentence imply! Let her be furious, then, as furious as she liked.

Her voice, just outside his door, interrupted his meditation. 'Only a moment, Rollo, it will only take me a moment!'

And Rollo's reply, spoken in a tone as urgent as hers, but louder:

'I tell you there isn't time: we shall miss the train.'

He seemed to hustle her away downstairs, poor Vera. She had really been kind to Jimmy, in spite of her preposterous claims on his affection. He was glad he would see her again tomorrow. . . . Verdew was so much nicer than London. . . . He began to doze.

On the way back from the woods there was a small low church with a square tower and two bells—the lower one both cracked and flat. You could see up into the belfry through the slats in the windows. Close by the church ran a stream, choked with green scum except where the cattle went down to drink, and crossed by a simple bridge of logs set side by side. Jimmy liked to stand on the bridge and listen to the unmelodious chime. No one heeded it, no one came to church, and it had gone sour and out of tune. It gave Jimmy an exquisite, slightly morbid sense of dereliction and decay, which he liked to savour in solitude; but this afternoon a rustic had got there first.

'Good-day,' he said.

'Good-day,' said Jimmy.

'You're from the castle, I'm thinking?' the countryman surmised.

'Yes.'

'And how do you find Mr. Verdew?'

'Which Mr. Verdew?'

'Why, the squire, of course.'

'I think he's pretty well,' said Jimmy.

'Ah, he may appear to be so,' the labourer observed; 'but them as has eyes to see and ears to hear, knows different.'

'Isn't he a good landlord?' asked Jimmy.

'Yes,' said the old man. 'He's a tolerably good landlord. It isn't that.' He seemed to relish his mysteriousness.

'You like Mr. Rollo Verdew better?' suggested Jimmy.

'I wouldn't care to say that, sir. He's a wild one, Mr. Rollo.'

'Well, anyhow, Mr. Randolph Verdew isn't wild.'

'Don't you be too sure, sir.'

'I've never seen him so.'

'There's not many that have. And those that have—some won't tell what they saw and some can't.'

'Why won't they?'

'Because it's not their interest to.'

'And why can't the others?'

'Because they're dead.'

There was a pause.

'How did they die?' asked Jimmy.

'That's not for me to say,' the old man answered, closing his mouth like a trap. But this gesture, as Jimmy had already learned, was only part of his conversational technique. In a moment he began again:

'Did you ever hear of the Verdew murders?'

'Something.'

'Well, 'twasn't only dogs that was killed.'

'I know.'

'But they were all killed the same way.'

'How?'

'With a knife,' said the old man. 'Like pigs. From ear to ear,' he added, making an explanatory gesture; 'from ear to ear.' His voice became reminiscent. 'Tom Presland was a friend o' mine. I seed him in the evening and he said, he says, "That blamed donkey weren't worth a ten-pound fine." And I said, "You're lucky not to be in prison," for in case you don't know, sir, the Bench here don't mind fellows being a bit hasty with their animals, although Mr. Verdew is the chairman. I felt nigh killing the beast myself sometimes, it was that obstinate. "But, Bill," he says, "I don't feel altogether comfortable when I remember what happened to Jack Didwell." And sure enough he was found next morning in the ditch with his throat gapin' all white at the edges, just like poor old Jack.

And the donkey was a contrary beast, that had stood many a knock before, harder than the one what killed him.'

'And why is Mr. Verdew suspected?'

'Why, sir, the servants said he was in the castle all night and must have been, because the bridge was drawed. But how do they know he had to use the bridge? Anyhow, George Wiscombe swears he saw him going through Nape's Spinney the night poor old Tom was done in. And Mr. Verdew has always been cruel fond of animals, that's another reason.'

How easy it is, thought Jimmy, to lose one's reputation in the country!

'Tell me,' he said, 'how does Mr. Verdew satisfy his conscience when he eats animals and chickens, and when he has slugs and snails killed in the garden?'

'Ah, there you've hit it,' said the old man, not at all nonplussed. 'But they say Mr. Rollo Verdew has helped him to make a mighty great list of what may be killed and what mayn't, according as it's useful-like to human beings. And anybody kills anything, they persuade him it's harmful and down it goes on the black list. And if he don't see the thing done with his own eyes, or the chap isn't hauled up before the Bench, he doesn't take on about it. And in a week or less it's all gone from his mind. Jack and Tom were both killed within a few days of what they'd done becoming known; so was the collie dog what was found here a fortnight back.'

'Here?' asked Jimmy.

'Close by where you're standing. Poor beast, it won't chase those b——y cats no more. It was a mess. But, as I said, if what you've done's a week old, you're safe, in a manner of speaking.'

'But why, if he's really dangerous,' said Jimmy, impressed in spite of himself by the old man's tacit assumption of Randolph's guilt, 'doesn't Mr. Rollo Verdew get him shut up?' This simple question evoked the longest and most pregnant of his interlocutor's pauses. Surely, thought Jimmy, it will produce a monstrous birth, something to make suspicion itself turn pale.

'Now don't you tell nothing of what I'm saying to you,' said the old man at length. 'But it's my belief that Mr. Rollo don't want his brother shut up; no, nor thought to be mad. And why? Because if people know he's mad, and he goes and does another murder, they'll just pop him in the lunatic asylum and all his money will go to government and charity. But if he does a murder like you or me might, and the circumstances are circumstantial, he'll be hanged for it, and all the money and the castle and the coal-mine will go into the pockets of Mr. Rollo.'

'I see,' said Jimmy. 'It sounds very simple.'

'I'm not swearing there's anything of the sort in Mr. Rollo's mind,' said the old man. 'But that's the way I should look at it if I was him. Now I must be getting along. Good-night, sir.'

'Good-night.'

Of course it wasn't really night, only tea-time, five o'clock; but he and his acquaintance would meet no more that day, so perhaps the man was right to say good-night. Jimmy's thoughts, as he worked his way up the castle mound, were unclear and rather painful. He didn't believe a tithe of what the old man said. It was not even a distortion of the truth; it was ignorant and vulgar slander, and had no relation to the truth except by a kind of contiguity. But it infected his mood and gave a disagreeable direction to his thoughts. He was lonely; Randolph had not appeared at lunch, and he missed Rollo, and even more he missed (though this surprised him) Rollo's wife. He hadn't seen much of them, but suddenly he felt the need of their company. But goodness knows where they are, thought Jimmy; I can't even telephone to them. In the midst of these uneasy reflections he reached his bedroom door. Walking in, he could not for a moment understand why the place looked so strange. Then he realised; it was empty. All his things had been cleared out of it.

'Evidently,' thought Jimmy, 'they've mistaken the day I was going away, and packed me!' An extraordinary sensation of relief surged up into his heart. Since his luggage was nowhere to be seen, it must have been stacked in the hall, ready for his departure by the evening train. Picturing himself at the booking-office of Verdew Grove station buying a ticket for London, Jimmy started for the hall.

William cut short his search.

'Were you looking for your things, sir?' he asked, with a slight smile. 'Because they're in the Onyx Room. We've moved you, sir.'

'Oh,' said Jimmy, following in the footman's wake. 'Why?'

'It was Mr. Verdew's orders, sir. I told him the light was faulty in your bedroom, so he said to move you into the Onyx Room.'

'The room next his?'

'That's right, sir.'

'Couldn't the fuse be mended?'

'I don't think it was the fuse, sir.'

'Oh, I thought you said it was.'

So this was the Onyx Room—the room, Jimmy suddenly remembered, that Rollo had meant him to have in the beginning. Certainly its colours were dark and lustrous and laid on in layers, but Jimmy didn't care for them. Even the ceiling was parti-coloured. Someone must have been given a free hand here; perhaps Vera had done the decoration. The most beautiful thing in the room was the Chinese screen masking the door that communicated, he supposed, with Randolph's bedroom. What a clatter it would make if it fell, thought Jimmy, studying the heavy, dark, dully-shining panels of the screen. The door opening would knock it over. He heard the footman's voice.

'Is it for one night or more, sir? I've packed up some of your things.'

'I'm not sure yet,' said Jimmy. 'William, will this screen move?'

The footman took hold of the screen with both hands and telescoped it against his chest. There was revealed an ordinary looking door covered with green baize. Jimmy could see the point of a key-head, so the door was probably not very thick.

'This used to be the dressing-room,' William volunteered, as though making a contribution to Jimmy's unspoken thoughts.

'Thank you,' said Jimmy, 'and would you mind putting the screen back? . . . And, William!'

The footman stopped.

'There's still time to send a telegram?'

'Oh yes, sir. There's a form here.'

All through his solitary tea Jimmy debated with himself as to whether he should send the telegram—a telegram of recall, of course, it would be. The message presented no difficulty. 'Wire if Coxford case opens Tuesday.' He knew that it did, but his attendance was not at all necessary. He was undoubtedly suffering from a slight attack of nerves; and nowadays one didn't defy nerves, one yielded to them gracefully. 'I know that if I stay I shall have a bad night,' he thought; 'I might as well spend it in the train.' But of course he hadn't meant to go at all; he had even promised Rollo to stay. He had wanted to stay. To leave abruptly tonight would be doubly rude: rude to Randolph, rude to Rollo. Only Vera would be pleased. Vera, whose clumsy attempt to lure him to London he had so easily seen through. Vera, whose 'I shall be furious if you don't come' rankled whenever he thought of it. Every moment added its quota to the incubus of indecision that paralysed his mind. Manners, duty, wishes, fears, all were contradictory, all pulled in different directions. A gust of apprehension sent him hot-foot to the writing-table. The telegram was ready written when, equally strong, an access of self-respect came and made him tear it up. At last he had an idea. At six o'clock he would send the telegram; the office might still be open. There might still be time to get a reply. If, in spite of his twofold obstacle he had an answer, he would take it as the voice of fate, and leave that night. . . .

At half-past seven William came in to draw the curtains; he also brought a message. Mr. Verdew begged Mr. Rintoul to excuse him, but he felt a little unwell, and was dining in his own room. He hoped to see Mr. Rintoul tomorrow to say goodbye. 'You are going, then, sir?' added the footman.

Jimmy blindfolded his will, and took an answer at random from among the tablets of his mind.

'Yes. And—William!' he called out.

'Sir?'

'I suppose it's too late now for me to get an answer to my telegram?'

'I'm afraid so, sir.'

For a second Jimmy sunned himself in a warm flow of recovered self-esteem. Luck had saved him from a humiliating flight. Now his one regret was that his nerves had cheated him of those few extra days at Verdew. 'If there had been a bolt on my side of the green door,' he said to himself, 'I should never have sent that telegram.'

How like, in some ways, was the last evening to the first. As bedtime approached, he became acutely conscious of his surroundings—of the stone floors, the vaulted passages, the moat, the drawbridge—all those concrete signs which seemed to recall the past and substitute it for the present. He was completely isolated and immured; he could scarcely believe he would be back in the real, living world tomorrow. Another glass of whisky would bring the centuries better into line. It did; and, emboldened by its heady fumes, he inspected, with the aid of his candle (for the ground-floor lights had been turned out) the defences of door and window, and marvelled anew at their parade of clumsy strength. Why all these precautions when the moat remained, a flawless girdle of protection?

But was it flawless? Lying in bed, staring at the painted ceiling, with its squares and triangles and riot of geometrical designs, Jimmy smiled to remember how Rollo had once told him of a secret entrance, known only to him. He had promised to show it to Jimmy, but he had forgotten. A nice fellow Rollo, but he didn't believe they would ever know each other much better. When dissimilar natures come together, the friendship blossoms quickly, and as quickly fades. Rollo and Jimmy just tolerated each other—they didn't share their lives, their secrets, their secret passages. . . .

Jimmy was lying on his back, his head sunk on the brightly lit pillow, his mind drowsier than his digestion. To his departing consciousness the ceiling looked like a great five of diamonds spread over his head; the scarlet lozenges moved on hinges, he knew that quite well, and as they moved they gave

a glimpse of black and let in a draught. Soon there would be
a head poking through them all, instead of through this near
corner one, and that would be more symmetrical. But if I
stand on the bed I can shut them; they will close with a click.
If only this one wasn't such a weight and didn't stick so. . . .

Jimmy awoke in a sweat, still staring at the ceiling. It
heaved and writhed like a half-dead moth on the setting-
board. But the walls stood still, so that there was something
more than whisky at the back of it. And yet, when he looked
again, the ceiling did not budge.

The dream was right; he could touch the ceiling by standing
on the bed. But only with the tips of his fingers. What he
needed was a bar of some kind with which to prise it open.
He looked round the room, and could see nothing suitable but
a towel-horse. But there were plenty of walking-sticks downstairs. To light his candle and put on his dressing-gown and
slippers was the work of a moment. He reached the door in
less time than it takes to tell. But he got no further, because
the door was locked.

Jimmy's heart began to beat violently. Panic bubbled up
in him like water in a syphon. He took a wild look around the
room, ran to the bed-head, and pressed the bell-button as
though he meant to flatten it in its socket. Relief stole in his
heart. Already he heard in imagination the quick patter of
feet in the corridor, the hurried, whispered explanations, the
man's reassuring voice: 'I'll be with you in a moment, sir.'
Already he felt slightly ashamed of his precipitate summons,
and began to wonder how he should explain it away. The
minutes passed, and nothing happened. He need not worry
yet; it would take William some time to dress, and no doubt
he had a long way to come. But Jimmy's returning anxiety
cried out for some distraction, so he left the edge of the bed
where he had been sitting, fetched the towel-horse, and, bal-
ancing unsteadily on the mattress, began to prod the ceiling.
Down came little flakes and pellets of painted plaster; they
littered the sheets, and would be very uncomfortable to sleep
on. . . . Jimmy stooped to flick them away, and saw from the
tail of his eye that since he rang five minutes had gone by.

He resumed the muffled tattoo on the ceiling. Suddenly it gave; the red diamond shot upwards and fell back, revealing a patch of black and letting in a rush of cool air.

As, stupefied, Jimmy lowered his eyes, they fell upon the screen. It was moving stealthily outwards, toppling into the room. Already he could see a thin strip of the green door. The screen swayed, paused, seemed to hang by a hair. Then, its leaves collapsing inwards upon each other, it fell with a great crash upon the floor. In the opening stood Randolph, fully dressed; he had a revolver in his right hand, and there was a knife between his teeth. It was curved and shining, and he looked as though he were taking a bite out of the new moon.

The shot missed Jimmy's swaying legs, the knife only grazed his ankle, and he was safe in the darkness of the attic, with the bolt of the trap-door securely shut. He ran trembling in the direction the draught came from, and was rewarded first by a sense of decreasing darkness, and then by a glimpse, through a framed opening in the roof, of the stars and the night sky.

The opening was low down, and to climb out was easy. He found himself in a leaden gully, bounded on one side by a shallow parapet two feet high, and on the other, as it seemed, by the slope of the roof. Finding his way along the gully, he was brought up sharp against an octagonal turret, that clearly marked the end of the building. The moat was directly below him. Turning to the left, he encountered another similar turret, and turning to the left again he found himself up against a wall surmounted by tall chimneys. This wall appeared to be scored with projections and indentations—soot-doors he guessed them to be; he hoped to be able to use them to climb the wall, but they were awkwardly spaced, close to the parapet, and if he missed his footing he ran the risk of falling over its edge.

He now felt a curious lightheartedness, as though he had shuffled off every responsibility: responsibility towards his pyjamas, which were torn and dirty, towards his foot, which was bleeding, towards trains, letters, engagements—all the petty and important demands of life. Cold, but not unhappy, he sat down to await daybreak.

The clock had just chimed three-quarters, which three-quarters he did not know, when he heard a scraping sound that seemed to come from the corresponding parapet across the roof. He listened, crouching in the angle between the chimney wall and the battlement. His fears told him that the sound was following the track by which he had come; the shuffling grew indistinct, and then, the first turret passed, began to draw nearer. It could only be Randolph, who clearly had some means of access to the roof other than the trap-door in Jimmy's bedroom. He must have, or he could not have reached it to spy on his victim while he was asleep. Now he was turning the last corner. Jimmy acted quickly and with the courage of desperation. At the corner where he crouched there projected above the battlement three sides of an octagonal turret, repeating the design of the true turrets at the end. Grasping the stone as well as he could, he lowered himself into space. It was a terrible moment, but the cautious shuffle of Randolph's approach deadened his fear. His arms almost at their full stretch, he felt the dripstone underneath his feet. It seemed about six inches wide, with a downward curve, but it sufficed. He changed his grip from the plain stone band of the parapet to the pierced masonry beneath it, which afforded a better purchase, and held his breath. Randolph could not find him unless he leant right over the balustrade. This he did not do. He muttered to himself; he climbed up to the apex of the roof; he examined the flue-doors, or whatever they were. All this Jimmy could clearly see through the quatrefoil to which he was clinging. Randolph muttered, 'I shall find him when the light comes,' and then he disappeared. The clock struck four, four-fifteen, four-thirty, and then a diffused pallor began to show itself in the eastern sky.

The numbness that had taken hold of Jimmy's body began to invade his mind, which grew dull and sleepy under the effort of compelling his tired hands to retain their hold. His back curved outwards, his head sank upon his breast; the changes of which his cramped position admitted were too slight to afford his body relief. So that he could not at once look round when he heard close above his head the sound of an opening door and the sharp rattle of falling mortar. He recognised the figure as it passed him—Rollo's.

Jimmy restrained his impulse to call out. Why had Rollo come back? Why was he swaggering over the roofs of Verdew Castle at daybreak looking as though he owned it? It was not his yet. Rollo turned, and in the same leisurely fashion walked back towards Jimmy's corner. His face was set and pale, but there was triumph in his eyes, and cruelty, and the marks of many passions which his everyday exterior had concealed. Then his eyebrows went up, his chin quivered, and his under-lip shot out and seemed to stretch across his face. 'Just five minutes more, five minutes more; I'll give him another five minutes,' he kept muttering to himself. He leaned back against the wall. Jimmy could have touched the laces of his shoes, which were untied and dirty. 'Poor old Jimmy, poor old James!' Rollo suddenly chanted, in a voice that was very distinct, but quite unlike his own. To Jimmy's confused mind he seemed to be speaking of two different people, neither of whom was connected with himself. 'Never mind, Jimmy,' Rollo added in the conciliatory tone of one who, overcome by his better nature, at last gives up teasing. 'Anyhow, it's ten to one against.' He stumbled down the gully and round the bend.

Jimmy never knew how he summoned strength to climb over the parapet. He found himself sprawling in the gully, panting and faint. But he had caught sight of a gaping hole like a buttery hatch amid the tangle of soot-doors, and he began to crawl towards it. He was trying to bring his stiff knee up to his good one when from close by his left ear he heard a terrible scream. It went shooting up, and seemed to make a glittering arc of sound in the half-lit sky. He also thought he heard the words, 'Oh, God, Randolph, it's me!' but of this he was never certain. But through all the windings of Rollo's bolt-hole, until it discharged itself at the base of a ruined newel-staircase among the outbuildings, he still heard the agonised gasping, spasmodic, yet with a horrible rhythm of its own, that followed Rollo's scream. He locked the cracked paintless door with the key that Rollo had left, and found himself among the lanes.

Late in the evening of the same day a policeman asked to see Mrs. Verdew, who was sitting in a bedroom in the King's Head inn at Fremby, a market town ten miles from Verdew Castle. She had been sitting there all day, getting up from time to time to glance at a slip of paper pinned to one of the pillows. It was dated, '7.30 a.m., July 10th,' and said, 'Back in a couple of hours. Have to see a man about a car. Sorry— Rollo.' She wouldn't believe the constable when he said that her husband had met with an accident some time early that morning, probably about five o'clock. 'But look! But look!' she cried. 'See for yourself! It is his own handwriting! He says he went away at half-past seven. Why are all Englishmen so difficult to convince?'

'We have a statement from Mr. Randolph Verdew,' said the policeman gently. 'He said that he . . . he . . . he met Mr. Rollo at the castle in the early hours of the morning.'

'But how can you be so stupid!' cried Mrs. Verdew. 'It wasn't Rollo—it was Mr. Rintoul who . . .'

'What name is that?' asked the policeman, taking out his notebook.

Episode

IT was quite a small party because our hostess liked general conversation; we never sat down to dinner more than eight, and generally only six, and after dinner when we went up to the drawing-room the chairs were so arranged that it was impossible for two persons to go into a huddle in a corner and so break things up. I was glad on arriving to find that I knew everyone. There were two nice clever women besides our hostess and two men besides myself. One was my friend Ned Preston. Our hostess made it a point never to ask wives with their husbands, because she said each cramped the other's style and if they didn't like to come separately they needn't come at all. But since her food and her wine were good and the talk almost always entertaining they generally came. People sometimes accused her of asking husbands more often than wives, but she defended herself by saying that she couldn't possibly help it because more men were husbands than women were wives.

Ned Preston was a Scot, a good-humoured, merry soul, with a gift for telling a story, sometimes too lengthily for he was uncommonly loquacious, but with dramatic intensity. He was a bachelor with a small income which sufficed for his modest needs, and in this he was lucky since he suffered from that form of chronic tuberculosis which may last for years without killing you, but which prevents you from working for your living. Now and then he would be ill enough to stay in bed for two or three weeks, but then he would get better and be as gay, cheerful and talkative as ever. I doubt whether he had enough money to live in an expensive sanatorium and he certainly hadn't the temperament to suit himself to its life. He was worldly. When he was well he liked to go out, out to lunch, out to dinner, and he liked to sit up late into the night smoking his pipe and drinking a good deal of whisky. If he had been content to live the life of an invalid he might have been alive now, but he wasn't; and who can blame him? He died at the age of fifty-five of a haemorrhage which he had one night after coming home from some house where, he may well have flattered himself, he was the success of the party.

He had that febrile vitality that some consumptives have, and was always looking for an occupation to satisfy his desire for activity. I don't know how he heard that at Wormwood Scrubs they were in want of prison visitors, but the idea took his fancy, so he went to the Home Office and saw the official in charge of prisons to offer his services. The job is unpaid, and though a number of persons are willing to undertake it, either from compassion or curiosity, they are apt to grow tired of it, or find it takes up too much time, and the prisoners whose problems, interests and future they have been concerned with are left somewhat in the lurch. The Home Office people consequently are wary of taking on anyone who does not look as if he would persevere, and they make careful inquiries into the applicant's antecedents, character and general suitability. Then he is given a trial, is discreetly watched, and if the impression is unfavourable is politely thanked and told that his services are no longer required. But Ned Preston satisfied the dour and shrewd official who interviewed him that he was in every way reliable, and from the beginning he got on well with the governor, the warders and the prisoners. He was entirely lacking in class consciousness, so prisoners, whatever their station in life, felt at ease with him. He neither preached nor moralised. He had never done a criminal, or even a mean, thing in his life, but he treated the crime of the prisoners he had to deal with as though it were an illness like his own tuberculosis which was a nuisance you had to put up with, but which it did no good to talk about.

Wormwood Scrubs is a first offenders' prison and it is a building, grim and cold, of forbidding appearance. Ned took me over it once and I had goose-flesh as the gates were unlocked for us and we went in. We passed through the halls in which the men were working.

'If you see any pals of yours take no notice of them,' Ned said to me. 'They don't like it.'

'Am I likely to see any pals of mine?' I asked drily.

'You never can tell. I shouldn't be surprised if you had had friends who'd passed bad cheques once too often or were caught in a compromising situation in one of the parks. You'd be surprised how often I run across chaps I've met out at dinner.'

One of Ned's duties was to see prisoners through the first difficult days of their confinement. They were often badly shaken by their trial and sentence; and when, after the preliminary proceedings they had to go through on entering the jail, the stripping, the bath, the medical examination and the questioning, the getting into prison clothes, they were led into a cell and locked up, they were apt to break down. Sometimes they cried hysterically; sometimes they could neither eat nor sleep. Ned's business then was to cheer them, and his breezy manner, his natural kindliness, often worked wonders. If they were anxious about their wives and children he would go to see them and if they were destitute provide them with money. He brought them news so that they might get over the awful feeling that they were shut away from the common interests of their fellow men. He read the sporting papers to be able to tell them what horse had won an important race or whether the champion had won his fight. He would advise them about their future, and when the time approached for their release see what jobs they were fitted for and then persuade employers to give them a chance to make good.

Since everyone is interested in crime it was inevitable that sooner or later, with Ned there, the conversation should turn upon it. It was after dinner and we were sitting comfortably in the drawing-room with drinks in our hands.

'Had any interesting cases at the Scrubs lately, Ned?' I asked him.

'No, nothing much.'

He had a high, rasping voice and his laugh was a raucous cackle. He broke into it now.

'I went to see an old girl today who was a packet of fun. Her husband's a burglar. The police have known about him for years, but they've never been able to get him till just now. Before he did a job he and his wife concocted an alibi, and though he's been arrested three or four times and sent up for trial, the police have never been able to break it and he's always got off. Well, he was arrested again a little while ago, but he wasn't upset, the alibi he and his wife had made up was perfect and he expected to be acquitted as he'd been before. His wife went into the witness-box and to his utter amazement she didn't give the alibi and he was convicted. I went to see him. He wasn't so much worried at being in jail as puzzled by his wife not having spoken up, and he asked me to go and see her and ask what the game was. Well, I went, and d'you know what she said to me? She said: "Well, sir, it's like this; it was such a beautiful alibi I just couldn't bear to waste it." '

Of course we all laughed. The story-teller likes an appreciative audience, and Ned Preston was never disinclined to hold the floor. He narrated two or three more anecdotes. They tended to prove a point he was fond of making, that in what till we all got democratic in England were called the lower orders there was more passion, more romance, more disregard of consequences than could ever be found in the well-to-do and presumably educated classes, whom prudence has made timid and convention inhibited.

'Because the working man doesn't read much,' he said, 'because he has no great gift for expressing himself, you think he has no imagination. You're wrong. He's extravagantly imaginative. Because he's a great husky brute you think he has no nerves. You're wrong again. He's a bundle of nerves.'

Then he told us a story which I shall tell as best I can in my own words.

Fred Manson was a good-looking fellow, tall, well-made, with blue eyes, good features and a friendly, agreeable smile, but what made him remarkable so that people turned round in the streets to stare at him was that he had a thick head of hair, with a great wave in it, of a deep rich red. It was really a great beauty. Perhaps it was this that gave him so sensual a look. His maleness was like a heady perfume. His eyebrows were thick, only a little lighter than his hair, and he was lucky enough not to have the ugly skin that so often disfigures red-heads. His was a smooth olive. His eyes were bold, and when he smiled or laughed, which in the healthy vitality of his youth he did constantly, his expression was wonderfully alluring. He was twenty-two and he gave you the rather pleasant impression of just loving to be alive. It was inevitable that with such looks and above all with that troubling sexuality he should have success with women. He was charming, tender and passionate, but immensely promiscuous. He was not exactly callous or brazen, he had a kindly nature, but somehow or other he made it quite clear to the objects of his passing fancy that all he wanted was a little bit of fun and that it was impossible for him to remain faithful to anyone.

Fred was a postman. He worked in Brixton. It is a densely populated part of London, and has the curious reputation of harbouring more criminals than any other suburb because trams run to it from across the river all night long, so that when a man has done a job of housebreaking in the West End he can be sure of getting home without difficulty. Fred liked his job. Brixton is a district of innumerable streets lined with little houses inhabited by the people who work in the neighbourhood and also by clerks, shop-assistants, skilled workers of one sort or another whose jobs take them every day across the river. He was strong and healthy and it was a pleasure to him to walk from street to street delivering the letters. Sometimes there would be a postal packet to hand in or a registered letter that had to be signed for, and then he would have the opportunity of seeing people. He was a sociable creature. It was never long before he was well known on whatever round he was assigned to. After a time his job was changed. His duty then was to go to the red pillar-boxes into which the letters were put, empty them, and take the contents to the main post office of the district. His bag would be pretty heavy sometimes by the time he was through, but he was proud of his strength and the weight only made him laugh.

One day he was emptying a box in one of the better streets, a street of semi-detached houses, and had just closed his bag when a girl came running along.

'Postman,' she cried, 'take this letter, will you. I want it to go by this post most particularly.'

He gave her his good-natured smile.

'I never mind obliging a lady,' he said, putting down his bag and opening it.

'I wouldn't trouble you, only it's urgent,' she said as she handed him the letter she had in her hand.

'Who is it to—a feller?' he grinned.

'None of your business.'

'All right, be haughty. But I tell you this, he's no good. Don't you trust him.'

'You've got a nerve,' she said.

'So they tell me.'

He took off his cap and ran his hand through his mop of curling red hair. The sight of it made her gasp.

'Where d'you get your perm?' she asked with a giggle.

'I'll show you one of these days if you like.'

He was looking down at her with his amused eyes, and there was something about him that gave her a funny little feeling in the pit of her stomach.

'Well, I must be on my way,' he said. 'If I don't get on with the job pretty damn quick I don't know what'll happen to the country.'

'I'm not detaining you,' she said coolly.

'That's where you make a mistake,' he answered.

He gave her a look that made her heart beat nineteen to the dozen and she felt herself blushing all over. She turned away and ran back to the house. Fred noticed it was four doors away from the pillar-box. He had to pass it and as he did so he looked up. He saw the net curtains twitch and knew she was watching. He felt pleased with himself. During the next few days he looked at the house whenever he passed it, but never caught a glimpse of the girl. One afternoon he ran across her by chance just as he was entering the street in which she lived.

'Hulloa,' he said, stopping.

'Hulloa.'

She blushed scarlet.

'Haven't seen you about lately.'

'You haven't missed much.'

'That's what you think.'

She was prettier than he remembered, dark-haired, dark-eyed, rather tall, slight, with a good figure, a pale skin and very white teeth.

'What about coming to the pictures with me one evening?'

'Taking a lot for granted, aren't you?'

'It pays,' he said with his impudent, charming grin.

She couldn't help laughing.

'Not with me, it doesn't.'

'Oh, come on. One's only young once.'

There was something so attractive in him that she couldn't bring herself to give him a saucy answer.

'I couldn't really. My people wouldn't like me going out with a fellow I don't know. You see, I'm the only one they have and they think a rare lot of me. Why, I don't even know your name.'

'Well, I can tell you, can't I? Fred. Fred Manson. Can't you say you're going to the pictures with a girl friend?'

She had never felt before what she was feeling then. She didn't know if it was pain or pleasure. She was strangely breathless.

'I suppose I could do that.'

They fixed the night, the time and the place. Fred was waiting for her and they went in, but when the picture started and he put his arm round her waist, without a word, her eyes fixed on the screen, she quietly took it away. He took hold of her hand, but she withdrew it. He was surprised. That wasn't the way girls usually behaved. He didn't know what one went to the pictures for if it wasn't to have a bit of a cuddle. He walked home with her after the show. She told him her name. Grace Carter. Her father had a shop of his own in the Brixton Road, he was a draper and he had four assistants.

'He must be doing well,' said Fred.

'He doesn't complain.'

Gracie was a student at London University. When she got her degree she was going to be a school teacher.

'What d'you want to do that for when there's a good business waiting for you?'

'Pa doesn't want me to have anything to do with the shop—not after the education he's given me. He wants me to better myself, if you know what I mean.'

Her father had started life as an errand-boy, then become a draper's assistant and because he was hard-working, honest and intelligent was now owner of a prosperous little business. Success had given him grand ideas for his only child. He didn't want her to have anything to do with trade. He hoped she'd marry a professional man perhaps, or at least someone in the City. Then he'd sell the business and retire, and Gracie would be quite the lady.

When they reached the corner of her street Gracie held out her hand.

'You'd better not come to the door,' she said.

'Aren't you going to kiss me good-night?'

'I am not.'

'Why?'

'Because I don't want to.'

'You'll come to the pictures again, won't you?'

'I think I'd better not.'

'Oh, come on.'

There was such a warm urgency in his voice that she felt as though her knees would give way.

'Will you behave if I do?' He nodded. 'Promise?'

'Swop me bob.'

He scratched his head when he left her. Funny girl. He'd never met anyone quite like her. Superior, there was no doubt about that. There was something in her voice that got you. It was warm and soft. He tried to think what it was like. It was like as if the words kissed you. Sounded silly, that did, but that's just what it was like.

From then on they went to the pictures once or twice a week

After a while she allowed him to put his arm round her waist and to hold her hand, but she never let him go farther than that.

'Have you ever been kissed by a fellow?' he asked her once.

'No, I haven't,' she said simply. 'My ma's funny, she says you've got to keep a man's respect.'

'I'd give anything in the world just to kiss you, Gracie.'

'Don't be so silly.'

'Won't you let me just once?' She shook her head. 'Why not?'

'Because I like you too much,' she said hoarsely, and then walked quickly away from him.

It gave him quite a turn. He wanted her as he'd never wanted a woman before. What she'd said finished him. He'd been thinking of her a lot, and he'd looked forward to the evenings they spent together as he'd never looked forward to anything in his life. For the first time he was uncertain of himself. She was above him in every way, what with her father making money hand over fist and her education and everything, and him only a postman. They had made a date for the following Friday night and he was in a fever of anxiety lest she shouldn't come. He repeated to himself over and over again what she'd said: perhaps it meant that she'd made up her mind to drop him. When at last he saw her walking along the street he almost sobbed with relief. That evening he neither put his arm round her nor took her hand and when he walked her home he never said a word.

'You're very quiet tonight, Fred,' she said at last. 'What's the matter with you?'

He walked a few steps before he answered.

'I don't like to tell you.'

She stopped suddenly and looked up at him. There was terror on her face.

'Tell me whatever it is,' she said unsteadily.

'I'm gone, I can't help myself, I'm so stuck on you I can't see straight. I didn't know what it was to love like I love you.'

'Oh, is that all? You gave me such a fright. I thought you were going to say you were going to be married.'

'Me? Who d'you take me for? It's you I want to marry.'

'Well, what's to prevent you, silly?'

'Gracie! D'you mean it?'

He flung his arms round her and kissed her full on the mouth. She didn't resist. She returned his kiss and he felt in her a passion as eager as his own.

They arranged that Gracie should tell her parents that she was engaged to him and that on the Sunday he should come and be introduced to them. Since the shop stayed open late on Saturday and by the time Mr. Carter got home he was tired out, it was not till after dinner on Sunday that Gracie broke her news. George Carter was a brisk, not very tall man, but sturdy, with a high colour, who with increasing prosperity had put on weight. He was more than rather bald and he had a bristle of grey moustache. Like many another employer who has risen from the working class he was a slave-driver, and he got as much work out of his assistants for as little money as was possible. He had an eye for everything and he wouldn't put up with any nonsense, but he was reasonable and even kindly, so that they did not dislike him. Mrs. Carter was a quiet, nice woman, with a pleasant face and the remains of good looks. They were both in the early fifties, for they had married late after 'walking out' for nearly ten years.

They were very much surprised when Gracie told them what she had to tell, but not displeased.

'You are a sly one,' said her father. 'Why, I never suspected for a minute you'd taken up with anyone. Well, I suppose it had to come sooner or later. What's his name?'

'Fred Manson.'

'A fellow you met at college?'

'No. You must have seen him about. He clears our pillar-box. He's a postman.'

'Oh, Gracie,' cried Mrs. Carter, 'you can't mean it. You can't marry a common postman, not after all the education we've given you.'

For an instant Mr. Carter was speechless. He got redder in the face than ever.

'Your ma's right, my girl,' he burst out now. 'You can't throw yourself away like that. Why, it's ridiculous.'

'I'm not throwing myself away. You wait till you see him.'

Mrs. Carter began to cry.

'It's such a come-down. It's such a humiliation. I shall never be able to hold up my head again.'

'Oh, ma, don't talk like that. He's a nice fellow and he's got a good job.'

'You don't understand,' she moaned.

'How d'you get to know him?' Mr. Carter interrupted. 'What sort of a family's he got?'

'His pa drives one of the post office vans,' Gracie answered defiantly.

'Working-class people.'

'Well, what of it? His pa's worked twenty-four years for the post office and they think a lot of him.'

Mrs. Carter was biting the corner of her handkerchief.

'Gracie, I want to tell you something. Before your pa and me got married I was in domestic service. He wouldn't ever let me tell you because he didn't want you to be ashamed of me. That's why we was engaged all those years. The lady I was with said she'd leave me something in her will if I stayed with her till she passed away.'

'It was that money that gave me my start,' Mr. Carter broke in. 'Except for that I'd never have been where I am today. And I don't mind telling you your ma's the best wife a man ever had.'

'I never had a proper education,' Mrs. Carter went on, 'but I always was ambitious. The proudest moment of my life was when your pa said we could afford a girl to help me and he said then: "The time'll come when you have a cook *and* a house-maid," and he's been as good as his word, and now you're going back to what I come from. I'd set my heart on your marrying a gentleman.'

She began crying again. Gracie loved her parents and couldn't bear to see them so distressed.

'I'm sorry, ma, I knew it would be a disappointment to you, but I can't help it, I can't really. I love him so, I love him so terribly. I'm sure you'll like him when you see him. We're going for a walk on the Common this afternoon. Can't I bring him back to supper?'

Mrs. Carter gave her husband a harassed look. He sighed.

'I don't like it and it's no good pretending I do, but I suppose we'd better have a look at him.'

Supper passed off better than might have been expected. Fred wasn't shy and he talked to Gracie's parents as though he had known them all his life. If to be waited on by a maid, if to sup in a dining-room furnished in solid mahogany and afterwards to sit in a drawing-room that had a grand piano in it was new to him, he showed no embarrassment. After he had gone and they were alone in their bedroom Mr. and Mrs. Carter talked him over.

'He is handsome, you can't deny that,' she said.

'Handsome is as handsome does. D'you think he's after her money?'

'Well, he must know that you've got a tidy little bit tucked away somewhere, but he's in love with her all right.'

'Oh, what makes you think that?'

'Why, you've only got to see the way he looks at her.'

'Well, that's something at all events.'

In the end the Carters withdrew their opposition on the condition that the young things shouldn't marry until Gracie had taken her degree. That would give them a year, and at the back of their minds was the hope that by then she would have changed her mind. They saw a good deal of Fred after that. He spent every Sunday with them. Little by little they began quite to like him. He was so easy, so gay, so full of high spirits, and above all so obviously head over ears in love with Gracie, that Mrs. Carter soon succumbed to his charm, and after a while even Mr. Carter was prepared to admit that he didn't seem a bad fellow. Fred and Gracie were happy. She went to London every day to attend lectures and worked hard. They spent blissful evenings together. He gave her a very nice engagement ring and often took her out to dinner in the West End and to a play. On fine Sundays he drove her out into the country in a car that he said a friend had lent him. When she asked him if he could afford all the money he spent on her he laughed, and said a chap had given him a tip on an outsider and he'd made a packet. They talked interminably of the little flat they would have when they were married and the fun it would be to furnish it. They were more in love with one another than ever.

Then the blow fell. Fred was arrested for stealing money from the letters he collected. Many people, to save themselves the trouble of buying postal orders, put notes in their envelopes, and it wasn't difficult to tell that they were there. Fred went up for trial, pleaded guilty, and was sentenced to two years' hard labour. Gracie went to the trial. Up to the last moment she had hoped that he would be able to prove his innocence. It was a dreadful shock to her when he pleaded guilty. She was not allowed to see him. He went straight from the dock to the prison van. She went home, and locking herself up in her bedroom, threw herself on the bed and wept. When Mr. Carter came back from the shop Gracie's mother went up to her room.

'Gracie, you're to come downstairs,' she said. 'Your father wants to speak to you.'

Gracie got up and went down. She did not trouble to dry her eyes.

'Seen the paper?' he said, holding out to her the *Evening News*.

She didn't answer.

'Well, that's the end of that young man,' he went on harshly.

They too, Gracie's parents, had been shocked when Fred was arrested, but she was so distressed, she was so convinced that everything could be explained, that they hadn't had the heart to tell her that she must have nothing more to do with him. But now they felt it time to have things out with her.

'So that's where the money came from for those dinners and theatres. And the car. I thought it funny he should have a friend who'd lend him a car on Sundays when he'd be wanting it himself. He hired it, didn't he?'

'I suppose so,' she answered miserably. 'I just believed what he told me.'

'You've had a lucky escape, my girl, that's all I can say.'

'He only did it because he wanted to give me a good time. He didn't want me to think I couldn't have everything as nice when I was with him as what I've been used to at home.'

'You're not going to make excuses for him, I hope. He's a thief, that's what he is.'

'I don't care,' she said sullenly.

'You don't care? What d'you mean by that?'

'Exactly what I say. I'm going to wait for him and the moment he comes out I'm going to marry him.'

Mrs. Carter gave a gasp of horror.

'Gracie, you can't do a thing like that,' she cried. 'Think of the disgrace. And what about us? We've always held our heads high. He's a thief, and once a thief always a thief.'

'Don't go on calling him a thief,' Gracie shrieked, stamping her foot with rage. 'What he did he did just because he loved me. I don't care if he is a thief. I love him more than ever I loved him. You don't know what love is. You waited ten years to marry pa just so as an old woman should leave you some money. D'you call that love?'

'You leave your ma out of this,' Mr. Carter shouted. Then an idea occurred to him and he gave her a piercing glance. 'Have you *got* to marry the feller?'

Gracie blushed furiously.

'No. There's never been anything of that sort. And not through any fault of mine either. He loved me too much. He didn't want to do anything perhaps he'd regret afterwards.'

Often on summer evenings in the country when they'd been lying in a field in one another's arms, mouth to mouth, her desire had been as intense as his. She knew how much he wanted her and she was ready to give him what he asked. But when things got too desperate he'd suddenly jump up and say:

'Come on, let's walk.'

He'd drag her to her feet. She knew what was in his mind. He wanted to wait till they were married. His love had given him a delicacy of sentiment that he'd never known before. He couldn't make it out himself, but he had a funny sort of feeling about her, he felt that if he had her before marriage it would spoil things. Because she guessed what was in his heart she loved him all the more.

'I don't know what's come over you,' moaned Mrs. Carter. 'You was always such a good girl. You've never given us a day's uneasiness.'

'Stop it, ma,' said Mr. Carter violently. 'We've got to get this straight once and for all. You've got to give up this man, see? I've got me own position to think of and if you think I'm going to have a jail-bird for a son-in-law you'd better think again. I've had enough of this nonsense. You've got to promise me that you'll have nothing more to do with the feller ever.'

'D'you think I'm going to give him up now? How often d'you want me to tell you I'm going to marry him the moment he gets out?'

'All right, then you can get out of my house and get out pretty damn quick. And stay out.'

'Pa!' cried Mrs. Carter.

'Shut up.'

'I'll be glad to go,' said Gracie.

'Oh, will you? And how d'you think you're going to live?'

'I can work, can't I? I can get a job at Payne & Perkins. They'll be glad to have me.'

'Oh, Gracie, you couldn't go and work in a shop. You can't demean yourself like that,' said Mrs. Carter.

'Will you shut up, ma,' shouted Mr. Carter, beside himself now with rage. 'Work, will you? You that's never done a stroke of work in your life except that tomfoolery at the college. Bright idea it was of your ma's to give you an education. Fat lot of good it'll be to you when you've got to stand on your feet for hours and got to be civil and pleasant to a lot of old trouts who just try and give you all the trouble they can just to show how superior they are. I bet you'll like it when you're bawled out by the manageress because you're not bright and snappy. All right, marry your jail-bird. I suppose you know you'll have to keep him too. You don't think anyone's going to give him a job, do you, not with his record. Get out, get out, get out.'

He had worked himself up to such a pitch of fury that he sank panting into a chair. Mrs. Carter, frightened, poured out a glass of water and gave him some to drink. Gracie slipped out of the room.

Next day, when her father had gone to work and her mother was out shopping, she left the house with such effects as she could get into a suitcase. Payne & Perkins was a large department store in the Brixton Road, and with her good appearance and pleasant manner she found no difficulty in getting taken on. She was put in the ladies' lingerie. For a few days she stayed at the Y.W.C.A. and then arranged to share a room with one of the girls who worked with her.

Ned Preston saw Fred in the evening of the day he went to jail. He found him shattered, but only because of Gracie. He took his thieving very lightly.

'I had to do the right thing by her, didn't I? Her people, they didn't think I was good enough for her; I wanted to show them I was just as good as they were. When we went up to the West End I couldn't give her a sandwich and half of bitter in a pub, why, she's never been in a pub in her life, I *had* to take her to a restaurant. If people are such fools as to put money in letters, well, they're just asking for it.'

But he was frightened. He wasn't sure that Gracie would see it like that.

'I've got to know what she's going to do. If she chucks me now—well, it's the end of everything for me, see? I'll find some way of doing meself in, I swear to God I will.'

He told Ned the whole story of his love for Gracie.

'I could have had her over and over again if I'd wanted to. And I did want to, and so did she. I knew that. But I respected her, see? She's not like other girls. She's one in a thousand, I tell you.

He talked and talked. He stormed, he wept. From that confused torrent of words emerged one thing very clearly. A

passionate, a frenzied love. Ned promised that he would see
the girl.

'Tell her I love her, tell her that what I did I just did
because I wanted her to have the best of everything, and tell
her I just can't live without her.'

As soon as he could find time Ned Preston went to the
Carters' house, but when he asked for Gracie the maid who
opened the door told him that she didn't live there any more.
Then he asked to see her mother.

'I'll go and see if she's in.'

He gave the maid his card, thinking the name of his club
engraved in the corner would impress Mrs. Carter enough to
make her willing to see him. The maid left him at the door,
but in a minute or two asked him to come in. He was shown
into the stiff and little-used sitting-room. Mrs. Carter kept him
waiting for some time and when she came in, holding his card
in the tips of her fingers, he guessed it was because she had
thought fit to change her dress. The black silk she wore was
evidently a dress for occasions. He told her his connection
with Wormwood Scrubs and said that he had to do with a
man named Frederick Manson. The moment he mentioned
the name Mrs. Carter assumed a hostile attitude.

'Don't speak to me of that man,' she cried. 'A thief, that's
what he is. The trouble he's caused us. They ought to have
given him five years, they ought.'

'I'm sorry he's caused you trouble,' said Ned mildly. 'Perhaps if you'd give me a few facts I might help to straighten
things out.'

Ned Preston certainly had a way with him. Perhaps Mrs.
Carter was impressed because he was a gentleman. 'Class he
is,' she probably said to herself. Anyhow it was not long
before she was telling him the whole story. She grew upset as
she told it and began to cry.

'And now she's gone and left us. Run away. I don't know
how she could bring herself to do a thing like that. God knows,
we love her. She's all we've got and we done everything in the
world for her. Her pa never meant it when he told her to
get out of the house. Only she was so obstinate. He got in a

temper, he always was a quick-tempered man, he was just as upset as I was when we found she'd gone. And d'you know what she's been and gone and done? Got herself a job at Payne & Perkins. Mr. Carter can't abide them. Cutting prices all the time they are. Unfair competition, he calls it. And to think of our Gracie working with a lot of shop-girls—oh, it's so humiliating.'

Ned made a mental note of the store's name. He hadn't been at all sure of getting Gracie's address out of Mrs. Carter.

'Have you seen her since she left you?' he asked.

'Of course I have. I knew they'd jump at her at Payne & Perkins, a superior girl like that, and I went there, and there she was sure enough—in the ladies' lingerie. I waited outside till closing time and then I spoke to her. I asked her to come home. I said her pa was willing to let bygones be bygones. And d'you know what she said? She said she'd come home if we never said a word against Fred and if we was prepared to have her marry him as soon as ever he got out. Of course I had to tell her pa. I never saw him in such a state, I thought he was going to have a fit, he said he'd rather see her dead at his feet than married to that jail-bird.'

Mrs. Carter again burst into tears and as soon as he could Ned Preston left her. He went to the department store, up to the ladies' lingerie, and asked for Grace Carter. She was pointed out to him and he went up to her.

'Can I speak to you for a minute? I've come from Fred Manson.'

She went deathly white. For a moment it seemed that she could not utter a word.

'Follow me, please.'

She took him into a passage smelling of disinfectants which seemed to lead to the lavatories. They were alone. She stared at him anxiously.

'He sends you his love. He's worried about you. He's afraid you're awfully unhappy. What he wants to know really is if you're going to chuck him.'

'Me?' Her eyes filled with tears, but on her face was a look of ecstasy. 'Tell him that nothing matters to me as long as he loves me. Tell him I'd wait twenty years for him if I had to. Tell him I'm counting the days till he gets out so as we can get married.'

For fear of the manageress, she couldn't stay away from her work for more than a minute or two. She gave Ned all the loving messages she could get into the time to give Fred Manson. Ned didn't get to the Scrubs till nearly six. The prisoners are allowed to put down their tools at five-thirty, and Fred had just put his down. When Ned entered the cell he turned pale and sank on to the bed as though his anxiety was such that he didn't trust his legs. But when Ned told him his news he gave a gasp of relief. For a while he couldn't trust himself to speak.

'I knew you'd seen her the moment you came in. I smelt her.'

He sniffed as though the smell of her body were strong in his nostrils, and his face was as it were a mask of desire. His features on a sudden seemed strangely blurred.

'You know, it made me feel quite uncomfortable so that I had to look the other way,' said Ned Preston when he told us this, with a cackle of his shrill laughter. 'It was sex in its nakedness all right.'

Fred was an exemplary prisoner. He worked well, he gave no trouble. Ned suggested books for him to read and he took them out of the library, but that was about as far as he got.

'I can't get on well with them somehow,' he said. 'I start reading and then I begin thinking of Gracie. You know, when she kisses you ordinary like—oh, it's so sweet, but when she kisses you really, my God, it's lovely.'

Fred was allowed to see Gracie once a month, but their meetings, with a glass screen between, under the eyes of a warder, were so painful that after several visits they agreed it would be better if she didn't come any more. A year passed. Owing to his good behaviour he could count on a remittance of his sentence and so would be free in another six months. Gracie had saved every penny she could out of her wages, and now as the time approached for Fred's release she set about getting a home ready for him. She took two rooms in a house and furnished them on the hire purchase system. One room of course was to be their bedroom and the other the living-room and kitchen. There was an old-fashioned range in it and this she had taken out and replaced by a gas-stove. She wanted everything to be nice and new and clean and comfortable. She took pains to make the two little rooms bright and pretty. To do all this she had to go without all but the barest necessities of existence and she grew thin and pale. Ned suspected that she was starving herself and when he went to see her took a box of chocolates or a cake so that she should have at least something to eat. He brought the prisoner news of what Gracie was doing and she made him promise to give him accurate accounts of every article she bought. He took fond, more than fond, passionate messages from one to the other. He was convinced that Fred would go straight in future and he got him a job as a commissionaire from a firm that had a chain of restaurants in London. The wages were good and by calling taxis or fetching cars he would be able to make money on the side. He was to start work as soon as he came out of jail. Gracie took the necessary steps so that they could get married at once. The eighteen months of Fred's imprisonment were drawing to an end. Gracie was in a fever of excitement.

It happened then that Ned Preston had one of his periodical bouts of illness and was unable to go to the prison for three weeks. It bothered him, for he didn't like to abandon his prisoners, so as soon as he could get out of bed he went to the Scrubs. The chief warder told him that Manson had been asking for him.

'I think you'd better go and see him. I don't know what's the matter with him. He's been acting rather funny since you've been away.'

It was just a fortnight before Fred was due to be released. Ned Preston went to his cell.

'Well, Fred, how are you?' he asked. 'Sorry I haven't been able to come and see you. I've been ill, and I haven't been able to see Gracie either. She must be all of a dither by now.'

'Well, I want you to go and see her.'

His manner was so surly that Ned was taken aback. It was unlike him to be anything but pleasant and civil.

'Of course I will.'

'I want you to tell her that I'm not going to marry her.'

Ned was so astounded that for a minute he could only stare blankly at Fred Manson.

'What on earth d'you mean?'

'Exactly what I say.'

'You can't let her down now. Her people have thrown her out. She's been working all this time to get a home ready for you. She's got the licence and everything.'

'I don't care. I'm not going to marry her.'

'But why, why, why?'

Ned was flabbergasted. Fred Manson was silent for a bit. His face was dark and sullen.

'I'll tell you. I've thought about her night and day for eighteen months, and now I'm sick to death of her.'

When Ned Preston reached this point of his story our hostess and our fellow guests broke into loud laughter. He was plainly taken aback. There was some little talk after that and the party broke up. Ned and I, having to go in the same direction, walked along Piccadilly together. For a time we walked in silence.

'I noticed you didn't laugh with the others,' he said abruptly.

'I didn't think it funny.'

'What d'you make of it?'

'Well, I can see his point, you know. Imagination's an odd thing, it dries up; I suppose, thinking of her incessantly all that time he'd exhausted every emotion she could give him, and I think it was quite literally true, he'd just got sick to death of her. He'd squeezed the lemon dry and there was nothing to do but throw away the rind.'

'I didn't think it funny either. That's why I didn't tell them the rest of the story. I wouldn't accept it at first. I thought it was just hysteria or something. I went to see him two or three days running. I argued with him. I really did my damnedest. I thought if he'd only see her it would be all right, but he wouldn't even do that. He said he hated the sight of her. I couldn't move him. At last I had to go and tell her.'

We walked on a little longer in silence.

'I saw her in that beastly, stinking corridor. She saw at once that there was something the matter and she went awfully white. She wasn't a girl to show much emotion. There was something gracious and rather noble about her face. Tranquil. Her lips quivered a bit when I told her and she didn't say anything for a minute. When she spoke it was quite calmly, as though—well, as though she'd just missed a bus and would have to wait for another. As though it was a nuisance, you know, but nothing to make a song and dance about. "There's nothing for me to do now but put my head in the gas-oven," she said.

'And she did.'

Peasants

WHEN Michael John Cronin stole the funds of the Carricknabreena Hurling, Football and Temperance
Association, commonly called the Club, everyone said 'Divil's
cure to him!' ''Tis the price of him!' 'Kind father for him!'
'What did I tell you?' and the rest of the things people say
when an acquaintance has got what was coming to him. And
not only Michael John but the whole Cronin family, seed,
breed and generation, came in for it; there wasn't one of them
for twenty miles round or a hundred years back but his deeds
and sayings were remembered and examined by the light of
this fresh scandal. Michael John's father (the Heavens be his
bed!) was a drunkard who beat his wife, and his father before
him a land-grabber. Then there was an uncle or grand-uncle
who had been a policeman and taken a hand in the bloody
work at Mitchelstown long ago, and an unmarried sister of
the same whose good name by all accounts it would have
needed a regiment of husbands to restore. It was a grand
shaking-up the Cronins got altogether, and anyone that had a
grudge in for one of them, even if it was no more than a thirty-
third cousin, had rare sport, dropping a friendly word about
it and saying how sorry he was for the poor mother, till he
had the blood lighting in the Cronin eyes.

There was only one thing for them to do with Michael
John; that was to send him to America and let the thing blow
over, and that, no doubt, is what they would have done but
for a certain unpleasant and extraordinary incident.

Father Crowley, the parish priest, was chairman of the
committee. He was a remarkable man, even to look at; tall,
powerfully built but very stooped, with shrewd loveless eyes
that rarely softened except to two or three of the older people.
He was a strange man, well on in years, noted for his strong
political views which never happened to coincide with those

of any party, and as obstinate as the devil himself. Now what should Father Crowley do but try to force it down the necks of the committee that Michael John should be prosecuted?

The committee were all religious men who up to that had never as much as dared to question the judgements of a man of God; yes, faith, and if the priest had been a bully (which to give him his due he wasn't) he might have danced a horn-pipe on the backs of the lot of them and there would have been no complaint. Yet, a man has principles, and the like of this had never been heard of in the parish before. What? Put the police on a boy and he in trouble?

One by one the committee-men spoke up and said so. 'But he did wrong,' said Father Crowley, thumping the table. 'He did wrong and he must be punished.'

'Maybe so, father,' replied Con Norton, the vice-chairman, who acted as spokesman. 'Maybe so indeed; but is that any reason his poor mother should be punished too and she a widow-woman?'

'True for you!' chorused the others.

'Serve his mother right!' said the priest shortly. 'There's none of you but knows better than I do the way that young man was brought up. He's a rogue and his mother is a fool. Why didn't she beat Christian principles into him when she had him on her knee?'

'That may be, too,' agreed Norton mildly. 'I wouldn't say but you're right, but is that any reason his uncle Peter should be punished?'

'Or his uncle Dan?' asked another.

'Or his uncle James?' asked a third.

'Or his cousins, the Dwyers that keep the little shop in Lissnacarriga, as decent a living family as there is in the county Cork?' asked a fourth.

'No, father,' said Norton, 'the argument is against you.'

'Is it, indeed?' exclaimed the priest, growing cross. 'Is it so? What the devil has it to do with his uncle Dan or his uncle James? What are ye talking about? What punishment is it to them? Will ye tell me that? Ye'll be telling me next 'tis a punishment to me, and I a child of Adam like himself!'

'And do you mean, father,' asked Norton, ''tis no punishment to them, having one of their own blood made a public show? Erra, is it mad you think we are? Maybe 'tis a thing you'd like done to yourself?'

'There was none of my family ever a thief,' replied Father Crowley sternly.

'We don't know whether there was or not,' snapped a little man called Daly, a hot-tempered character from the hills.

'Aisy now! Aisy, Phil!' said Norton.

'What do you mean by that?' asked Father Crowley, rising and grabbing his hat and stick.

'What I mean,' said Daly, blazing up, 'is that I won't sit here and listen to insinuations about my native place from any foreigner. There are as many rogues and thieves and vagabonds and liars in Cullough as ever there were in Carricknabreena—ay, begod, and more, and bigger! That's what I mean.'

'No, no, no, no,' said Norton soothingly. 'That's not what he means at all, father. We don't want any bad blood. What he means is that the Crowleys may be a fine substantial family in their own country, but that's fifteen long miles away, and this isn't their country, and the Cronins are neighbours of ours since the dawn of history and time, and it would be a queer thing if at this hour of day we handed one of them over to the police. . . . And listen to me, father,' he went on, forgetting that he was supposed to be making a peaceful speech, and hitting the table as hard as the rest, 'if a cow of mine got sick in the morning, 'tisn't a Cremin or a Crowley I'd be asking for help, and damn the bit of use 'twould be if I did. And all knows I'm no enemy of the priests but a respectable farmer that pays his dues and goes to his duties regularly.'

'True for you! True for you!' agreed the committee.

'I don't give a button what you are,' replied the priest. 'And now listen to me, Con Norton. I bear young Cronin no grudge, nor his family either, which is more than some of you can say, but I know my duty and I'll do it in spite of the lot of you.'

He stood at the door and looked back. They were gazing blankly at one another. He shook his fist at them.

'Ye all know me,' he said. 'Ye know that all my life I'm fighting the long-tailed families. Now, with the help of God, I'll shorten the tail of one of them.'

Father Crowley's threat frightened them. They knew he was a determined man and had spent his time attacking what he called the 'corruption' of councils and committees, which was all very well as long as it happened outside your own parish. They dared not oppose him openly because he knew too much about them all, and in public at least had a lacerating tongue. The solution they favoured was a tactful one. They formed themselves into a Michael John Cronin Fund Committee, and canvassed the parishioners for subscriptions to pay off Michael John's debt. Regretfully they decided that the priest would hardly countenance a football match for the purpose.

Then with the defaulting treasurer, who wore a suitably contrite air, they marched up to the presbytery. Father Crowley was at his dinner but he told the housekeeper to show them in. He looked up in astonishment as his dining-room filled with the seven committee-men, pushing before them the cowed Michael John.

'Who the blazes are ye?' he asked, glaring at them over the lamp.

'We're the Club Committee, father,' replied Norton.

'Oh, are ye?'

'And this is the threasurer—the ex-threasurer, I should say.'

'I won't pretend I'm glad to see him,' said the priest.

'He came to say he's sorry, father. He's very sorry, true as God, and I'll tell you no lie, he is. . . .' Norton made two steps forward and in a dramatic silence laid a heap of notes and silver on the table.

'What's that?' asked Father Crowley.

'The money, father. 'Tis all paid back now, and you've no call to be black with us any more. Any little crossness there was we'll say no more about it, in the name of God.'

The priest looked at the money and then at Norton.

'Con,' he said, 'you'd better keep the soft word for the judge. Maybe he'll think more of it than I do.'

'The judge, father?' asked Norton stupidly.

'Ay, Con, the judge.'

For close on a minute there was silence. The committee stood there with open mouths in consternation.

'And is that what you're doing to us, father?' asked Norton, his voice trembling. 'Is it yourself is going to show us up before the whole country as a lot of robbers?'

'You foolish creatures, I'm showing up none of you.'

'You are then, father, and every man, woman and child in the parish,' said Norton savagely. 'And mark my words, 'twon't be forgotten for you.'

On the following Sunday Father Crowley spoke of the matter from the altar. He spoke for a full half-hour, without a trace of emotion on his grim old face, but his sermon was one long venomous denunciation of the 'long-tailed families', which, according to him, were the ruination of the country and made a mockery of truth, justice and charity. He was, as his congregation agreed, a shockingly obstinate old man who never knew when he was in the wrong.

After Mass he was visited in his sacristy by the committee. He gave Norton a terrible look from under his shaggy eyebrows which made that respectable farmer flinch.

'Father,' said Norton appealingly, 'we only want one word with you. One word and then we'll be going. You're a hard character, and you said some bitter things to us this morning, things we never deserved from you. But we're quiet, peaceable, poor men and we won't cross you any more.'

Father Crowley made a sound like a snort.

'We came to make a good bargain with you, father.'

'Well, what is it?'

'We'll say no more about the whole business if you'll do one little thing to oblige us.'

'The bargain?' said the priest impatiently. 'What's the bargain?'

'We'll leave the matter drop for good and all if you'll give the boy a character.'

'Yes, father,' cried the whole committee in chorus. 'Give him a character! Give him a character!'

'Give him a what?' cried the priest.

'Give him a character, father, for the love of God!' said Norton emotionally. 'If you speak up for him, the judge will leave him off, and then there'll be no stain on the parish.'

'Is it out of your minds you are, you half-witted *aindeiseoirs*?' asked the priest, his face suffused with blood, his head trembling. 'Here am I all these long years preaching to ye about decency and justice and truth and ye no more understand me than that wall there! Is it the way ye want me to perjure myself? Is it the way ye want me to tell a damned lie with the name of Almighty God on my lips? Answer me, every one of ye, is it?'

'Ah, what perjure!' said Norton impatiently. 'Sure, can't you say a few words for the boy? There's no one asking you to say much. What harm will it do you to tell the judge he's an honest, good-living, upright lad, and that he took the money without meaning any harm?'

'My God!' muttered the priest, running his hands distractedly through his grey hair. 'There's no talking to ye, no talking to ye, ye lot of sheep.'

When he was gone the committee-men turned and looked at one another.

'He's an awful trial,' said one.

'He's a tyrant,' said Daly, vindictively.

'He is indeed,' sighed Norton, scratching his head. 'But in God's holy name, boys, before we do anything, we'll give him one more chance.'

That evening while the priest was having his tea the committee-men called again. This time they looked very spruce and business-like and independent. Father Crowley glared at them.

'Are ye back?' he asked bitterly. 'Somehow I was thinking

ye would be, and I declare to goodness I'm sick of ye and yeer old committee, and I'm sorry to the Lord I ever joined it or had anything to do with it. Because, let me tell ye, it has my peace of mind destroyed.'

'Oh, we're not the committee, father,' said Norton stiffly.

'Oh, aren't ye?'

'No, we are not.'

'Well, all I have to say is ye look mighty like it. And if I'm not being impertinent, who the deuce are ye?'

'We're a deputation.'

'Oh! A deputation! Fancy that now! And a deputation from what?'

'A deputation from the parish. . . . So, now maybe you'll listen to us?'

'Oh, go on! I'm listening, I'm listening.'

'Well, now 'tis like this, father,' said Norton suddenly dropping his airs and graces and leaning against the table. ''Tis about that little business this morning. Now, father, maybe you didn't understand us and we didn't understand you. But we're quiet, simple, poor men that want to do the best we can by everybody, and a few words or a few pounds wouldn't stand in our way. Do you follow me now?'

'I declare,' said Father Crowley, resting his elbows on the table. 'I don't know whether I do or not.'

'Well, 'tis like this. We don't want any blame on the parish and on the Cronins, and you're the one man that can save us. Now all we ask of you is to give the boy a character——'

'Yes, father,' interrupted the others in chorus. 'Give him a character! Give him a character!'

'Give him a character, father, and you'll never be troubled with him again. Don't say no to me now till you hear me out! We won't ask you to go next, nigh or near the court. You have pen and ink there beside you, and one couple of lines is all we'll ask of you. The day he walks out of the court you can hand him his ticket to America and tell him never again to show his face in Carricknabreena. There's the price of it, father,' added Norton, clapping a bundle of notes on the table. 'Put the money in your pocket, and we've his mother's word and his own word that he'll go there when you bid him.'

'He can go to pot!' retorted the priest. 'What is it to me where he goes?'

'Now, now, father, just a minute! Just a minute! Sure, we know well 'tis no advantage to you or the parish, and that's the very thing we came to talk about. Now supposing—just supposing for the sake of argument, you do what we're suggesting, there's a few of us here, and between us we might be able to raise whatever little contribution to the building fund you'd think would be reasonable to cover the expense and trouble to yourself? Do you follow me now?'

'Con Norton,' said the priest, rising and holding the edge of the table with his hands, 'I follow you. This morning it was perjury, and now it's bribery, and the Lord knows what 'twill be next. I see I've been wasting my breath. . . . And I see, too,' he added savagely, leaning across the table towards them, 'a pedigree bull would be more use to ye than a priest.'

'What do you mean, father?' asked Norton in a quiet voice.

'What I say.'

'And that's a saying that will be remembered for you the longest day you live,' hissed Norton, leaning towards him till they were facing one another across the table.

'A bull,' gasped Father Crowley. 'Not a priest.'

''Twill be remembered!'

'Will it? Then remember this too. I'm an old man now I'm forty years a priest, and I'm not a priest for the money or power or glory of it, like others I know. I gave the best that was in me—maybe 'twasn't much, but 'twas more than many a better man would give, and at the end of my days . . .' Lowering his voice to a whisper he searched them with his terrible eyes, '. . . at the end of my days, if I did a wrong thing, or a bad thing, or an unjust thing, there isn't man or woman in this parish that would brave me to my face and call me a villain, and isn't that a poor story for an old man that tried to be a good priest?' His voice changed again, and he raised his head. 'Now get out before I kick you out!'

And true to his word and character not one word did he say in Michael John's favour the day of the trial, no more than if he was a heathen. Three months Michael John got and by all accounts he got off lightly.

When he came out of gaol he was a changed man. Downcast he was and dark in himself. There was no one but was sorry for him; people who had never spoken to him before spoke to him now, and to all he said, 'I'm very grateful to you, friend, for overlooking my misfortune.' He refused to go to America, so Norton and the committee made another whip-round, and between this and the money they had collected previously and what the Cronins had made up to send him to America, he found himself with enough to open a small shop. Then he secured a job on the County Council and an agency for some shipping company, and at last he was able to buy a public-house.

As for Father Crowley, till he was shifted, twelve months later, he never did a day's good in the parish. The dues went down and the presents went down, and people who had money to spend on Masses took it fifty miles away rather than leave it to him. They said it broke his heart.

He has left unpleasant memories behind him. Only for him, the people say, Michael John Cronin would be in America today. Only for him he would never have married a girl with a fortune, or had it to lend to poor people in the hard times, or ever sucked the blood of Christians. For as an old man said to me of him, 'A robber he is and was, and a grabber like his grandfather before him, and an enemy of the people like his uncle, the policeman; and though some say he'll dip his hand where he dipped it before, for myself I have no hope unless the mercy of God sends us another Moses or Brian Boru to cast him down and hammer him in the dust.'

V. S. PRITCHETT

The Aristocrat

I T was at two o'clock and after a good lunch that Mr.
Murgatroyd went into the Prince of Denmark and took his
stand four-square and defensive against the bar. The time
was seven minutes past two by the clock above the bottles,
but by his gold watch, which he slipped out of its chamois case,
it was two. He remarked upon this to Mrs. Pierce, the
publican, who was leaning with her fat forearms on the bar,
musing like a cat; and she croaked out a long story about her
husband winding up the clock on Saturday nights. The
usual people were on the bench in the small bar, crowded,
cheerful, and comfortable, Mr. Sanders with a red carnation
in his buttonhole, squeezing his little legs together with glee,
like a house-fly in the sun, in the midst of three women and
not sitting next to his wife. They all heard the conversation
with Mrs. Pierce and they heard her say:

'Bit of an 'eat wave isn't it, Mr. Murgatroyd?' nodding to
the first flakes of March snow in the street.

To this Mr. Sanders added his news:

'Couple of cases of sunstroke in the Theobald's Road they
tell me.'

The presence of Mr. Murgatroyd brought out Mr. Sanders's
wit. He was a dogged little man with a waxed moustache and
tobacco-stained fingers, one to nudge the ladies in the ribs
with his sharp elbows, a jumping cracker at three-ten a week
in the provision trade. And bald.

Mr. Murgatroyd was wearing a smart, new grey flannel suit.
A pair of yellow gloves drooped in one hand like the most
elegant banana-skins. He was a shy and important man. His
eloquence was in the breadth of his shoulders, in the thick
pink of his face after the first drink, in the full-moon expansion
of his stomach under the smooth waistcoat and in the polish

of his shoes. Mrs. Sanders, a woman pushed to the outskirts of everything and sitting on the extreme edge of the bench, was ashamed of her wriggling husband when Mr. Murgatroyd, blue-eyed, shy and impressive, stood with his lids lowered, gazing at the floor, secure and silent in his substance. The young Jewess who was always there on Saturday afternoon got up and opened her fur coat when Mr. Murgatroyd came in. She rested one hand on her hip, gave a long look into the mirror and began walking up and down, almost touching Mr. Murgatroyd when she turned. Mr. Murgatroyd lowered his eyes when she came, rolling her hips, humming and laughing towards him.

It was Mr. Sanders's round. Mr. Murgatroyd took a deep drink, faced the eyes of the dancing Jewess for a second, and then, as the beer sank down in him, grew heavy in the head, solid in his silence and vague in his vision.

It was at this moment when they were busy with their glasses, all talking at once, when Mr. Murgatroyd unbuttoned his new coat and was easing out his disclaiming stomach and when the Jewess gave it a tap on the fourth button, with the words: 'What you got in there, Mr. Murgatroyd?'—it was at this moment that a stranger came into the bar. He was a tall, white-haired man and was among them just as Mr. Sanders was pulling the money out of his pocket. Mr. Sanders was bobbing about, standing in his way.

'Jim,' whispered Mrs. Sanders, anxiously leaning across to pull her husband's coat-tails. 'There's a gentleman wants to get past.'

'Excuse me, mister,' said Mr. Sanders, holding a full glass in each hand and abashed by the height of the stranger. A quiet, slightly wavering voice replied and the stranger walked past them to the bar.

'A beer, if you please,' he said. He turned round, and all talk stopped. They saw the old man looking at them, counting them, giving each one of them a fine, quick calculating stab of his eyes. There were wet points of thawed snow on his long shabby green overcoat. Without a word he took his glass and walked slowly over to the mirror and put his glass down on the shelf. They watched him. His clothes were worn but they were carefully kept.

One hand was fidgeting in his overcoat pocket as he stood. He was an old man; he might have been seventy, even seventy-five. He was thin, rigid and austere, a soldierly old man with quick crafty eyes. His lips were pared away to two thin, stiff lines, he carried his chin high like a sentry. His nose was lean and aquiline and he wore a long, carefully clipped moustache which curled with a military flourish. It was the alertness of the grey threadbare eyes of the old man and something supple and gentle in him that silenced everyone.

Mr. Murgatroyd lowered his eyes and studied the old man's clothes. They were old and respectable. Mr. Sanders was silenced by the aristocratic curve, the disciplined richness of that white moustache. Mrs. Tagg jostled her various selves together within her corsets and stared. Mrs. Sanders timidly admired. The Jewess stood yielding, softening her gaiety before his white age.

'Cold day,' said the old man to them all. They were all surprised. Only the Jewess and Mrs. Tagg murmured a reply.

Although he stood still, he was a restless old man. He moved his feet a little as he stood, and one of his hands was continually fingering something hidden in his pocket. Everybody noted this. Then his eyes moved in soft, darting glances at them all, so that they shifted their eyes. By those razor-cut glances he seemed to observe not their faces but things on their persons. Mr. Sanders straightened his carnation after one of these looks and Mrs. Tagg felt for her black beads. When he turned to Mr. Murgatroyd he looked straight into the middle of Mr. Murgatroyd's fine grey flannel stomach. Mr. Murgatroyd leaned back rather more defensively against the bar; then he relented; being a very shy man, he could not resist the chance of a conversation when someone had got over the first difficulties.

'Was it snowing still?' Mr. Murgatroyd asked.

'It was,' said the old man.

Mr. Murgatroyd wagged his head impressively.

'This wind finds out all your weak spots,' said the old man. There was a movement of sympathy; he drew himself up with dignity to repel it.

Then the old man, with some deliberation, opened his over-coat and he was seen to be even thinner than he had at first appeared. His long hand went into the pocket of his carefully darned jacket and he drew out something which amazed them all.

It was a very large green silk handkerchief with a brilliant pattern of red and yellow suns on it, rich, exotic and expensive. Mrs. Tagg reckoned out the price at once. He let the hand-kerchief fall to its full length and caught it with his other hand. He gave it a small shake and gathered it up, clutching it tightly and watching it spring out and open like a gorgeous flower. Mr. Sanders had expected to see it lifted straight to the beads of foam on the old man's fine moustache; but now he was playing with it, showing it off, conjuring with its brilliant lightness in the snow darkness of the bar. Would it fall to the dirty floor?

But the old man did not let it fall. He lightly touched his moustache with it and put it not into the inner pocket, but into the outside pocket of his overcoat. It hung out and Mr. Murgatroyd looked down his own chest and gave a touch to his own handkerchief in his breast pocket. The old man took one of his economical drinks and then smiled a friendly, faintly triumphant smile.

Mrs. Tagg smiled back at him. She was gazing at the handkerchief hanging far out of the pocket.

'Mind you don't drop that handkerchief of yours,' said Mr. Murgatroyd with great difficulty.

The old man, still smiling, drew back before this friendliness and straightened himself.

'You don't want to lose a nice one like that,' said Mrs. Tagg.

The old man surveyed them all and murmured something impatiently as if resenting interference. Rebuked, they watched. Presently, eyeing them all, he drew out of his other pocket the thing he had been fingering for so long. It was a short smooth stick about a foot long, like a wooden whistle.

It was not a whistle, but merely a stick. He took it out and ran it through his hands, smoothing it and stroking it, and with every touch his thin, stiff hands seemed to become lighter and softer and more pliable. He passed the stick from one hand to the other, sometimes holding it only between the tips of his two forefingers. The Jewess came forward to watch this.

'Nice bit of wood,' said Mr. Murgatroyd enquiringly.

'Uh,' grinned the old man and then with a severe look put the stick back in his pocket. There was disappointment in the wondering eyes of Mrs. Sanders. But the old man was fumbling and muttering:

'Yes, yes,' and went on fumbling.

'Your handkerchief is in the other pocket,' said Mr. Sanders eagerly. The Jewess looked admiringly at Mr. Sanders for being so quick to read her thoughts.

'I know,' said the old man, giving him a severe glance, and still fumbling and frowning now with irritation.

Mr. Murgatroyd expanded and said with amusement:

'Lost something?'

The old man looked round sharply.

'Have you got a sixpence?' he jerked.

Mr. Murgatroyd's smile died in his soul but remained fixed on his face. He coloured. He moved his lips. He concealed a swallow. He leaned farther back against the counter. Everyone was watching the crisis in Mr. Murgatroyd.

'I want a sixpence,' said the old man and appealed to the others. 'A sixpence,' he said quickly. And at the same time he drew out the brilliant handkerchief and caught it with the other hand.

'I'll show you something. I'll show you what I can do with this handkerchief.'

His whole manner had changed. He had become sharp and assertive.

The Jewess saw it at once. Her eyes woke up.

'You are going to do a trick,' she said.

He looked at her with contempt and a smile on the tail of it.

'A conjuring trick?' asked Mr. Murgatroyd, widening his eyes. 'What are you going to do? Sixpence and a handkerchief?' he said deprecatingly.

'You know it?' said the old man.

'Everyone knows it. Everyone sees it. The vanishing sixpence.'

'There's nothing new in that,' laughed Mr. Sanders. 'Eh, ma?' he said.

They all laughed. God, the old man was a conjurer. Mrs. Pierce, without unfolding her arms, slid them farther down the bar. The old man's eyes glittered.

'I'll bet you a tanner,' said the old man, 'you don't see it.' And he stared full and unanswerably at Mr. Murgatroyd. Mr. Murgatroyd stared back with all his might. He entrenched himself against the counter. Mrs. Pierce stepped nearer on her side and he entrenched himself against the support of Mrs. Pierce and the bar. He went very red and a mist came into his eyes.

'You want my sixpence,' he said in a stupor, strenuously defending himself.

'No. I'll make a bet,' the old man said, 'with anyone.' He snapped his fingers at them all. 'You'll get it back,' he said softly, smiling. They were ashamed of their suspicions. They gazed with command at Mr. Murgatroyd hemmed in against the bar. He was obliged to hand the old man a sixpence.

The old man looked at the sixpence on the pink palm of Mr. Murgatroyd's hand. Very reluctantly he took it and held it in his fingers.

'It's a funny thing,' he said, 'but you see all kinds of handkerchief tricks, but no one sees this.'

'Let's see it,' interrupted Mr. Murgatroyd and was frowned on for interrupting.

'Some of these men you see on the halls are quick.' He chattered away and he told them of ways of doing the trick, ways of folding the handkerchief and of concealing the coin.

'There, hold it a minute,' he said, giving the sixpence back to Mr. Murgatroyd to the astonishment of all. And his fingers captivated them with the play of his handkerchief as he illustrated his points.

They all leaned forward.

'Well, let's see it,' said Mr. Murgatroyd from his defence. But the old man went on talking. And then he insisted on Mr. Murgatroyd holding the handkerchief. The Jewess came forward and wanted to hold it too.

'Now watch,' said the old man. And he took back the sixpence and placed it in the handkerchief and began to knot it in. Mr. Murgatroyd held one end of the handkerchief while the old man got to work with both his nimble hands. He folded and knotted. He stopped to explain.

'Get on with it,' said Mr. Sanders.

'Shut up. You watch,' said Mrs. Tagg, sitting vast in nervous judgement.

'Well, there you are,' said the old man. 'The sixpence is in there, isn't it? You saw me put it in.'

'I saw it,' said Mr. Murgatroyd very hot.

'It was his sixpence, he ought to know,' said Mr. Sanders.

The old man smiled along his lips. Mrs. Sanders gazed sadly at her husband. The Jewess watched like a jackdaw for brightness.

'Feel it,' said the old man.

Reluctantly, ashamed of suspicion, Mr. Murgatroyd put out his hand. He could feel the hard round coin.

'It's there,' he said to the others.

'Oh!' said the old man coldly, whipping the handkerchief open.

It was empty. There was no sixpence. The beautiful rich, green handkerchief with the yellow suns on it waved. Mrs. Sanders was glad the poor old gentlemen had a beautiful silk handkerchief.

'There!' said Mrs. Pierce gloomily from the bar.

'That's done it,' said Mr. Sanders, screwing up his legs.

Mrs. Tagg made more room for herself on the bench and then breathed deeply.

'A man who can do that,' she frowned, 'is a clever man.'

'He had it in his hand all the time,' said the Jewess.

The old man showed her his empty hands.

'Eh?' said the old man, faintly smiling. He began absently to fold up the handkerchief with his rippling hands which never ceased in their movements.

'Yes,' said Mr. Murgatroyd, rather proud of himself. 'Yes,' he said, shaking his head.

The handkerchief was whipped open again and there was the sixpence in it.

'You see!' Mrs. Pierce murmured miserably.

They all began to talk at once.

The old man put his handkerchief back into his pocket and reached for his drink. He listened to the arguments and explanations.

'Oh, I must give you your sixpence,' he said to Mr. Murgatroyd. But Mr. Murgatroyd recoiled. He was shamed by the sight of his coin. He thickened with generosity, his skin gleamed with admiration and the flush of his second pint. He felt he was the leader of a delegation, the master of ceremonies, the mayor of a town; but too much of a man of the world to show it crudely. He condescended in a knowing, intimate, chatty way with the sparse of speech old man.

'No, that's your sixpence,' said Mr. Murgatroyd casually. 'You won it.'

'Oh . . .' the old man hesitated.

'Yes, go on. You take it. Go on,' said Mrs. Tagg firmly, shaking her head. Mrs. Tagg was proud of being out for justice.

The old man drew the stick from his pocket and began sliding it to and fro and shyly pocketed the sixpence. Mrs. Sanders smiled wistfully and gladly at him when he did this.

'There's nothing in it,' said the old man. 'It's all a swindle. The quickness of the hand deceiving the eye and human nature,' he said. 'Take the stick and tumbler trick.' He picked up an empty glass and rammed the stick several times at the bottom of it. The third or fourth time it appeared to go through.

'Gawd,' said Mr. Sanders with admiration. 'That's clever. See how he done that? Do it again! There now.'

'Dear me. Look at that,' said Mrs. Tagg.

They all saw it. They all felt warm and intimate.

'There's a trick in everything,' said the old man.

'A man with a brain can diddle anyone,' said Mr. Sanders, nodding intimately to the old man, whose eye faintly fluttered and then ignored him.

Somehow a ring had come into the old man's hand. The Jewess was the first to notice it.

'A ring and a stick,' said the old man. 'Get it off without moving your hands.' He slid the ring up and down the stick and then slipped it off.

It was the maddening way of this old man to start a trick and then stop and talk and begin all over again.

Now he was off again and he got Mr. Murgatroyd to hold one end of the stick, while he took out his handkerchief again. He covered the stick up. The ring was on it. The handkerchief in all its colours covered the stick and Mr. Murgatroyd's hand was resting pressed against his waistcoat. The old man kept altering the position of Mr. Murgatroyd's hand, pulling the stick away to show the ring was still on it, and then giving it back again.

'The chair trick now,' he was saying. 'They tie a man up to a chair with his arms behind his back. You can go up and see he's properly knotted, and yet he just steps out of it. What's the explanation? Trick knots.'

'They're not real knots, then?' accused Mr. Sanders.

'He's knotted up,' said the old man.

'But not with real knots,' said the Jewess.

'They're knots all right,' said the old man. 'He's got a couple of tapes up his sleeve coming out in slits in his coat.'

They exclaimed. He was fidgeting all the time, straightening out his handkerchief. He even gave Mr. Murgatroyd a tap in the ribs and said he was sorry. Mr. Murgatroyd smiled pityingly at the poor fussy old conjuror with all his tricks. Suddenly the old man said 'Look!' and whipped off the handkerchief. There was no ring on the stick.

'What are you drinking?' said Mr. Murgatroyd with embarrassment.

The old man hesitated. 'No, thank you,' he said. 'Not before my dinner. I haven't had my dinner yet.'

'Oh, I see,' murmured Mr. Murgatroyd with embarrassment.

No dinner! What did he mean, no dinner? Did he mean he was earning his dinner? They were all very comfortable people with full stomachs. It was embarrassing to sit there full of food while an old man going on for seventy-five stood there empty, a fine old man like that. An aristocratic old man and nothing inside him. Mr. and Mrs. Sanders, they had had a stew. Mrs. Tagg had had a nice bit of crab and a Guinness. Crab didn't agree with the Jewess. 'It isn't that it repeats, but, you know, I know I've had it.' So she had had spaghetti. As for Mr. Murgatroyd, he had been built up on steak and two vegetables and raisin roll. They were diffusing their goodness in him.

All were touched when the old man gave a short bow and murmured in his quavering dignified voice that an old soldier would be grateful for a copper or two. His quick eyes watched their hands.

A handsome old man like that doing this for a living! Mrs. Sanders signalled to her husband. The Jewess opened her handbag.

'An old soldier did you say?' asked Mrs. Tagg on behalf of everyone.

'The East Kents,' said the old man, straightening.

'The Buffs!' she smiled with sudden reminiscent warmth, imperiousness vanishing in a glitter of long-forgotten gaiety.

'Yes, that's it. The Buffs,' the old man repeated mechanically. His thin, long, clever, hungry hands.

'Steady, the Buffs!' exclaimed Mrs. Tagg, with a shake of her head and tears of pleasure in her eyes.

'Oh, ah . . .' murmured the old man.

'Chatham?' said Mr. Sanders. 'Nice place. The Bells, Chatham. Know that?'

'Twenty-five years' service,' said the old man. 'Not so young now.'

'I could tell you was an old soldier,' said Mrs. Tagg with pride.

He stood there talking to them as he put the few coppers in his pocket. Mr. Sanders began to remember the good old days at Chatham during the war.

'I was talking about the Boer War,' said the old man.

Mrs. Sanders raised her head high in shame for her husband. She was proud of the heroic old man.

'Well,' he said, after a while. 'I suppose I'd better be moving along to my dinner.'

They were sad. But they understood. They realized he was a hungry old man.

'Good day, and I thank you,' he said.

Mr. Murgatroyd put out his hand. The old man was surprised by this handshake. It was the only time he had been taken aback. Raising his hat, he went slowly out of the bar. The swing door bumped after him and Mrs. Pierce raised herself from the counter and went to the window to see the tall, upright figure walk away. When she came back she said: 'It's snowing hard now.'

They all sat in silence staring into the tops of their glasses. Except the Jewess, who took off her hat and combed her hair by the mirror. There on the mantelpiece was the froth-laced glass the old man had used.

'Well, well,' said Mr. Murgatroyd uncomfortably. He relaxed from the slanting position into which he had recoiled before the old man. 'He gets a living,' said Mr. Murgatroyd.

There was a long silence. The bar seemed to be much darker now that the old man had gone. They were thinking about Mr. Murgatroyd's words. Mr. Murgatroyd was all right, he had a new suit of clothes, gloves in his hand, a fountain-pen in his pocket, a car outside and a new Trilby hat. But everyone had to get a living. Mrs. Sanders moved to the end of the bench and pulled up the collar of her coat with a shiver.

'Hunger,' said Mrs. Sanders in her timid voice. 'That's the worst thing.'

They all looked at her with curiosity and reproof for speaking that word.

And that uncomfortable word reminded Mr. Murgatroyd

of something. His shyness and importance were moving inside him. It was his round.

'What's everyone having?' he said at last, looking away up at the clock among the bottles. Mrs. Pierce looked up, too.

'Guinness, ma'am. Time for another, I think. Your clock's fast, Mrs. Pierce. . . .'

And his hand went down his waistcoat for his watch. Down and down it went. And as it went down he seemed to feel a nudge in his stomach and a look of consternation came on his face. The watch was not there. His hand dug in his other pocket.

'Well, I'm . . .' he said aloud. The watch had gone.

His eyes popped wide and hard, his jaw dropped. He went very pale and then flushed to the colour of a beetroot.

'Here,' he blurted out, starting from the counter. 'My watch. It was here. I know it was. It's gone. You saw it, Mrs. Pierce. You saw me take it out. It's gone. That artful old swine has pinched my watch!'

He glared at them all.

'Where is he?' he shouted. 'Which way did he go? Look for him! Of all the thieves . . .'

Unable to do more because of the vast heaving and of his rage, Mr. Murgatroyd looked as though he would burst.

V. S. PRITCHETT

The Scapegoat

THERE were long times when we were at peace and when
the world left us alone. We could go down Earl Street and,
although we did not like the place and it felt strange to us and
the women stared down from the windows and a child here
and there might call out a name after us, we just walked on
thinking of something else. But we were always more at ease
and more ourselves, even in the quietest times of truce, when
we had turned the corner by the hop-warehouse and had got
back into Terence Street, which was our own. The truth is
that you can't live without enemies, and the best enemies are
the ones nearest home; and though we sometimes went out to
the Green to boo the speakers and some of our lads went after
the Yids or joined a procession up West, that was idleness and
distraction. The people we hated were not a mile away on the
main road where the trams and the buses are and you don't
know one man from the next; no, the people we hated were
round the corner, next door, in Earl Street. They were, we
used to say, a different class of people from ourselves altogether.

I don't know why, but if there was any trouble in the world,
we turned out and attacked them. I don't know either how
these things began. You would know there was trouble
coming when you heard the voices of the children getting
shriller and more excited, until their cries became rhythmic
like the pulse of native war-cries in the forest. We were,
indeed, lost in a *jungle* of streets. Somehow the children would
have sticks, old pieces of board and stones in their hands, and
they would be rushing in groups to the hop-warehouse and
jeering and then scattering back. A similar thing would be
happening in Earl Street. Usually this happened in the warm
long evenings of the summer. Then, after the children, the
thing got hold of the women and they came down from their

windows where they had been watching and scratching their arms, very hot and restless, and would stand at their doorsteps and start shouting at their children. A stone would fly up and then the women would be down in the middle of the street.

It might take a day to work up or it might take longer. You would get the Earl Street girls going down our street talking in loud voices daring us, and our young lads would stand by saying nothing until the girls got to the corner. And then those girls would have to bolt. Towards closing time the Gurneys, the fighting family in Earl Street, would be out and we had our Blackers and then it was a question of who came out of the Freemasons and how he came out. But perhaps nothing would happen and we would just go down Earl Street after dark and merely kick their milk-bottles down the basements.

This has been going on ever since the old people can remember. When the war came we knew everyone in Earl Street was a spy or a Hun or a Conchie. The Great War, for us, was between Earl Street and Terence Street. They had a V.C. and we hadn't, though we had a bunch of other stuff and one man who escaped from the Turks and was in the papers; and, though we did our best, the tea we gave was nothing to the tea they did in Earl Street for their V.C. Where they got the money from was the puzzle. Thirty-two pounds. Some of our women said the Earl Street girls must have been on the streets; and at the Freemasons the men said half of Earl Street were nothing but bloody pensioners. The police came in before we had the question settled. But when the war ended, things changed. Half of our lot was out of work and when we went down Earl Street we would see half of their lot out of work too, and Earl Street did not seem quite so strange to us. One street seemed to blend into the other. This made some of our lot think and they gave their steps an extra clean to show there was a difference between Earl Street and Terence Street after all.

In the years that followed, sometimes we were up on Earl Street, sometimes we were down. We were waiting for some big event. It did not come for a long time and a stranger might have thought that the old frontiers had gone and the reign of universal peace was upon us. It was not. The Jubilee came and we saw our chance. Earl Street had collected thirty-two pounds for its V.C.'s tea-party. We reckoned we would top that for the Jubilee. We would collect forty.

There was a red-haired Jew in our street called Lupinsky. He was a tailor. He was round-shouldered from bending over the table and his eyes were weak from working by gas at night. In the rush season he and his family would be up past midnight working. He was a keen man. He came out in pimples —he was so keen. Lupinsky saw everything before any of us. He saw the Jubilee before the King himself. He had got his house full of bunting and streamers and Union Jacks. 'Get in at the early doors,' he said. 'What'll you have?' he used to say to us when we went to his shop. 'Rule Britannia or God Save the King?' 'Who's that?' we said. 'The King of the Jews?' 'Getcha,' said Lupinsky. 'He's dead. Didn't you hear?' He raked in the money. They had another Jew in Earl Street doing the same. 'I say!' called Lupinsky. 'I say!'— we used to call him. 'I-say-what'll-you-have'—'Cohen's sold 120 yards to Earl Street and you've only done 70.' So we doubled. 'I say,' says Lupinsky. 'I say. When you going to start collecting? They got ten quid in Earl Street and you haven't started.'

And this was true. The trouble was we couldn't agree upon who should collect. We had had a nasty experience with the Club a few years back. And then Lupinsky was hot for doing it himself. He'd got the bunting. He'd seen it coming. He'd even got boxes. He'd thought of everything. We had nothing against Lupinsky, but when we saw him raking in the money on his God Saves and Kiss-me-quicks and his flags of all the nations, we thought he was collecting enough as it was. He might mix up the two collections. 'No,' we said to Lupinsky. 'You're doing your bit, we'll do the rest.' 'That's O.K.,' Lupinsky said. He never bore resentment, he was too keen. 'But I hear Earl Street's up to twelve ten.' He wasn't upset with us, but he couldn't bear to see us shilly-shallying around while Earl Street walked away with it. 'If you don't trust me,' he said, 'can't you trust yourselves? I don't know what's happened to this street.' And he spat from the top of his doorstep into the gutter.

Lupinsky was wrong about us. We trust each other. There is not a man in Terence Street you cannot trust. In that nasty business we had with the Club, the man was not a Terence Street man. We could trust one another. But we were frightened. Forty pounds! We thought. That's a big sum. We didn't like the handling of it. There wasn't one of us who had seen forty pounds in his life. The Blackers, a good fighting lot, were terrified. Albert Smith and his uncle were the most likely, but they said they were single and didn't like the idea. And we, for some reason, thought a single man wasn't right for the job. And the wives, the married ones, though eagerly wanting their husbands to do it, were so afraid the honour would go to someone else, that they said to give it to a married man was tempting Providence. Lupinsky went down the street almost in tears, saying Earl Street had touched seventeen ten.

Then suddenly we saw the right man had been staring us in the face all the time. He was not single and he was not married. He was a widower, made serious by death: Art Edwards. We chose Art Edwards, and he agreed.

Art Edwards was a man of forty-seven, and the moment he agreed we were proud of him. He was a grey-haired man, not very talkative and of middle height, very patient and looked you straight in the face. He lived with his sister, who looked after his two children, he had a fruit stall in the main road— he had been there for twenty years—and every Sunday he used to go alone with a bunch of flowers for his wife's grave at the cemetery. The women admired him very much for doing this. He never changed. His house was the neatest house in our street and he never seemed to get richer or poorer. He just went on the same.

He had been a widower a good long time, too, and some thought he ought to marry again. The women were curious about him and said you couldn't but respect a man who didn't take a second, and Art was held up as a model. This didn't prevent many of them running after him and spreading the rumour afterwards that his sister was a woman who wouldn't let a man call his soul his own. But the way Art mourned for the dead and kept faithful to The First, the ONE AND ONLY, as the women said, was striking. Some of the men said that being a model wasn't healthy and that if they had been in Art's shoes they would muck around on the quiet. They wondered why the hell he didn't, yet admired him for his restraint. Some of us couldn't have lived with temptation all those years without slipping up.

Art had put a black band on his sleeve when his wife died and had worn it ever since. But when he started collecting for the tea we had the feeling he had put off his mourning and had come alive again. We were pleased about this because, with his modest, retiring ways, we hardly knew him. 'It will bring him out,' we said. He came round with his little red book and his tin and we said, 'What's it now, Art? How we doin'?' Art was slow at adding up, but accurate. He told us. We made a big effort and we touched the ten-pound mark pretty soon.

This woke us up and made us feel good, but Lupinsky came round and said it wasn't any bloody good at all. They'd touched nineteen pounds in Earl Street. So one of the women said they'd help Art. He didn't want this, or his sister didn't. So she joined in, too, to keep the other women off him. They knocked at his door at all hours and stopped him in the street. And when she saw this his sister put on her best hat and coat and went round and stopped their men. The result was everyone was collecting and came round to Art and said:

'Here y'are, Art. One and eight,' or 'Here y'are, Art, eight and six.'

And two of the Blacker girls had a fight because one said the other wasn't collecting fair, but was cheapening herself to get the money. For we touched seventeen and went on to twenty-one.

The night we passed Earl Street some of our girls went out and just walked down Earl Street telling them. They

didn't like it. A crowd from Earl Street came round and
called 'Down with the Yids' outside Lupinsky's. Then Earl
Street picked up and passed us again. We went round to Art
and planked down more money. Art got out his book and
he couldn't write it down fast enough.

'Where do you keep it, Art?' we said.

He showed us a box in the cupboard. It was a fine sight all
that money. His sister said:

'Art's picked up a bit in the High Street.' We looked at
him as if he were a hero. ''Slike business,' he said. 'You've
got to go out for it.'

We looked with wonder at him. We had chosen the right
man. It was bringing him out. And he had ideas too. He got
some of the kids to go out at night with tins.

We passed Earl Street and they passed us. Then we passed
them again. It was ding-dong all the time. Lupinsky flew in
and out with the latest like a wasp and stung us to more. Art
Edwards, he said, had no life in him. After this, it became
madness. People got out their savings.

There was a funny case at Harry Law's. He was a boozer,
a big, heavy man, very particular in the house and very
religious. Some nights when he was bad he used to beat his
wife and we used to look down into their basement window
wondering what would be happening inside, for something
usually was happening. There were often shouts and curses
and screams coming from that room and then times, which
made you uncomfortable, when everything was quiet.
Harry Law was often out of a job. Mrs. Law was a timid
woman and everyone was sorry for her. She used to go up to
the Freemasons and look through the door at him. She was
a thin, round-shouldered woman, always anxious about her
husband and sorry that he made a fool of himself, for he got
pompous when he was drunk and she hated the way people
laughed at him. He used to say she had no ambition and he
had dragged her out of the gutter. She said, '*Down* into the
gutter, you mean.' They used to have guilty arguments like
this for hours, each boasting they were better than the other
and wondering all the time why they had got into their

present situation. Then Harry Law would go to church so as
to feel good and find out why, and his wife used to stop at
home and think about it too. She would put her arms round
him and love him when he came back. And he would be all
right for a few days until he got some scheme into his head for
making money. When he had the scheme he would go out
and get drunk again.

Harry Law wanted to show everyone that he was a man of
ideas and ambitions, and better than the rest of us in Terence
Street. He used to dress up on Sundays. He used to say he
had been better off once and had had a shop. The truth was,
as his wife bitterly told everyone, he'd always been the same;
up and down all his life. She couldn't bear other people
laughing at him, but she used to tear his reputation to bits
herself and get great pleasure out of doing it.

It was just at the height of our madness that he came into
the Freemasons and, instead of cadging for drinks, began to
order freely. A funny thing had happened, he said. And he
said, in his lordly voice, 'I want Art Edwards.' It turned out
that he had been going across the room while his wife was out
and had tripped up on something on the floor. There was a
bump in the lino. Being a very inquisitive man who never had
anything to do, he knelt down and felt the lump. 'I thought
it was dirt,' he said. One of the things he always said about
his wife was that she was dirty. He was a very clean man
himself. He decided to take up the lino, and underneath he
found a lump of money wrapped up in notes. It was his wife's
savings.

That was why Harry Law was lording it at the Freemasons.
He had hardly given a penny to the Collection, but now, when
everyone was present, he was going to make a great gesture
and show his greatness. When Art came in, he said, 'Here,
Art. Have a fiver.'

We all stared. Harry Law was leaning against the bar with
the notes in the tips of his fingers as if they were dirt, like a
duke giving a tip.

At that moment his wife came in.

'That's mine,' she screamed. 'It's mine.'

There was a row and Art wouldn't take the money. Everyone said that a man hadn't the right to take his wife's money. But Harry said, 'What!' Wasn't his money as good as anybody's? and we said, 'Yes, Harry, but that belongs to your missus.' She was crying, and he kept saying, 'Go home. I'll teach you to come round here. It is my money. I earned it.'

This was awkward. Between her tears, with her hands covering her face, Mrs. Law was saying she had saved it. He was always ruining them, so she had to save. Still, if he'd earned it, it was his.

'Take that money,' said Harry, dropping it like a lord on the floor. The notes fell down, we all looked at them and no one moved. Mr. Bell of the Freemasons got a laugh by saying we were littering up his bar with paper. Then Harry turned his back and we picked it up and were going to give it to Mrs. Law, but Harry said in a threatening voice, 'That's Art's. For the Collection. I reckon I got Earl Street knocked silly.'

That part of the statement was irresistible. While we hesitated, Art said:

'Give it here then. I'll look after it.' Lupinsky, who had been sitting there all the time clutching his hands and his eyes starting out of his head with misery at the sight of money lying in the sand, gave a shout.

'That's the boy,' he said. 'We've got 'em.'

We all felt uncomfortable with Harry and we went away in ones and twos and Mrs. Law went out still crying. After she went out Art went too, and when we got down the street Art stopped and told Mrs. Law he wasn't going to take the money and he made her take it back. She clutched it with both hands and looked at him like a dog with gratitude.

That night half the men in Terence Street wanted to take up their lino and sat up late arguing with their wives; but the madness was still in the air, especially when Earl Street, hearing our news, sent all their kids up West and passed us. There was a fight in the High Street between our kids and the Earl Street kids and one of ours lost her box. But there was nothing in it except stones. They put stones in to make a rattle so that people would think they were doing well. If there had been any money in that box there wouldn't have been a pane of glass in Earl Street left.

'They've passed us,' the cry went down our street. In the middle of this Mrs. Law came over to Art and gave him back the money. She made him take it.

'Your husband made you,' says Art.

'Him,' she said scornfully. 'He don't know anything about it. I told him you gave it me back and he said, "A good thing too." He's feeling sorry for himself. I'll teach him to touch my money, I said. If there's going to be any giving in this house, it's me that's got the money. I'm going to teach my husband a lesson,' she said.

This surprised Art, for he had been very sorry for poor Mrs. Law, and had shown it. But I've no doubt she was tired of being pitied. That money was all she had. She was going to show us that the Laws had their pride and she wasn't going to let them down. Only *she* was going to give it.

Her eyes shone and were sharp. They were greenish, miserly grey eyes, yet she was not miserly. Now she was proud and not bedraggled with tears and misery, she looked jubilant and cunning. She had been a gay, quick-tongued woman in her time.

'I kept it under the floor. That was wrong of me,' she said. 'I oughter have put it in the Post Office.'

She said she knew her husband was right. It was not right to hide money.

Everyone in Terence Street had supposed Mrs. Law to be a poor, timid, beaten soul, and Art had always thought the same, he said; but now he said that she had some spirit. She had opened her heart to him because he had been kind to her and now she said, very proudly, that he should come and have a chat with her husband. She took Art triumphantly to her basement just to show her husband there were other men in the world. Old Harry Law saw this at once—he was always on his dignity—so he just talked largely to Art about the shops he had had, the ups and downs, his financial adventures.

Investments, he called them. We had all heard of investments, but none of us had ever had any. If he had his life over again, Harry Law said, he'd invest every penny.

'There's a man,' Art said when he went, 'who doesn't practise what he preaches.' But he respected Harry's preaching, though he despised him a bit. And Harry said, 'There's a man who stays the same all his life. Never made a penny, never lost a penny. The only money he's got,' said Harry, 'isn't his—this collection.'

And Harry asked him how much it was. There were some thirty-odd pounds, Art said.

Harry respected him when he heard that and said with a sigh, 'Money makes money.'

When Art got back, his sister was short with him. 'Going after other men's wives,' she said. And she lectured him about Mrs. Law. It had been such a warm, pleasant, friendly evening over at Harry Law's that Art was hurt about this.

'Him and her,' he said, 'has got more brains than you think. They've lived, all right. They've had their ups and downs.'

'He's a boozer.'

'We've all got our faults. He's had his ups and downs.'

And that was the phrase that he kept repeating. It fascinated him. He felt generous. It came to him that he had never felt anything for years. He had just gone on standing in the High Street by the stall. He had never taken a holiday. He had never bought himself anything he wanted. He had never done anything. It startled him—but he suddenly didn't want his wife who was in the grave. The street had chosen him, singled him out above all others, and there he stood naked, nothing. He was shy about his nonentity. He felt a curious longing for ups and downs.

You will say, 'How did we know what Art Edwards thought?' That was the strange thing: we did know. We knew as if he had told us, as if we were inside him. You see, because we had singled him out he was, in a sense, ourselves. We could see him thinking and feeling and doing what we would. He had taken the burden off us. By doing that he had become nearer and more precious to us than any other person.

And there was Terence Street two pounds ahead of Earl Street, drunk with the excitement of it. Art used to get the money out and count it—it was the biggest sum of money he had ever seen—and a sober pride filled him. He had done this. People like Mrs. Law had just thrown in all they had. He had put in his bit cautiously, but everyone had scraped and strained and just wildly thrown in the cash. It made him marvel. He marvelled at us, he marvelled—as his hands trembled over the money—that he had been picked out by us to hold it.

We went round once or twice to look at the money too. What a nest egg, what an investment! Over thirty pounds! We said we wished it was ours. We said we wished we could give more, or double it. We all wanted to double it. We looked at it sadly. 'If that thirty pounds had been on the winner today,' someone said. 'Or on the dogs.'

We laughed uneasily. And we dreamed. The more we looked at that money the more we thought of things you could do with it—mad things like backing a horse or sensible things like starting a business or having a holiday.

When we got up in Art's kitchen and saw him put the money in the cupboard and lock the door, we nodded our heads sadly. It was like burying the dead.

'It's sad it's got to go,' we thought.

And it seemed fitting that Art, who had buried the dead and who was a dour man with iron-grey hair and level-looking eyes, should have the grim task of keeping that money, like some sexton. And we were glad to have him doing it, to have him be responsible instead of us. For some of us had to admit we'd go mad at times with temptation tingling in our fingers and hissing like gas in coal in our hearts.

When we left him we felt a kind of sorrow for Art for bearing our burden, for being the custodian of our victory over Earl Street.

It made us all very friendly to Art. The time went by. We used to stop and have a word with him in the street. And Art became friendly too. But he wasn't at the Freemasons much. He went over to Mrs. Law's. And Harry Law didn't go on the booze. He stayed at home talking largely to Art. Once or twice Art went out in the evenings with Mr. and Mrs. Law. Lupinsky used to see them up at the Pictures.

Lupinsky was our reporter of everything, and gradually, expressing no doubt the instinct of the street, he had become our reporter on Art Edwards. We wanted a friendly eye kept on him not because he was valuable but because he was— well, as you would keep an eye on a sick man, say, a man who might have a heart attack or go dizzy in the street. When Lupinsky came back and said, 'I see Art Edwards getting on a tram,' we used to look up sharply and then, annoyed with ourselves, say 'What of it? What was he doing, having a ride?'

That Jew used to make us tired. And he'd started worrying already about the catering. They'd started arranging about the catering already in Earl Street. 'It's a funny thing,' we said, 'about the Yids. He's only been here fifteen years and you'd think he'd been here for ever. Anyone'd think he'd been born in the street. You'd bloody well think it was Jerusalem.'

We had been born there, most of us, and we said:

'It *will* be Jerusalem soon.'

But we would have been nowhere without Lupinsky.

And then one morning he came along and said:

'Seen Art?'

'No,' we said.

'He's not up in the High Street,' said Lupinsky. 'And he's not at his house.'

'What of it?' we said.

Lupinsky was breathless. All the pimples on his face seemed about to burst. He had the kind of red hair that is coarse and stands up on end and thick arched eyebrows which were raised very high but were now higher for his eyes were starting out of his head. There were always bits of cotton from tailoring on his clothes and he was, as I have said, rather hump-backed from leaning all day over his machine.

'I saw him last night at the station. Nine o'clock. He took a ticket on the North London and hasn't been back.'

'Smart baby,' we said. But we were thinking of Lupinsky. We didn't believe him and yet we did believe him. 'What were you doing up at the station—brother had another fire?' we said. Lupinsky's brother was always having fires.

But it was true. Art hadn't been home that night and his sister was very shifty when we went to see her. We never liked Art's sister and we grinned to think he'd got away from her for a night.

'Art had to go away on business,' she said.

Theirs was a tidy house and Art's sister worked hard in it. The window-sills were hearth-stoned. That woman never stopped. She always came to the door with an iron in her hand or a scrubbing-brush or with something she was cleaning or cooking. She was a tall, straight-nosed woman and she had the best teeth I've ever seen, but there was no thickness in her, no give.

She used to say, 'I've never had justice done me.'

And Art used to sigh and say, 'I can never do justice to her.'

'What about it now?' said Lupinsky, who was waiting for us.

'Art can go away if he likes,' we said. 'Why not?'

'Sure, yes, why not?' said Lupinsky. 'What are you worrying about?'

Later on Lupinsky came and told us Art was still away. His stall was still in the lock-up and he hadn't been down to the market. Lupinsky had a friend who had told him. Then Lupinsky had another friend who said he'd seen Art at Wembley.

'Too many Yids here,' said Albert Blacker. 'You can't move but you catch one in your clothes. What's up with Wembley?'

We went over to Mrs. Law's and called down to her. She was ironing in the light of the window.

'Seen Art Edwards?' we said.

'No,' she said. 'He hasn't been here for two or three days.'

'Oh,' we said.

Then Harry Law got up from his chair by the stove and said:

'Art gone?'

'We're just looking for him. Thought he might be with you?'

Mrs. Law gazed at us and then she looked at her husband. She was one of those women who when anything serious or unexpected happens, when they don't know what to think, when they are bewildered, always turn to their husbands; as if by studying him she would always know the worst about any event in the world and would be prepared. It was like looking up something in a book or gazing into a crystal. And when she had gazed at her husband and thought about him, she said:

'Oh dear.' And she put down her iron and her shoulders hunched up. She looked accusingly at her husband and he lowered his eyes. He knew she could read him like that.

We did not think so at the time, but afterwards we said we had the feeling that when Mrs. Law looked at her husband in that accusing way, she knew something about Art Edwards that we did not know. It turned out that she did not know. I looked out of the window that night when I went to bed. It was a warm night. I work in a fur-warehouse and the air had the close, dead, laid-out smell of ladies' furs. There was a cold hollow lilac light over the roofs from the arc-lamps in the High Street. At night our street is quiet and often you can hear the moan of a ship's siren from the river like the hoarse voice of someone going away. But the commonest sound is the clinking of shunting trucks on the railway—a sound that is meaningless as if someone who couldn't play the piano had struck the keys anyhow, trying to make a tune. It is a sound which makes you think the city has had an attack of nerves. As I stood there on one leg, undoing my boots, I heard quick footsteps coming along. They were Lupinsky's. Lupinsky was always up late.

'I say. I say,' he called up to me. 'Art's come back. I just seen him. He came back and let himself in.'

That night Art Edwards went into the lock-up in his yard and, attaching his braces to a hook in the roof, he hanged himself. The box in the cupboard was empty. He had gone off to Wembley and lost all the money on the dogs.

We went out into the street in the morning and stood outside the house and stared at the windows. The people from Earl Street came too. All the children came and stared and no one said anything in the street. Albert Blacker went into the yard at the back and Lupinsky was there with the police. Mrs. Law would not leave her house, but stood on her doorstep holding the railing tightly, watching from a distance. Harry Law would not come out. He walked up and down the room and called up to his wife to come down. He could not bear being left alone. She was afraid to leave her house and yet, I thought, wanted to be with Art.

'The bloody twister,' we said between our teeth.

'That bloody widower,' we said.

'Takes our money and has a night out. Our savings! Our money!'

'The rotten thief.'

We muttered like this standing in front of the house. We were sorry for the police who had to touch the body of a man like that.

'You wouldn't trust me,' Lupinsky said.

We looked at him. We turned away. We couldn't bear the sight of that man's pimples.

'I'm used to money,' Lupinsky said.

I could not repeat all the things we said. I remember clearly the red, white, and blue streamers drooping over the street and looking dirty, with 'God Save the King' on them. 'God Save Art Edwards,' said Harry Law, coming up. He was tight.

We thought of the spirit of Art Edward's sister being humbled. All down the street, at all the windows, the women leaned on their bare arms thinking about this. They cuffed their children and the children cried. There was the low

murmur of our voices in the street and then the whining voices
of children. Presently a couple of women came down, pushed
their way through the crowd and went in to help Art's sister.
We gaped at them.

And then Lupinsky, who gave the lead to everything and
always knew what we were thinking underneath, said:

'They're jeering at us in Earl Street.'

They were. We set our teeth. Kids came round shouting,
'Who swiped the money box! Who swiped the money box!'
Our kids did nothing for a long time. Then they couldn't
stand it. Our kids went for the Earl Street kids. Some of our
women came down to pull their kids off and this drew out the
Earl Street women. In half an hour Albert Blacker came out
of the Freemasons with his sleeves rolled up, just when the
Earl Street men were getting together, and then Harry Law
came out roaring. Mrs. Law ran towards him. But it was too
late. A stone went and a window crashed and that brought
out the rest of the Blacker family. We got it off our chests
that night and we crowded into Earl Street. Half their milk-
bottles had gone before the police whistles went.

And then it was clear to us. We knew what to do. Lupinsky
headed it. Art Edwards was suddenly our hero. We'd kill the
man who said anything against Art Edwards. In our hearts
we said, it might have been ourselves. Thirty pounds. We
remembered the sight of it! We even listened to Harry Law.

'He was trying to double it at the dogs,' he said. 'Investing
it. Every man has . . .'

His wife pulled his coat and tried to stop him.

'Every man,' continued Harry Law, 'has his ups and
downs.'

And to show Earl Street what we were and to show the
world what we thought of Art Edwards, we got up the biggest
funeral that has ever been seen in our street. He was ourselves, our hero, our god. He had borne our sins. You
couldn't see the hearse for flowers. The street was black with
people. The sun shone. We'd been round and got every stall-
holder, every barrow-man in the neighbourhood. The procession was a mile long when it got going. There was a

Jubilee for you, covered in red, white and blue wreaths. Art Edwards our king. It looked like a wedding. The great white trumpets of the lilies rocked thick on the coffin. Earl Street couldn't touch that. And Lupinsky collected the money.

WILLIAM SANSOM

The Girl on the Bus

Since to love is better than to be loved, unrequited love may be the finest love of all. If this is so, then the less requited the finer. And it follows that the most refined passion possible for us must finally be for those to whom we have never even spoken, whom we have never met. The passing face, the anguish of a vision of a face, a face sitting alone in front of you so endearing and so moving and so beautiful that you are torn and sick inside with hope and despair, instant despair . . . for it is hopelessly plain that no word can ever be spoken, those eyes will never greet yours, in a few minutes the bell will ring, the bus will shudder to a stop, and down some impersonal side street she will be gone. Never to be seen again. Gone even is the pain of listening to where she will book for—a fourpenny, or a threehalfpence ticket?

It is due to such an encounter that I find engaging the story of my friend Harry. Only Harry's girl was not on a bus, she passed on skis.

It was one late January afternoon when Harry was walking out at Haga. The snow lay thick, and everywhere over the fine rolling park groups of Stockholmers had sought out the best slopes for an afternoon's ski-ing. The sun was already low and yellow over the firs, it sent a cold tired dusk across the snow—and one could feel the pleasantly weary, flushed trudge of the skiers making their last climb before nightfall. Harry walked about tasting this air of a winter's day ending, enjoying the rich smell of birchwood burning, watching the first yellow lights square in the cream-coloured palace, tasting his own frosted breath. Up on the highest ridge stood the line of cavalry barracks, the fantastic line of false medieval war-tents—their great carved wooden folds were draped to the snow, a last glint of the sun flashed the gold emblems on their snow-domed roofs. From such an elegant extravagance it must have been fine to see the blue-cloaked cavalry ride forth steaming and jangling onto snowy hills. But now it was a ghost-house: and as if in evocation of its ghosts, every so often through the tall erect firs black-crouched skiers would glide, swift as shadows, like trees themselves flickering downward home.

It was some time then, in this bright half-light, that Harry turned and saw on the path behind him the figure of a girl trudging up on skis. He walked down towards her, enjoying the precision of her slender erect shape slide-stepping along towards him. Skiers walk with a beautifully controlled motion, feet always close together on the long hickory, pressing so lightly forward in long strides, pausing it seems invisibly between each forward motion, listening to a music playing somewhere in their shoulders—and always in firm endeavour, as on some enviable purposed unhurried quest pondering seriously forward.

Harry was looking down at her skis as she came up, taking pleasure from the movement and the slimness of her stride. So that not until she was nearly parallel with him and about to pass did he glance up at her face.

What he saw then took his breath away, he drew in a deep astounded breath and this then disappeared, so that there was nothing inside him at all.

Poor Harry did not have even a bus-ride's worth, not a threeha'pence worth. He had the length of two long ski-strides' worth. But that, he said, was in its expanded way enough. Not as much as he wanted—that would have amounted to a lifetime—but enough to provoke the indelible impression such passing visions may leave for a lifetime.

It would be useless to describe her. When Harry told me he talked of 'beauty' and of a colour of hair and a grace of cheek-bone and an expression of lips. But what he said did not amount to a concrete image, and particularly she did not necessarily fit the blue-print of my own imagined vision, should such a one ever chance to pass. Each to his own. Suffice it that this woman's face and manner and whatever she evoked

was for Harry perfection: was beyond what he thought might
be perfection: was absolute.

He was so shocked he nearly stopped, he certainly hesitated
and half turned his body—heavily coated and thus making
what must have been a most noticeable movement to follow
his wide-eyed worshipping glance. But in the same short time,
perhaps on her second stride forward, she suddenly turned
her face to him. Terrified, he looked away. He never knew
whether she saw him staring, or saw him at all, or looked past
or through him—he only felt a surge of embarrassment out of
all proportion to the occasion. He felt small, despairing, hopeless, and above all horrified that she might have caught his
eye and thought it the eye of an intruder.

She passed. It was a long time before Harry could bring
himself to turn round. But by then she was a black speck
among others in the lengthening snow, she was irretrievable.

For the next minutes Harry walked on and out of the park,
elated in spite of his distress. He was elated in the way a man
is when he has suddenly come face to face with a giddying
good work of art. The feeling was universal—it made to say:
'Good, good—so there are still such things in the world!' It
was a feeling of hope.

But of no practical hope. He knew that he would never see
the girl again. However, she had sent his spirits up . . . but
soon, it was apparent, too far. For once outside the park, her
park, the world proclaimed itself again. And it looked exceedingly bare and dull. The tram-ride home, among skiers now
wet and drab in the electric light, was lowering. His hotel,
white-walled as a sanatorium, primed with red corridor lights
and reticent switches, appalled him with its sterile gloom. He
took a glass of aquavit and telephoned a friend for dinner.

They went to a large old-fashioned restaurant. There were
many hundreds of people, an orchestra of twenty players
blared music to the farthest microphoned corner, waiters
bobbed and slid like black dolphins in the white sea of table-
cloth, and all around and up to the roof, high as an exhibition
hall, the gilded ornament twisted and plushly glittered. There
were palms, flowers, flags and chandeliers.

But here also Strindberg had kept his private dining-room: and it was with something of the same pessimist eye that Harry now allowed his spirits to sink below the level of the night-faring populace about. A tarnish shadowed the gilt, a dull propriety seemed to stuff the people. The band played ballad music of the 'nineties—and he felt no nostalgia, but a vehement disgust at the stuffed rose-love-garden pomp the song pictured for him. The diners, sitting too erect and quiet and uncomfortably unlaughing, began to look like the awkward guests at a staff-dinner. Two Salvation Army lasses, in fur bonnets, threaded their way through the tables. When the band began suddenly to play a gay Spanish march it was no better, it sounded too slow. And there were too many fiddles.

Now if you knew Harry as I know Harry, you would know that Harry then began to worry. He began to theorize. 'The sight of that girl,' he told himself, 'has coloured my whole life. By a hundredth chance I was in Stockholm, by a hundredth chance I went to Haga, by another hundredth I happened to be passing that path at that moment—and I had to see *her*. Now forever I am left with a standard of beauty which my world will always slightly fail. My relationships with women will never seem quite so keen, all other pursuits will seem henceforth without quite so much purpose. Of course, I shall enjoy myself in degree. But perfection has been trifled with. This kind of thing goes deeper than one thinks. . . . Oh why in hell did I go to Haga? And it is not as if I was as young as I was.'

He was still considering her on the train next morning at Malmö: 'The woman was always destined to be unattainable —and it is significant that I am leaving the city today. I suppose this will result in a fixation on Stockholm for the rest of my life. God knows how many superior contracts in other towns I shall discard for the subconscious opportunity of getting back to this blasted place.'

The train drew into Norrköping and lunch was served. It was difficult, sitting wedged with three other men, to know how much of each small dish to take for himself, so he took too little of each. But rather much of the one he liked most.

In guilty despondence, he looked out at the short orange trams circling the Norrköping neatnesses. How plain life could be! And these men eating in front and to the side of him were so large and well-conditioned! He felt himself smaller against their giant, businessy, grey-suited size. None of them spoke. They exchanged the dishes with little bows, and then relapsed into their erect selves. But as the train drew slowly out of Norrköping a group of children waved from behind railings. As one man, the three leaned slightly forward and made small flutterings with their white heavy hands. And without a word re-addressed themselves to their food.

Hell, thought Harry looking down at his own hand and seeing that it had not even the initiative to join in such a dull nice action. Hell, he thought, I shall have to wake myself up. And it was then that he decided on a new course of life, a disciplined course of self-indulgence. He would drink more, seek out more people, spend more money and work less.

The lowlands of Sweden rolled by. The sky hung grey and wet, the mossy turf with its scattering of huge time-smoothed boulders looked very ancient. Sometimes these boulders had been rolled to the edge of a field, but often they were too heavy to be moved, and lay still in the centre proclaiming their great, icy age. It was very difficult for Harry, wedged in now with his coffee, to see how to start on his new programme. It would have been ostentatious, he felt, to order a few brandies. But when one of the men asked for an after-dinner sherry, he did the same. One of these was enough. He felt slightly sick. The business-men, in their hard girth and with their large pale faces, began to look very like boulders.

But at Malmö a difference charged the air. At first this might have passed for the ambrosia of arrival—a search for luggage, the disturbing sea-air, the genial sheds and asphalt of docks. The delight of safe danger. But no—once aboard the ferry what had come upon people was evident. A glance into the smoke-room told much of the tale. Already, five minutes after the train had arrived, they were singing in the smoke-room. Tables were already massing empty bottles.

The three silent, kind, well-conditioned, Swedish business men were laughing together and sitting spread and easy. But it was not only a matter of alcohol—although the free dispensation of this, after a severely restricted country, proved in every way intoxicating. It was a broader sense of freedom. A shedding of propriety, of reserve—a change of manners, not from good to bad, but from good to good of another kind. Geniality and tolerance warmed the air.

Waiters hurried up with plates of enormous Danish sandwiches. In the very sandwiches there could be felt the difference between the two countries parted by a mile of water. Gone were the elegant and excellent Swedish confections, here were thick slabs of appetitious meat and fish piled hugely helter-skelter on a token of bread: Smörgåsbord had become Smørrebrød. And when they landed and he walked about the Danish train, Harry noticed immediately how the people had lost height and gained thickness: and how the porters wore dirtier, easier clothes. And standing in the street there was a beggar.

But although at first Harry responded to this interesting new brightness, he soon found he was the only one on the train who had no reason to be elated. He sank into greater gloom. He tried to revive his spirits with a fine meal and a night out in Copenhagen. But even when friendly Copenhageners, seeing him sitting alone, asked him to sit with them, plied him with food and drink, joked and prompted him in every way to enjoy himself—his mood remained. He felt nervous, frustrated, dull.

The next day, a little freshened by the morning, he boarded a midday boat train for Esbjærg and England. After all, he felt, things might be better. He was a fool to have taken a passing emotion so seriously. In fact, it was only an emotion and as such ephemeral and replaceable.

So that when they came to the Great Belt, and the train trundled aboard the ferry that was to take it across that wide flat water—Harry took to regarding his fellow-passengers with more interest. There is always an excitement when a compartmented train turns out its passengers to walk about and make a deckful. One has grown used and even loyal to one's own compartment: one knows the number of the carriage, it seems to be the best number of all! one even feels a sympathetic acquaintanceship with people seen through the glass of adjoining compartments and with those in the corridor. But there, on the boat, one must face a rival world—the world of other carriages. One resents their apparent assumption of equality—yet, inimical or not, it is a source of wonder that here are so many fellow-travellers of whose existence one was ignorant. One notes them with interest. One must watch and sniff.

Almost the first person Harry noted was the girl from Haga.

It could not be, it could, it was. Harry's heart jumped and his stomach sank. He turned furtively away.

He walked twenty yards down the deck, took out a cigarette and pretended that it was necessary to turn to light this against the wind. Then he backed against the cabin wall and, thus hidden, watched her. His emotion beat so strong that he imagined every passenger on the boat must recognize it, there would be a conspiracy aboard to smile about him. And consequently, though in the past days he had reproved himself for not having taken more courageous action at their first encounter—he had imagined all kinds of calm, forceful gallantry—his instinct now was for instant flight. However, common sense and a suspicion of the ridiculous strengthened him. And he was able to compromise by watching her from a distance.

She stood for a few minutes on deck, not watching the wide grey water but engrossed in her bag and some process of putting her coat and scarf and hat in order. These affairs she conducted with a tranquil efficiency. She was detached and sure, removed from all the others. She never raised her eyes to look at other people.

Then she turned and walked along to the luncheon saloon. Carefully Harry followed, pausing and looking away as if in search of somebody or something else, and chose a table about three away from hers. There he munched his enormous pork cutlet and kept her surveyed. Every time he dared to look at

her it seemed a stolen, intrusive moment. But he congratulated himself on his discretion. He told himself there was time,
she must be going aboard for the Harwich boat. There, with
a day and a night to stroll about the large saloons, opportunity
would present itself. He stole another glance. With horror he
found her looking straight at him, frowning a little. She
knew!

He left, and went down the steel staircase to where the train,
strangely tall and of such dark heavy metal, stood waiting.
He sat smoking and unnerved, alone in the carriage. But in a
few minutes the ferry docked, and soon the train was rumbling
out onto Jutland and the last stretch to Esbjærg.

The ship, white and clean and smiling with stewardesses,
welcomed them from the smoke and cramp of the train. But
the weather was beginning to blow, a freshness of pounding
black waves echoed in from the North Sea and storm clouds
raced ragged across a dark sky. Harry hurried aboard, estab-
lished his cabin, and went up to watch the other passengers
come up the gangway. He waited for half an hour, watched
the last arrivals drift in from the lighted sheds across the gritty
dark quay. But he had missed her. In some panic, and in her
absence growing more self-assured each moment, he searched
the ship. Up and down the steep stairways, in and out of
strange saloons, into the second class and once, daring all, by
intentional mistake into the ladies' rest room. But she was
nowhere. And the ship sailed.

Harry saw how he had missed his second chance. He looked
back at that hour on the ferry and cursed his ineptitude. He
despised himself, as he saw himself independent and adult
and assured yet baulking at the evident chance. He swore
that if ever again . . . but when she appeared in the lounge
after dinner he plunged his hand out for a coloured engineer-
ing gazette. All his fears returned. One does not necessarily
learn from experience.

The smoking-room was large and furnished with fresh,
modern, leather arm-chairs. The tables were ridged: and on
that evening the ridges were necessary, and then not always
high enough—for it was a very stormy night, and the ship was

rolling badly. Glasses and cups slid slowly about like moti-
vated chessmen, and more than once the ship gave a great
shuddering lurch that threw everything smashing to the floor.
Harry, behind his gazette, prayed that his coffee would not be
shot off clownishly across the saloon. He did not think then
what a good excuse that might make to smile at her. He only
prayed not to look a fool.

For her part, she sat serenely writing a letter. For some
reason her glass of brandy never slid an inch. It seemed to
borrow composure from her. Harry concentrated on an
advertisement for dozers. And, curiously, this calmed him.
It seemed so absurd, it showed up the moment: life is so very
various, nothing has quite such a unique importance as we
give it.

The storm grew in force. High waves smashed themselves
with animal force against the windows, and the ship rolled
more thunderously than ever. Stewards staggered, the arm-
chairs tugged at their floor-chains. Perhaps the smoke-room
was half-full when coffee began: but now it was emptying,
people who had resisted so far began to feel sick, and for others
it had become difficult to read or to talk or, among those
tilting tables, to think. As they went swaying and skidding
through the doors some laughed like people at a funfair:
others dared not open their mouths. And so there came a
moment, in spite of the drumming sea-noises outside, when
Harry noticed a distinct quiet in the room. He looked round
and saw that the room was nearly empty. There had descended the well-kept void dullness, the perceptible silence of a
waiting-room. Two business men sat apart reading. Their
smallest movement in that polished quiet attracted attention.
The girl wrote calmly on. The panic rose again in Harry's
chest. It would be so easy to go over and pick a magazine
from the case at her side. There were even magazines lying
on her own table! With no possibility of offence he could ask
her permission to read one.

He knew it was then or never. He began instantly to invent
excuses. For the first time he tried to reason. There, Harry
said to himself, is this girl whose appearance has knocked me

silly. But I know that a hundred to one her personality will never match this illusory loveliness. How do I know she won't be an utter fool? A bitch? A moron? . . . And then I'll have spoiled this—he could almost sigh with romantic detachment—beautiful experience. I have sipped—and that is forever more satisfying than the gross full draught. Then he looked at her again, and the detachment left him.

All right, he groaned, then at least there is the curse of classification. That has not yet disappeared. Suppose she answered me too genteelly? Or too broadly? Or in this accent or that—he heard in his ears those for which he held a deep, illogical antipathy. Then he remembered she was Swedish. It would not happen.

He looked back at the dozers. He saw they were described in refined lettering as 'earth-moving equipment'. He flung the magazine aside and in pale apprehension rose to his feet. The ship gave a lurch. He steadied himself. And then with great difficulty moved towards her.

Half-way across, exactly opposite the door, he who never did began to feel sea-sick. It was as if the paleness he had felt come over his face was spreading through him, and now with every roll of the ship a physical quease turned his stomach. It may have begun as a sickness of apprehension, but it took on all the symptoms of a sickness of sea. He felt weak, wretched and unsure of what next. He turned out through the door and balanced down the stairway to his cabin. In the lower bunk his cabin-companion lay pale and retching. The room smelled richly of sick. Harry added to it.

But only a little later, weak and having forgotten all about the girl, he fell into a deep, unmolested sleep. Twice in the night he woke—once when his heavy suitcase slid thudding from one end of the cabin to the other, once when he himself was nearly rolled out of the bunk. But he was no longer sick.

He woke late, feeling well and hungry. The ship was still pitching as heavily as before. He shaved with difficulty, watching his face swing in and out of the mirror, chasing with his razor the water that rolled in the opposite direction to that chosen by the ship. Then upstairs to breakfast. The whole ship was deserted. Harry looked at his watch, wondering whether he had misread the time and if it was perhaps still early—but his watch and the purser's clock made it already eleven o'clock. The notion smiled through him that the company had taken to the boats in the night, he was in a well-equipped ghost-ship with steam up. And indeed, walking through the deserted saloons, it felt like that. But in the dining-room three waiters were sitting.

During a breakfast that he could only eat by holding his cup in one hand and both cutting and forking his ham with the other, a waiter told him they were having one of the worst crossings he had ever known. Waves, even in such a great modern ship, had smashed plate-glass in the night. A settee had broken its chains, raced across the smoking-lounge and had run over a steward, breaking his leg. Of course, it was quite safe, but the ship would be about six hours late. They had made no headway at all during the night, they had simply sat rolling in the middle of the North Sea.

Harry wandered out along the passages and into the smoke-room. It was vexing to be so late. He was in no exact hurry, but an empty ship in stormy weather is a most tedious ordeal, and the long tossing day stretched out grey and eventless. One cannot easily write, it is difficult even to read, getting drunk is simpler but as aimless as the crashing glasses. To be sick is dreadful, but to spend a day lurching among lurching things, with never a level moment, is if not unendurable of the deepest, most troublesome tedium.

For a while Harry watched the waves. Some seemed higher than the ship itself, it seemed impossible not to be capsized. A sudden wet wall of grey running water would erect itself high as a housefront over the valley of the smoke-room window: then at the last moment up would go the ship on another unseen wave. All blew cold grey, but there was no mist—a gale wind whipped spray from the waves and tore the dish-cloth smoke to pieces. Low clouds scudded too fast to notice the ship, the horizon was no more than a jagged encampment of near waves. Not a bird, not a ship in sight.

Harry's thoughts naturally centred on what was still at the back of his mind. Breakfast over, he brought her foremost. And found to his surprise that he was no longer apprehensive of her. He welcomed the probability of her appearance, he welcomed the emptiness of the ship. She was obviously not the sea-sick type, she was likely to appear. And with an empty ship there would be more opportunity to speak—and at the same time nobody to smile behind his back if she snubbed him. It seemed that his sickness of the night before had proved in all ways cathartic.

He welcomed the luncheon gong, and in his expectant joy remembered with a smile the Swedish word for this: gonggong. But she did not appear at luncheon. And gradually his spirits falling and his stomach swelling, Harry ploughed in these difficult seas through the enormous and exquisite Danish meal.

The afternoon was terrible. Nothing, nothing happened. A few odd men came lurching through. Two young Danish fellows sat for a long time laughing over their drinks. Harry went down to pack, but was forced by the state of his companion to complete this as quickly as possible.

An hour before the ship was due in people began to come up exhausted or rested from the sanctuary of their cabins. The ship was steaming close against the English littoral, and the seas were much calmer. Disconsolate, Harry rose from his armchair, threw aside the paper on which he had been reduced to writing lists of all the vegetables he knew beginning with the letter 'p', and walked round to the little bar for a drink. There she was, bright as a bad penny, perched up on a stool between those two laughing young men.

His heart sank, but he went grimly to the other end of the bar and, with his back turned, ordered a dobbeltsnaps. He could not hear what was said, for between high laugher they spoke in the low intimate voices of people telling anecdotes: but he could watch them in a slice of mirror. And . . . So there! What had he told himself? Hadn't he been right? She was just an ordinary flirt! She hadn't talked to these men until five minutes before, and now she was going it hell-for-leather! Easy as pie, pie-in-the-sky! And that's why (subconsciously of course) he hadn't gone up to her. . . . But through this Harry knew deeply and quite consciously that he envied the young men and deprecated his own drivelling loutish cowardice. He turned and took one last look at her. She was wonderful . . . yes, she was wonderful.

He went downstairs and made ready to leave. In a while the ship docked. He took his bags and shuffled down among the line of passengers to the rail-lined dock. It was a curious relief to feel the land under one's feet, it brought what felt like a light unheard buzzing to the ears. Then the familiar smells and a further shuffle through the customs.

Suddenly, going through the doorway to the platform, he saw her again. She was clutching the arm of a large ugly elderly man. She was stroking this man. Together the two, the elegant fresh young girl and that obscene old figure, passed through the door. Harry believed his eyes and he was disgusted.

He had to pass them. They stood in the wan light of the old-fashioned station, she fingering about in her bag and at every moment flashing her eyes up at him, he bloated, gloat-eyed, mumbling heaven-knew-what salivary intimacies. It crossed Harry's mind how strange was the phenomenon of these ship-board passengers one never sees until the last moment, these cabined mysteries—and it struck him again horribly how this applied to those two, the old slug lying down there in the comfortable depths of the ship with his fair, fresh girl. . . .

The girl looked up and met Harry's eyes. She immediately smiled, it seemed in relief, and came up to him. She spoke excitedly, apologetically in Swedish:

—Oh, please do excuse me . . . but it's funny I remember distinctly I once saw you in Haga, you speak Swedish? You see, my father and I—we've lost our seat reservations. Could you tell me what is best to do? . . . We're new here. . . .

Harry's heart leapt. The lights in the station seemed to turn up, it was suddenly almost sunny. With delight he showed them to the end of the train where he knew there were empty carriages. Together they travelled to London and never stopped talking. He insisted on driving them to their hotel.

Harry and his lady have now been married some seven years. He has never, so far as can be known, regretted the requital.

DYLAN THOMAS

A Visit to Grandpa's

IN the middle of the night I woke from a dream full of whips and lariats as long as serpents, and runaway coaches on mountain passes, and wide, windy gallops over cactus fields, and I heard the old man in the next room crying, 'Gee-up!' and 'Whoa!' and trotting his tongue on the roof of his mouth.

It was the first time I had stayed in grandpa's house. The floorboards had squeaked like mice as I climbed into bed, and the mice between the walls had creaked like wood as though another visitor was walking on them. It was a mild summer night, but curtains had flapped and branches beaten against the window. I had pulled the sheets over my head, and soon was roaring and riding in a book.

'Whoa there, my beauties!' cried grandpa. His voice sounded very young and loud, and his tongue had powerful hooves, and he made his bedroom into a great meadow. I thought I would see if he was ill, or had set his bedclothes on fire, for my mother had said that he lit his pipe under the blankets, and had warned me to run to his help if I smelt smoke in the night. I went on tiptoe through the darkness to his bedroom door, brushing against the furniture and upsetting a candle-stick with a thump. When I saw there was a light in the room I felt frightened, and as I opened the door I heard grandpa shout, 'Gee-up!' as loudly as a bull with a megaphone.

He was sitting straight up in bed and rocking from side to side as though the bed were on a rough road; the knotted edges of the counterpane were his reins; his invisible horses stood in a shadow beyond the bedside candle. Over a white flannel nightshirt he was wearing a red waistcoat with walnut-sized brass buttons. The over-filled bowl of his pipe smouldered among his whiskers like a little, burning hayrick on a stick. At the sight of me, his hands dropped from the reins and lay blue and quiet, the bed stopped still on a level road, he muffled his tongue into silence, and the horses drew softly up.

'Is there anything the matter, grandpa?' I asked, though the clothes were not on fire. His face in the candlelight looked like a ragged quilt pinned upright on the black air and patched all over with goat-beards.

He stared at me mildly. Then he blew down his pipe, scattering the sparks and making a high, wet dog-whistle of the stem, and shouted: 'Ask no questions.'

After a pause, he said slyly: 'Do you ever have nightmares, boy?'

I said: 'No.'

'Oh, yes, you do,' he said.

I said I was woken by a voice that was shouting to horses.

'What did I tell you?' he said. 'You eat too much. Who ever heard of horses in a bedroom?'

He fumbled under his pillow, brought out a small, tinkling bag, and carefully untied its strings. He put a sovereign in my hand, and said: 'Buy a cake.' I thanked him and wished him good night.

As I closed my bedroom door, I heard his voice crying loudly and gaily, 'Gee-up! gee-up!' and the rocking of the travelling bed.

In the morning I woke from a dream of fiery horses on a plain that was littered with furniture, and of large, cloudy men who rode six horses at a time and whipped them with burning bed-clothes. Grandpa was at breakfast, dressed in deep black. After breakfast he said, 'There was a terrible loud wind last night,' and sat in his arm-chair by the hearth to make clay balls for the fire. Later in the morning he took me for a walk, through Johnstown village and into the fields on the Llanstephan road.

A man with a whippet said, 'There's a nice morning, Mr. Thomas,' and when he had gone, leanly as his dog, into the short-treed green wood he should not have entered because of the notices, grandpa said: 'There, do you hear what he called you? Mister!'

We passed by small cottages, and all the men who leant on the gates congratulated grandpa on the fine morning. We passed through the wood full of pigeons, and their wings broke the branches as they rushed to the tops of the trees. Among the soft, contented voices and the loud, timid flying, grandpa said, like a man calling across a field: 'If you heard those old birds in the night, you'd wake me up and say there were horses in the trees.'

We walked back slowly, for he was tired, and the lean man stalked out of the forbidden wood with a rabbit held as gently over his arm as a girl's arm in a warm sleeve.

On the last day but one of my visit I was taken to Llanstephan in a governess cart pulled by a short, weak pony. Grandpa might have been driving a bison, so tightly he held the reins, so ferociously cracked the long whip, so blasphemously shouted warning to boys who played in the road, so stoutly stood with his gaitered legs apart and cursed the demon strength and wilfulness of his tottering pony.

'Look out, boy!' he cried when we came to each corner, and pulled and tugged and jerked and sweated and waved his whip like a rubber sword. And when the pony had crept miserably round each corner, grandpa turned to me with a sighing smile: 'We weathered that one, boy.'

When we came to Llanstephan village at the top of the hill, he left the cart by the 'Edwinsford Arms' and patted the pony's muzzle and gave it sugar, saying: 'You're a weak little pony, Jim, to pull big men like us.'

He had strong beer and I had lemonade, and he paid Mrs. Edwinsford with a sovereign out of the tinkling bag; she inquired after his health, and he said that Llangadock was better for the tubes. We went to look at the churchyard and the sea, and sat in the wood called the Sticks, and stood on the concert platform in the middle of the wood where visitors sang on midsummer nights and, year by year, the innocent of the village was elected mayor. Grandpa paused at the churchyard and pointed over the iron gate at the angelic headstones and the poor wooden crosses. 'There's no sense in lying there,' he said.

We journeyed back furiously: Jim was a bison again.

I woke late on my last morning, out of dreams where the Llanstephan sea carried bright sailing-boats as long as liners; and heavenly choirs in the Sticks, dressed in bards' robes and brass-buttoned waistcoats, sang in a strange Welsh to the departing sailors. Grandpa was not at breakfast; he rose early. I walked in the fields with a new sling, and shot at the Towy gulls and the rooks in the parsonage trees. A warm wind blew from the summer points of the weather; a morning mist climbed from the ground and floated among the trees and hid the noisy birds; in the mist and the wind my pebbles flew lightly up like hailstones in a world on its head. The morning passed without a bird falling.

I broke my sling and returned for the midday meal through the parson's orchard. Once, grandpa told me, the parson had bought three ducks at Carmarthen Fair and made a pond for them in the centre of the garden; but they waddled to the gutter under the crumbling doorsteps of the house, and swam and quacked there. When I reached the end of the orchard path, I looked through a hole in the hedge and saw that the parson had made a tunnel through the rockery that was between the gutter and the pond and had set up a notice in plain writing: 'This way to the pond.'

The ducks were still swimming under the steps.

Grandpa was not in the cottage. I went into the garden, but grandpa was not staring at the fruit-trees. I called across to a man who leant on a spade in the field beyond the garden hedge: 'Have you seen my grandpa this morning?'

He did not stop digging, and answered over his shoulder: 'I seen him in his fancy waistcoat.'

Griff, the barber, lived in the next cottage. I called to him through the open door: 'Mr. Griff, have you seen my grandpa?'

The barber came out in his shirtsleeves.

I said: 'He's wearing his best waistcoat.' I did not know if it was important, but grandpa wore his waistcoat only in the night.

'Has grandpa been to Llanstephan?' asked Mr. Griff anxiously.

'We went there yesterday in a little trap,' I said.

He hurried indoors and I heard him talking in Welsh, and he came out again with his white coat on, and he carried a striped and coloured walking-stick. He strode down the village street and I ran by his side.

When we stopped at the tailor's shop, he cried out, 'Dan!' and Dan Tailor stepped from his window like an Indian priest but wearing a derby hat. 'Dai Thomas has got his waistcoat on,' said Mr. Griff, 'and he's been to Llanstephan.'

As Dan Tailor searched for his overcoat, Mr. Griff was striding on. 'Will Evans,' he called outside the carpenter's shop, 'Dai Thomas has been to Llanstephan, and he's got his waistcoat on.'

'I'll tell Morgan now,' said the carpenter's wife out of the hammering, sawing darkness of the shop.

We called at the butcher's shop and Mr. Price's house, and Mr. Griff repeated his message like a town crier.

We gathered together in Johnstown square. Dan Tailor had his bicycle, Mr. Price his pony trap. Mr. Griff, the butcher, Morgan Carpenter, and I climbed into the shaking trap, and we trotted off towards Carmarthen town. The tailor led the way, ringing his bell as though there were a fire or a robbery, and an old woman by the gate of a cottage at the end of the street ran inside like a pelted hen. Another woman waved a bright handkerchief.

'Where are we going?' I asked.

Grandpa's neighbours were as solemn as old men with black hats and jackets on the outskirts of a fair. Mr. Griff shook his head and mourned: 'I didn't expect this again from Dai Thomas.'

'Not after last time,' said Mr. Price sadly.

We trotted on, we crept up Constitution Hill, we rattled down into Lammas Street, and the tailor still rang his bell and a dog ran, squealing, in front of his wheels. As we clip-clopped over the cobbles that led down to the Towy bridge, I remembered grandpa's nightly noisy journeys that rocked the bed and shook the walls, and I saw his gay waistcoat in a vision and his patchwork head tufted and smiling in the candlelight. The tailor before us turned round on his saddle, his bicycle wobbled and skidded. 'I see Dai Thomas!' he cried.

The trap rattled on to the bridge, and I saw grandpa there; the buttons of his waistcoat shone in the sun, he wore his tight, black Sunday trousers and a tall, dusty hat I had seen in a cupboard in the attic, and he carried an ancient bag. He bowed to us. 'Good morning, Mr. Price,' he said, 'and Mr. Griff and Mr. Morgan and Mr. Evans.' To me, he said: 'Good morning, boy.'

Mr. Griff pointed his coloured stick at him.

'And what do you think you are doing on Carmarthen bridge in the middle of the afternoon,' he said sternly, 'with your best waistcoat and your old hat?'

Grandpa did not answer, but inclined his face to the river wind, so that his beard was set dancing and wagging as though he talked, and watched the coracle men move, like turtles, on the shore.

Mr. Griff raised his stunted barber's pole. 'And where do you think you are going,' he said, 'with your old black bag?'

Grandpa said: 'I am going to Llangadock to be buried.' And he watched the coracle shells slip into the water lightly, and the gulls complain over the fish-filled water as bitterly as Mr. Price complained:

'But you aren't dead yet, Dai Thomas.'

For a moment grandpa reflected, then: 'There's no sense in lying dead in Llanstephan,' he said. 'The ground is comfy in Llangadock; you can twitch your legs without putting them in the sea.'

His neighbours moved close to him. They said: 'You aren't dead, Mr. Thomas.'

'How can you be buried, then?'

'Nobody's going to bury you in Llanstephan.'

'Come on home, Mr. Thomas.'

'There's strong beer for tea.'

'And cake.'

But grandpa stood firmly on the bridge, and clutched his bag to his side, and stared at the flowing river and the sky, like a prophet who has no doubt.

EVELYN WAUGH

Mr. Loveday's Little Outing

I

'You will not find your father greatly changed,' remarked
Lady Moping, as the car turned into the gates of the
County Asylum.

'Will he be wearing a uniform?' asked Angela.

'No, dear, of course not. He is receiving the very best
attention.'

It was Angela's first visit and it was being made at her own
suggestion.

Ten years had passed since the showery day in late summer
when Lord Moping had been taken away; a day of confused
but bitter memories for her; the day of Lady Moping's annual
garden party, always bitter, confused that day by the caprice
of the weather which, remaining clear and brilliant with
promise until the arrival of the first guests, had suddenly
blackened into a squall. There had been a scuttle for cover;
the marquee had capsized; a frantic carrying of cushions and
chairs; a table-cloth lofted to the boughs of the monkey-
puzzler, fluttering in the rain; a bright period and the cautious
emergence of guests on to the soggy lawns; another squall;
another twenty minutes of sunshine. It had been an abomin-
able afternoon, culminating at about six o'clock in her father's
attempted suicide.

Lord Moping habitually threatened suicide on the occasion
of the garden party; that year he had been found black in the
face, hanging by his braces in the orangery; some neighbours,
who were sheltering there from the rain, set him on his feet
again, and before dinner a van had called for him. Since then
Lady Moping had paid seasonal calls at the asylum and
returned in time for tea, rather reticent of her experience.

Many of her neighbours were inclined to be critical of Lord

Moping's accommodation. He was not, of course, an ordinary inmate. He lived in a separate wing of the asylum, specially devoted to the segregation of wealthier lunatics. These were given every consideration which their foibles permitted. They might choose their own clothes (many indulged in the liveliest fancies), smoke the most expensive brands of cigars and, on the anniversaries of their certification entertain any other inmates for whom they had an attachment to private dinner parties.

The fact remained, however, that it was far from being the most expensive kind of institution; the uncompromising address, 'COUNTY HOME FOR MENTAL DEFECTIVES,' stamped across the notepaper, worked on the uniforms of their attendants, painted, even, upon a prominent hoarding at the main entrance, suggested the lowest associations. From time to time, with less or more tact, her friends attempted to bring to Lady Moping's notice particulars of seaside nursing homes, of 'qualified practitioners with large private grounds suitable for the charge of nervous or difficult cases', but she accepted them lightly; when her son came of age he might make any changes that he thought fit; meanwhile, she felt no inclination to relax her economical régime; her husband had betrayed her basely on the one day in the year when she looked for loyal support, and was far better off than he deserved.

A few lonely figures in great-coats were shuffling and loping about the park.

'Those are the lower-class lunatics,' observed Lady Moping. 'There is a very nice little flower garden for people like your father. I sent them some cuttings last year.'

They drove past the blank, yellow brick façade to the doctor's private entrance and were received by him in the 'visitors' room', set aside for interviews of this kind. The window was protected on the inside by bars and wire netting; there was no fireplace; when Angela nervously attempted to move her chair further from the radiator, she found that it was screwed to the floor.

'Lord Moping is quite ready to see you,' said the doctor.

'How is he?'

'Oh, very well, very well indeed, I'm glad to say. He had rather a nasty cold some time ago, but apart from that his condition is excellent. He spends a lot of his time in writing.'

They heard a shuffling, skipping sound approaching along the flagged passage. Outside the door a high peevish voice, which Angela recognized as her father's, said: 'I haven't the time, I tell you. Let them come back later.'

A gentler tone, with a slight rural burr, replied, 'Now come along. It is a purely formal audience. You need stay no longer than you like.'

Then the door was pushed open (it had no lock or fastening) and Lord Moping came into the room. He was attended by an elderly little man with full white hair and an expression of great kindness.

'That is Mr. Loveday who acts as Lord Moping's attendant.'

'Secretary,' said Lord Moping. He moved with a jogging gait and shook hands with his wife.

'This is Angela. You remember Angela, don't you?'

'No, I can't say that I do. What does she want?'

'We just came to see you.'

'Well, you have come at an exceedingly inconvenient time. I am very busy. Have you typed out that letter to the Pope yet, Loveday?'

'No, my lord. If you remember, you asked me to look up the figures about the Newfoundland fisheries first?'

'So I did. Well, it is fortunate, as I think the whole letter will have to be redrafted. A great deal of new information has come to light since luncheon. A great deal. . . . You see, my dear, I am fully occupied.' He turned his restless, quizzical eyes upon Angela. 'I suppose you have come about the Danube. Well, you must come again later. Tell them it will be all right, quite all right, but I have not had time to give my full attention to it. Tell them that.'

'Very well, Papa.'

'Anyway,' said Lord Moping rather petulantly, 'it is a matter of secondary importance. There is the Elbe and the

Amazon and the Tigris to be dealt with first, eh, Loveday? . . .
Danube indeed. Nasty little river. I'd only call it a stream
myself. Well, can't stop, nice of you to come. I would do
more for you if I could, but you see how I'm fixed. Write to
me about it. That's it. *Put it in black and white.*'

And with that he left the room.

'You see,' said the doctor, 'he is in excellent condition. He
is putting on weight, eating and sleeping excellently. In fact,
the whole tone of his system is above reproach.'

The door opened and Loveday returned.

'Forgive my coming back, sir, but I was afraid that the
young lady might be upset at his Lordship's not knowing her.
You mustn't mind him, miss. Next time he'll be very pleased
to see you. It's only to-day he's put out on account of being
behindhand with his work. You see, sir, all this week I've been
helping in the library and I haven't been able to get all his
Lordship's reports typed out. And he's got muddled with his
card index. That's all it is. He doesn't mean any harm.'

'What a nice man,' said Angela, when Loveday had gone
back to his charge.

'Yes. I don't know what we should do without old Loveday.
Everybody loves him, staff and patients alike.'

'I remember him well. It's a great comfort to know that
you are able to get such good warders,' said Lady Moping;
'people who don't know, say such foolish things about asylums.'

'Oh, but Loveday isn't a warder,' said the doctor.

'You don't mean he's cuckoo, too?' said Angela.

The doctor corrected her.

'He is an *inmate*. It is rather an interesting case. He has been
here for thirty-five years.'

'But I've never seen anyone saner,' said Angela.

'He certainly has that air,' said the doctor, 'and in the last
twenty years we have treated him as such. He is the life and
soul of the place. Of course he is not one of the private
patients, but we allow him to mix freely with them. He plays
billiards excellently, does conjuring tricks at the concert,
mends their gramophones, valets them, helps them in their
crossword puzzles and various—er—hobbies. We allow them

to give him small tips for services rendered, and he must by now have amassed quite a little fortune. He has a way with even the most troublesome of them. An invaluable man about the place.'

'Yes, but why is he here?'

'Well, it is rather sad. When he was a very young man he killed somebody—a young woman quite unknown to him, whom he knocked off her bicycle and then throttled. He gave himself up immediately afterwards and has been here ever since.'

'But surely he is perfectly safe now. Why is he not let out?'

'Well, I suppose if it was to anyone's interest, he would be. He has no relatives except a step-sister who lives in Plymouth. She used to visit him at one time, but she hasn't been for years now. He's perfectly happy here and I can assure you *we* aren't going to take the first steps in turning him out. He's far too useful to us.'

'But it doesn't seem fair,' said Angela.

'Look at your father,' said the doctor. 'He'd be quite lost without Loveday to act as his secretary.'

'It doesn't seem fair.'

2

Angela left the asylum, oppressed by a sense of injustice. Her mother was unsympathetic.

'Think of being locked up in a looney bin all one's life.'

'He attempted to hang himself in the orangery,' replied Lady Moping, '*in front of the Chester-Martins*.'

'I don't mean Papa. I mean Mr. Loveday.'

'I don't think I know him.'

'Yes, the looney they have put to look after Papa.'

'Your father's secretary. A very decent sort of man, I thought, and eminently suited to his work.'

Angela left the question for the time, but returned to it again at luncheon on the following day.

'Mums, what does one have to do to get people out of the bin?'

'The bin? Good gracious, child, I hope that you do not anticipate your father's return *here*.'

'No, no. Mr. Loveday.'

'Angela, you seem to me to be totally bemused. I see it was a mistake to take you with me on our little visit yesterday.'

After luncheon Angela disappeared to the library and was soon immersed in the lunacy laws as represented in the encylopaedia.

She did not reopen the subject with her mother, but a fortnight later, when there was a question of taking some pheasants over to her father for his eleventh Certification Party she showed an unusual willingness to run over with them. Her mother was occupied with other interests and noticed nothing suspicious.

Angela drove her small car to the asylum and, after delivering the game, asked for Mr. Loveday. He was busy at the time making a crown for one of his companions who expected hourly to be annointed Emperor of Brazil, but he left his work and enjoyed several minutes' conversation with her. They spoke about her father's health and spirits. After a time Angela remarked, 'Don't you ever want to get away?'

Mr. Loveday looked at her with his gentle, blue-grey eyes. 'I've got very well used to the life, miss. I'm fond of the poor people here, and I think that several of them are quite fond of me. At least, I think they would miss me if I were to go.'

'But don't you ever think of being free again?'

'Oh yes, miss, I think of it—almost all the time I think of it.'

'What would you do if you got out? There must be *something* you would sooner do than stay here.'

The old man fidgeted uneasily. 'Well, miss, it sounds ungrateful, but I can't deny I should welcome a little outing, once, before I get too old to enjoy it. I expect we all have our secret ambitions, and there *is* one thing I often wish I could do. You mustn't ask me what. . . . It wouldn't take long. But I do feel that if I had done it, just for a day, an afternoon even, then I would die quiet. I could settle down again easier, and devote myself to the poor crazed people here with a better heart. Yes, I do feel that.'

There were tears in Angela's eyes that afternoon as she drove away. 'He *shall* have his little outing, bless him,' she said.

3

From that day onwards for many weeks Angela had a new purpose in life. She moved about the ordinary routine of her home with an abstracted air and an unfamiliar, reserved courtesy which greatly disconcerted Lady Moping.

'I believe the child's in love. I only pray that it isn't that uncouth Egbertson boy.'

She read a great deal in the library, she cross-examined any guests who had pretensions to legal or medical knowledge, she showed extreme goodwill to old Sir Roderick Lane-Foscote, their Member. The names 'alienist,' 'barrister' or 'government official' now had for her the glamour that formerly surrounded film actors and professional wrestlers. She was a woman with a cause, and before the end of the hunting season she had triumphed. Mr. Loveday achieved his liberty.

The doctor at the asylum showed reluctance but no real opposition. Sir Roderick wrote to the Home Office. The necessary papers were signed, and at last the day came when Mr. Loveday took leave of the home where he had spent such long and useful years.

His departure was marked by some ceremony. Angela and Sir Roderick Lane-Foscote sat with the doctors on the stage of the gymnasium. Below them were assembled everyone in the institution who was thought to be stable enough to endure the excitement.

Lord Moping, with a few suitable expressions of regret, presented Mr. Loveday on behalf of the wealthier lunatics with a gold cigarette case; those who supposed themselves to be emperors showered him with decorations and titles of honour. The warders gave him a silver watch and many of the non-paying inmates were in tears on the day of the presentation.

The doctor made the main speech of the afternoon. 'Remember,' he remarked, 'that you leave behind you nothing but our warmest good wishes. You are bound to us by ties that none will forget. Time will only deepen our sense of debt to you. If at any time in the future you should grow tired of your life in the world, there will always be a welcome for you here. Your post will be open.'

A dozen or so variously afflicted lunatics hopped and skipped after him down the drive until the iron gates opened and Mr. Loveday stepped into his freedom. His small trunk had already gone to the station; he elected to walk. He had been reticent about his plans, but he was well provided with money, and the general impression was that he would go to London and enjoy himself a little before visiting his step-sister.

It was to the surprise of all that he returned within two hours of his liberation. He was smiling whimsically, a gentle, self-regarding smile of reminiscence.

'I have come back,' he informed the doctor. 'I think that now I shall be here for good.'

'But, Loveday, what a short holiday. I'm afraid that you have hardly enjoyed yourself at all.'

'Oh yes, sir, thank you, sir, I've enjoyed myself *very much*. I'd been promising myself one little treat all these years. It was short, sir, but *most* enjoyable. Now I shall be able to settle down again to my work here without any regrets.'

Half a mile up the road from the asylum gates, they later discovered an abandoned bicycle. It was a lady's machine of some antiquity. Quite near it in the ditch lay the strangled body of a young woman, who, riding home to her tea, had chanced to overtake Mr. Loveday, as he strode along, musing on his opportunities.

ANGUS WILSON

Realpolitik

JOHN HOBDAY sat on the edge of his desk and swung his left leg with characteristic boyishness. He waited for the staff to get settled in their seats and then spoke with careful informality.

'I know how frightfully busy you are. As a matter of fact I am myself,' he said with the half-humorous urchin smile that he used for such jokes. Only his secretary, Veronica, gave the helpful laugh he expected. It was not going to be an easy meeting, he decided. 'So I'm not going to waste your time with a lot of talk' he went on 'I just thought . . .' He paused and beat with his pencil against the desk whilst Mrs. Scrutton moved her chair fussily out of the sunlight. 'Ready?' he asked with an over-elaborate smile 'Right. Then we'll start again. As I was saying, we're all very busy, but all the same I thought it was time we had a little meeting. I've been here a week now and although I've had some very helpful chats with each of you in turn, we've never had a chance to get together and outline our plans'. None of the three who formed his audience made any response. Veronica, who remembered him taking over new departments at the Ministry during the war, thought he hasn't got the right tone, he doesn't realize that he's coming up against deeper loyalties with these people, loyalties to scholarship and ideas. She almost felt like letting him fend for himself, but old habits were too strong.

'I'm sure it's what everybody's been wanting' she said in her deep voice. She had gauged rightly, his moment of uncertainty had gone, her faithful bark had guided him at the crucial moment. Mrs. Scrutton tried to discomfort him. She rustled the papers on her lap and whispered audibly to Major Sarson 'Our plans. *His* plans for us would be more honest'.

But it was too late, she had missed her chance. John merely frowned at the interruption and it was Mrs. Scrutton who was left with burning cheeks, hiding her embarrassment by lighting a fresh cigarette.

'As you know' John went on, and Veronica could tell by the loud, trumpeting, rhetorical note of his voice that he was once more the confident salesman lost in the dream world of the grandiose schemes he was putting before them 'I've got some very big ideas for the Gallery. I'm not an expert in any way as you people are, but I think that's possibly why Sir Harold's executors chose me for the job. They felt the Gallery had already got its full weight of scholars and experts, what it needed was a man with administrative experience, whose training had led him to take an over all view of things, to think, shall I say, widely rather than deeply. That's why they got me in. But I'm going to be absolutely frank with you' tossing a lock of brown, wavy hair from his forehead, he stared at his audience with a wide-eyed appeal 'I need *your* help, without my staff I can get nowhere.'

Major Sarson winced slightly. All this theatricality and the loud pitch of John's voice got on his nerves, besides he could feel a draught round his legs. It's like some damned Methodist preacher fellow, he thought.

'You've been grand in this first week' John went on 'absolutely grand. I don't mind telling you now that when I arrived I was dead scared. You'd all been here for years, you knew the collections backwards, you had your own ways of running the place, and above all you'd had the inestimable advantage of knowing Sir Harold, of hearing exactly what was in his mind when he bought this picture or that object, of knowing what his ideals were in giving the public the benefit of his taste and experience. I felt sure you were bound to resent me as an outsider, and I knew I'd have done the same in your place'.

The faces in front of him were quite unresponsive. He isn't going to get anywhere with sentimental appeals, thought Veronica, these people are idealists, there's nothing more hardboiled. The damned fools, thought John, they have the chance of turning this tin pot, cranky provincial gallery into a national institution and they won't play ball. Well if they can't see which way their own chances lie, they're not getting in the way of mine. They'll have to come to heel or go. His voice became a little sharper, a shade less ingenuous and friendly.

'You've all told me your views in our various little chats. Sometimes we've agreed, sometimes we haven't. You've inclined to the feeling that all is for the best in the best of all possible worlds, I've felt that some changes were needed, that the scope of the work here wanted broadening, that the organization wanted, let's face it, bringing up to date a bit, and in all this the Board has agreed with me'.

Tony Parnell's baby face had grown steadily more pouting and scowling as John had been speaking. To think of this mountebank in charge of the Gallery, a professional careerist, who understood nothing of Sir Harold's ideas and aims, who had even laughed when he'd spoken to him of the metaphysical aspects of technique in painting. He had banked so much on becoming Curator. Sir Harold had spoken so often of him as 'my torchbearer, the youngest member of our staff', and now these awful business men who had got control of the estate had put this creature in. Major Sarson and Mrs. Scrutton were too old to fight these changes, he had promised before the meeting that *he* would make the challenge. Now was his opportunity. Red in the face, he opened his mouth, but in his nervousness his voice emerged a high falsetto. John smiled across at Veronica.

'The Board haven't had much opportunity of agreeing with us since they haven't heard our views' Tony squeaked.

'My dear Parnell' said John, and his tone was purposely patronizing and offensive. The old ones he regarded without rancour as dead wood to be cleared away, but Tony he disliked personally for his assumptions of scholarly disinterestedness and moral superiority. 'Don't let that worry you. As soon as you've got your ideas clear come along and push them at the Board as much as you like. I shouldn't use too much of your favourite art jargon if I was you; the Board are anxious to help but they're only ordinary business men and they might not understand. If you follow my advice you'll come down to earth a bit, but of course that's entirely your affair'.

Mrs. Scrutton fingered the buttons on her checked tweed coat nervously. 'There's no need to bully Mr. Parnell' she said.

'Oh, come' said John jocosely 'if Parnell's going to have the ladies on his side I shall have to surrender'. To his delight he saw that Tony was frowning with annoyance.

'Do let me deal with this in my own way' he said to Mrs. Scrutton, whose lip began to tremble.

So that severe grey bobbed hair and man's collar and tie could dissolve early into tears, thought John, so much the better.

'Mrs. Scrutton was only trying to help you, Parnell' said Major Sarson 'Don't let us forget our manners, please'.

John yawned slightly 'When the little civil war's over' he said 'I'd just like to outline our main functions. As I see them they're these: Relations with the Public, that's you, Parnell; Display, Mrs. Scrutton; Research, Major Sarson. Miss Clay' he indicated Veronica 'is maid of all work. And I, well, I'm the Aunt Sally, ready to stop the bricks and pass on the bouquets'.

Major Sarson looked at his watch impatiently. 'I quite agree, with you, Major,' said John 'the sooner we get finished the better. No true gentlemen continue to hold meetings after opening time'. The old man's face twitched violently, no one before had referred overtly to his notorious weakness.

'I'd like to take the public first' said John. 'You've done a first-rate job, Parnell—within its limits. But you haven't gone far enough. You've got real enthusiasm and that's half the battle—but only half. You give the public first-rate value in lectures and catalogues when they get here, but you don't try to get them to come. I know what you're going to say "They'll come if they're interested." But aren't you being a bit hard on the poor, tired, pushed around public of today?

They've got to be told about the place. You've got to com-
pete with the cinema, the football team *and* the fireside radio.
In short you've got to advertise and you can't do that unless
you have figures.' Here John paused and picked up a file of
papers.

'You have all the figures there' said Tony sulkily.

'I know' said John 'but don't you think they're just a bit
too general? "So many people visited the Gallery on August
5th; so many on November 3rd" But what sort of people?
Who are we catering for? Were they Chinamen, shop-girls,
farmers, or just plain deaf-mutes? To tell us anything these
figures want breaking down into groups—so many foreigners,
so many over-forties, so many under-twenties. That's the way
to build up a picture. Now supposing you run over these
figures in the way that I suggest and we'll talk again.'

Tony was about to protest that this task was impossible, but
John held up his hand. 'No, no, time's very short and there's
one more point I want to raise before we pass on to display'.
Mrs. Scrutton drew her coat tightly round her. 'It's about the
lecture-room. Sir Louis Crippen was saying something at the
last Board meeting about its not being free for his archaeo-
logical society when he needed it. Do you know anything
about that?'

Tony Parnell hesitated. 'Well, actually' he said 'Mrs.
Scrutton makes all the lecture hall arrangements'.

'But isn't it the P.R.O.'s pigeon?' asked John.

'Yes' said Tony. 'But . . . well . . . Mrs. Scrutton . . .'

'I see' said John coldly. 'Perhaps you'd enlighten me, then,
Mrs. Scrutton.'

The grey bob shook as she answered, an involuntary shake
that was to prove the prelude to age's palsy. 'Sir Louis asked
for Tuesday and Tuesdays are always booked by Miss
Copley' she said.

'Miss Copley?'

Mrs. Scrutton guessed that he knew the answer and her
reply attempted a rebuke. 'Miss Copley is an old and true
friend to the Gallery' she said. 'She's been giving her lectures
to Schools on Tuesdays for many years.'

'No doubt' said John 'but I still think Sir Louis should have preference'.

'I don't agree at all' said Major Sarson 'it would be most unfair'.

'Yes, why should Sir Louis receive special treatment?' asked Mrs. Scrutton.

'Well, frankly,' replied John 'because although Miss Copley may be a very old friend, Sir Louis is a very influential one and the Gallery needs influential friends.'

Before Mrs. Scrutton there floated Sir Harold's features, like Erasmus she had thought him, the last of the humanists. Major Sarson too, remembered his old friend's handshake and his firm clear voice 'Sarson' he had said 'this money came to me through false standards, false distinctions. There shall be no distinctions in its use but those of scholarship'. The eyes of both these old people filled with tears.

John turned to Veronica. 'You've nothing to do, Miss Clay' he said. 'In future you will take on the lecture hall arrangements. Anything important you'll refer to me.' Mrs. Scrutton made a gesture of protest. 'No, no' said John. 'I'm not going to let you wear yourself out on these minor details, you're far too valuable to the Gallery. Besides, you've got more than a full time job with Display if it's properly carried out.'

Tony Parnell half rose from his chair 'I thought the Lecture Hall arrangements came under Public Relations?'

'So did I' said John 'until you disillusioned me.

'Next we come to Display. I suppose no side of our work has been more revolutionized in recent years. The Philadelphia report, you know, and the Canadian Association series' he went on, smiling at Mrs. Scrutton. She suddenly felt very tired, she had seen these documents but had never been able to bring herself to read them. 'But there's no need for me to mention these things to you' John continued. 'Your arrangement of the miniature collection . . .' and he sighed in wonder. 'Well, I'm going to pay you a great compliment there. Your arrangement of the miniatures not only makes one want to look at them, it makes it impossible for one not to look at them.

I'm sure, Mrs. Scrutton, you'll agree with my wish that some other sides of the collection had the same advantages as the miniatures—the jewellery, for instance, and the armour. But that's not your fault. There's just too much for one person, that's all there is to it. The same applies to the research. I'm not going to embarrass Major Sarson by talking about his position as a scholar' he waved his hand towards the old man who went red round the ears 'suffice it to say what we all know, that the Gallery is honoured by the presence of the world's greatest authority on the Dutch school, and a great scholar of painting generally. Though I doubt, by the way, whether the Major's exactly fond of the moderns. I sometimes wish that the Gallery possessed only paintings, I'm sure Major Sarson does. Unfortunately that isn't the case. I fully sympathized with him when he spoke to me as he did of "those wretched pots and pans,"' here John laughed patronizingly 'but I doubt if a ceramics man would. Frankly' he said, turning to Major Sarson 'I consider it disgraceful that a scholar of your calibre should be taken off your real work in this way. Now how, you may ask, do I suppose to remedy the situation? Well the answer is that I propose to treble the staff. From next month new staff will begin to arrive—some students from the Universities, some more experienced men from other galleries and museums.'

There was silence for a minute, then Mrs. Scrutton spoke. 'Does the Board know of this?'

'Yes' said John 'they fully approve the scheme'.

'Do they realize the expense involved?' asked Tony, the practical man.

'The Board are business men' said John 'they know that outlay must precede returns'. He looked round at their faces. 'Well, I think that's all' he said. 'I know you will give the new members of the staff the same co-operation you have given me, whether it is a question of instructing and training them, or in some cases of working under them'. His tone was openly sarcastic.

'Do I understand that people will be put over us?' asked Mrs. Scrutton.

'In cases where experts are brought in, it may be necessary to make revisions in seniority' said John.

'You realize, of course, that in such an eventuality we should resign' said Major Sarson.

'That would be a great loss to the Gallery, but we could not, of course, control your decisions,' replied John, and opening the door, he bowed them out.

'Golly' said Veronica 'you do tell some lies, don't you? Or have the Board ratified your staff changes?'

'How many more times must I tell you, Veronica, that truth is relative' said John.

Veronica looked down for a minute 'I'll make you some coffee' she said.

'Yes' said John 'Victory always makes me thirsty. I cannot help being satisfied when I think of the well merited unpleasant few weeks those three are going to have. The punishment of incompetence is always satisfactory.'

'Mmm' said Veronica doubtfully.

'What's that mean? You've not fallen for this sentimental stuff about Sir Harold, have you?'

'Good Lord, no' said Veronica. 'It's not those misfits I'm worrying about, it's you.'

'Me?' said John. 'Why?'

'You're getting too fond of bullying' said Veronica 'it interferes with your charm, and charm's essential for your success'. She went out to make the coffee.

What Veronica said was very true, thought John, and he made a note to be more detached in his attitude. All the same these criticisms were bad for his self-esteem. For all her loyalty Veronica knew him too well, got too near home. Charm was important to success, but self-esteem was more so. His imagination began to envisage further staff changes, perhaps a graduate secretary would really be more suitable now.

BIOGRAPHICAL NOTES

BOWEN, ELIZABETH (1899-1973). Born in Dublin and educated at Downe House School in Kent. Her published works include: *The Last September*; *To the North*; *The House in Paris*; *The Death of the Heart*; *Bowen's Court*; *The Heat of the Day*, and *A World of Love*.

CARY, JOYCE (1888-1957). Born in Donegal and educated at Clifton and Trinity College, Oxford. Studied art in Edinburgh. Fought in the Balkan War, 1912-13. Served in Sir Horace Plunkett's Irish Co-operative Organization and in the Nigerian Political Service from 1913 to 1920. Fought with the Nigeria Regiment in the Cameroons 1915-16. Author of many novels, including *Herself Surprised*; *To be a Pilgrim*; *The Horse's Mouth*; *Mr. Johnson*; *A Fearful Joy*; *Prisoner of Grace*; *Except the Lord*, and *Not Honour More*.

DE LA MARE, WALTER (1873-1956). Best known as a poet, but author of stories and novels also. His published works include: *The Return*; *Peacock Pie*; *Memoirs of a Midget*; *The Riddle*; *Broomstick*; *Behold, This Dreamer*; *The Traveller*; *Winged Chariot*, etc.

GREENE, GRAHAM (1904). Educated Berkhamsted and Balliol College, Oxford. Served on staff of *The Times* and the *Spectator*. Foreign Office, 1941-44. Director: Eyre and Spottiswoode Ltd., 1944-8; Bodley Head, 1958-68. His published works include: *It's a Battlefield*; *England Made Me*; *The Basement Room*; *Brighton Rock*; *The Power and the Glory*; *The Heart of the Matter*; *The End of the Affair*, and *The Quiet American*.

HARTLEY, LESLIE POLES (1895-1972). Educated Harrow and Balliol College, Oxford. His published works include: *The Killing Bottle*; *The Shrimp and the Anemone*; *The Sixth Heaven*; *Eustace and Hilda*; *The Go-Between*, and *A Perfect Woman*.

MAUGHAM, WILLIAM SOMERSET (1874-1965). Educated at King's School, Canterbury, Heidelberg University, and St. Thomas's Hospital. Author of novels, plays, and short stories. Officer of the Legion of

Honour. His published works include: *Liza of Lambeth*; *Mrs. Craddock*; *The Moon and Sixpence*; *Ashenden*; *Cakes and Ale*; *The Summing Up*; *The Razor's Edge*; *A Writer's Notebook*. Among his plays are: *A Man of Honour*; *Lady Frederick*; *The Circle*; *Our Betters*; *The Constant Wife*; *For Services Rendered*.

O'CONNOR, FRANK (1903-66). Born in Cork and educated by the Christian Brothers. His published works include: *Guests of the Nation* and *Bones of Contention* (stories); *The Saint and Mary Kate* (novel); *The Wild Bird's Nest* and *Lords and Commons* (verse), and *The Big Fellow* (biography).

PRITCHETT, SIR VICTOR SAWDON (1900). Educated at Alleyn's School. Director of *New Statesman* and *Nation*. Holder of various academic posts since 1953. His published works include: *Marching Spain*; *The Spanish Virgin*; *Nothing Like Leather*; *Dead Man Leading*; *Mr. Beluncle*; *Collected Short Stories*, and a biography of Turgenev, *The Gentle Barbarian*.

SANSOM, WILLIAM (1912-76). Educated Uppingham and in Europe. His publications include: *Fireman Flower*; *Something Terrible, Something Lovely*; *The Body*; *The Passionate North*; *The Face of Innocence*, and *A Bed of Roses*.

THOMAS, DYLAN (1914-53). Educated Swansea. His published works include: *Deaths and Entrances*; *The Map of Love*; *Portrait of the Artist as a Young Dog*; *Under Milk Wood*; *The Doctor and the Devils*; *Quite Early One Morning*; *Collected Poems*.

WAUGH, EVELYN (1903-66). Educated at Lancing and Hertford College, Oxford. Was in Royal Marines and Royal Horse Guards during 1939-45 War. His publications include: *Decline and Fall*; *Vile Bodies*; *Black Mischief*; *A Handful of Dust*; *Edmund Campion*; *Brideshead Revisited*; *The Loved One*; *Men at Arms*, and *Officers and Gentlemen*.

WILSON, ANGUS (1913). Educated at Westminster School and Merton College, Oxford. Foreign Office, 1942-6; Deputy Superintendent of Reading Room, British Museum, 1949-55; Lecturer 1963-66, and Professor of English Literature since 1966, at the University of East Anglia. His published works include: *The Wrong Set; Such Darling Dodos; Emile Zola; Hemlock and After; Anglo-Saxon Attitudes, The Old Men at the Zoo*, and *The World of Charles Dickens*.

ACKNOWLEDGEMENTS

We are grateful for permission to reproduce the following copyright stories:

Elizabeth Bowen: 'Ivy Gripped the Steps'. Copyright 1946 and renewed 1974 by Elizabeth Bowen. Reprinted from *The Demon Lover* by permission of Jonathan Cape Ltd. on behalf of the Estate of Elizabeth Bowen and from *The Collected Stories of Elizabeth Bowen* by permission of Alfred A. Knopf, Inc.

Joyce Cary: 'The Good Investment' and 'Umaru'. Copyright 1950 Joyce Cary. Reprinted by kind permission of Curtis Brown Ltd.

Walter de la Mare: 'Seaton's Aunt' from *The Best Stories of Walter de la Mare*. Reprinted by permission of The Literary Trustees of Walter de la Mare and The Society of Authors as their representative.

Graham Greene: 'When Greek Meets Greek' from *Collected Stories*, copyright 1947, renewed © 1975 by Graham Greene. All rights reserved. (London: William Heinemann Ltd., and The Bodley Head; New York: Viking.) Reprinted by permission of Laurence Pollinger Ltd., and Viking Penguin, Inc.

L. P. Hartley: 'The Killing Bottle' from *The Travelling Grave* in *The Complete Short Stories of L. P. Hartley*. Copyright © The Exectutors of the Estate of the late L. P. Hartley. Reprinted by permission of Hamish Hamilton Ld.

W. Somerset Maugham: 'Episode'. Copyright 1946 by Fawcett Publications, Inc. Reprinted from *Creatures of Circumstance* by permission of Doubleday, a division of Bantam, Doubleday, Dell Publishing Group, Inc., and William Heinemann, Ltd.

Frank O'Connor: 'Peasants'. Copyright 1936 by Frank O'Connor. Reprinted from *Stories of Frank O'Connor* by permission of A. D. Peters & Co. Ltd., and from *Collected Stories* by permission of Alfred A. Knopf, Inc.

V. S. Pritchett: 'The Aristocrat' and 'The Scapegoat'. Reprinted from *You Make Your Own Life* by permission of Chatto & Windus Ltd., and from *Collected Stories* (Random House Inc.) by permission of A. D. Peters & Co.

William Sansom: 'The Girl on the Bus' from *The Passionate North*. Copyright 1950 by William Sansom. Reprinted by permission of Elaine Greene Ltd.

Dylan Thomas: 'A Visit to Grandpa's' from *Portrait of the Artist as a Young Dog*. Reprinted by permission of David Higham Associates Ltd.

Evelyn Waugh: 'Mr Loveday's Little Outing'. Reprinted from *Work Suspended* (London: Chapman & Hall Ltd) by permission of A. D. Peters & Co., Ltd. Published in the United States in *Mr Loveday's Little Outing and Other Sad Stories* (Boston: Little, Brown & Co.). US Copyright handled by Harold Matson Literary Agency.

Angus Wilson: 'Realpolitik' from *The Wrong Set*. Copyright © Angus Wilson 1949. Reprinted by permission of Secker & Warburg Ltd., and Curtis Brown Ltd., London.

Every effort has been made to contact copyright holders before publication. However in some cases this has not been possible. If contacted the publisher will ensure that full credit is given at the earliest opportunity.